North Side
of the Tree

Also by Maggie Prince for older readers

Raider's Tide
Memoirs of a Dangerous Alien
Pulling the Plug on the Universe
Here Comes a Candle to Light You to Bed

PRAISE FOR *RAIDER'S TIDE*

'...plenty of period flavour, along with characters you care a great deal about. This book will surely become a firm favourite.' *Bookseller*

'First person, present-tense narrative gives immediacy to the story... vivid evocation of landscape and domestic detail, and a heroine whose desire for independence will strike chords with teenage girls.' *TES*

'This brilliant, pacey and stylish historical novel crackles with tension and secrets.' *J-17*

'page-turning excitement with a warm strong story of a young woman's first love at its heart.' *Jonathan Douglas, Library Association*

North Side

of the Tree

MAGGIE PRINCE

Collins

An imprint of HarperCollinsPublishers

*My warmest thanks for items of historical information go to
Christo Groenewald, David Pile, Lindsay Warden,
Susan Wilson of Lancaster Reference Library and Local History Archive,
Andrew White of Lancaster Museum Services,
Andrew Thynne of Preston Public Records Office and
the staff of Aylesbury Library and Senate House Library.
Special thanks for valuable feedback and opinions go to Deborah
Groenewald, Daniel Groenewald, Sarah Molloy and Alison Stanley.*

First published in Great Britain by Collins in 2003
Collins is an imprint of HarperCollins*Publishers* Ltd,
77–85 Fulham Palace Road, Hammersmith, London W6 8JB

The HarperCollins website address is www.**fire**and**water**.com

1 3 5 7 9 6 4 2

Printed and bound in England by
Clays Ltd, St Ives plc

For Chris, always

*In transposing Beatrice's story into modern English,
the tone and content of her original narrative
have been preserved throughout,
and her exact words wherever possible.*

It is the late 1500s. Queen Elizabeth I is on the throne of England...

Chapter 1

I walk the Old Corpse Road again. In the dawn light the woods are full of birdsong and the waking voices of sheep. Around me, oak and hazel trees are turning to red and gold and ruin.

I am on my way to visit my sister who is living at Wraithwaite Parsonage in order to avoid being killed by my father. I move carefully amongst the trees, because this is the way he may be coming home, tired and edgy from a night's robbery on The King's Strete, some miles to the east of us.

I do not wish to meet my father, but I am not in a position to criticise him, because I too have a secret. I am a traitor. Three people know it, and their silence is all that stands between me and being burnt at the stake.

I reach the rockface that makes the Old Corpse Road

such a quick but difficult short-cut to our neighbouring village, and climb the steps cut into it, breathing in the earthy smells of autumn. Stunted yews and clumps of heather grow out of clefts in the limestone, and I hold on to them to haul myself up. At the top I nearly collapse with fright. Two strange men are asleep amongst the roots of a beech tree, perilously close to the edge of the escarpment. They have swords and axes at their sides. I tiptoe past them. These must be some of the men who walked from all over the district to march on Scotland with my father. Last spring we were raided by Scots, as we often are in this part of the country. Our men were to have raided them back, but this has now been put off until next spring, since our enemies have been forewarned by a fugitive Scot who hid for months in a hermit's cottage in the woods, and discovered our plans.

Oh Robert, where are you now? Are you safe? You may be gone from here, but I wish very much that you could be gone from my mind too.

As I set off through the thinning trees, on to the heathland which surrounds Wraithwaite, I glance back at the two men and silently wish them well. I'm glad this raid has been abandoned, and that they do not have to go to war. Maybe the raid on Scotland will be forgotten altogether now. With Robert gone, and all the preparations for winter needing to be made, anti-Scottish feeling along the border is dying down.

I pass the first cottages along the track to Wraithwaite. A woman is hanging out her washing. We call, "Good morrow, mistress," to each other, and she glances at the sky and adds, "I'm tempting fate. It's going to rain."

A flurry of wind blows the fallen leaves into a spiral ahead of me, and I nod in agreement. "You're right, mistress."

Sometimes, relief just washes over me. Little exchanges like this feel such a luxury, after being on the wrong side of the law for so long. I can pretend to be a respectable member of the community again, working the family farm, preparing to become betrothed to Cousin Hugh. Robert is gone. He wasn't caught, and neither was I. My narrow escape makes me want to be very, very good indeed, even to the extent of marrying Hugh, my childhood playmate, as is expected of me, no matter how ludicrous it might feel.

The parsonage stands on the far side of Wraithwaite Green. It is a beautiful stone house, but in poor repair. There is worm in its doorposts, and its roof slates are pushed out of kilter by tuffets of bright green moss. John Becker, our young and beautiful parson, was my teacher until I turned sixteen earlier this year. He knows my secret. He also saved me from drowning a month back. The warmth which once developed between us during long afternoons in a drowsy classroom has many a time teetered on the verge of becoming something more. I daren't look too closely at my feelings for John Becker, if I am indeed to redeem myself by marrying Hugh.

I walk up to the front of the house. Over the door, carved into the lintel, are the words *Truth and grace be to*

this place. I can hear someone chopping wood behind the house, so when no one answers my knock, I walk round to the back. John is chopping logs. He is shirtless and in coarse woven breeches and leather jerkin. He looks most unlike a priest. He hasn't seen me. I pull my cloak tightly round me and watch him swinging the axe at log after log, splitting them with the grace of long practice. The back of his neck is running with sweat. His dark curls look chaotic and unkempt.

I say softly, "Hello John..." and he turns. He is not an easy person to catch unawares, but I do so then. He stares at me for a moment, then secures the axe with a gentle chop into a new log, and comes over to me. I start to say, "Verity sent word that she wants to see me..." but the words dry in my throat as John Becker holds me by the shoulders and kisses me full on the lips. I feel a shock of such proportions that for a moment I scarcely know where I am. I look up at him. Next to us in the stables his black horse, Universe, stamps and snorts.

John says, "I refuse to go on pretending. I know it's probably too soon after your Scot, Beatie, but..."

There are footsteps behind me, and someone whistling. I turn. It is my sister, Verity.

"Beatie!" She comes out of the house and hugs me, then glances curiously from one to the other of us. "Well, I do declare," she murmurs.

Universe is now trying to kick the stable door down. John unbars the top half of it. "I'd better let him out into

12

the meadow. You two go in." He smiles at Verity. "You have matters to discuss, I think. I'll join you later."

My sister has been here for many weeks now, after angering my father by her desire to marry not her Cousin Gerald, as the family decreed, but James Sorrell, a young neighbouring farmer. James also had to take refuge here from my father's wrath for a while, but is now back tending his own farm, protected by two sturdy bodyguards, George and Martinus. They were once my father's henchmen before they too angered him and were sent away. Many people anger my father. Most end up elsewhere.

I go into the kitchen to greet Mother Bain, John's deaf, elderly housekeeper, then follow Verity up the narrow wooden stairs and along the landing to her room. The parsonage is in even worse fettle inside than out. The beams over our heads are crumbling to dust in places, and the door is so warped that it gapes against its frame when I shut it behind me. Verity's bed, though, is beautiful: pale old oak carved with scrolls and animals, and hung about with fine grey velvet curtains. She climbs up against the heap of bolsters at the head of the bed, and I sit on the end. The feather mattress shifts comfortably to the shape of my legs. Verity is still in her nightsmock, a vast linen article of smothering decency. Her day clothes lie on a cedar chest by the wall. "Don't you want to get dressed?" I ask her.

She twists a corner of the linen sheet round her finger, staring at it. "Nay, Beatie. I have to have some new clothes made. I can't get into these any more. Will you send Germaine over to measure me? I have to tell you this, and I want you to tell Mother, but no one else. I'm with child."

Verity, at fifteen, is a year younger than me. I gape at my younger sister and feel many things. I feel impressed. She has done what I have not. I feel jubilant. There is to be a new life in the family, and myself an aunt. Most of all, I feel terrified. What fearsome things Verity has ahead of her – my father's rage, the whisperings of neighbours, the dangers of childbirth.

"Oh Verity." For a moment I can think of nothing else to say. She is looking at me intently, looking for my reaction. I add stupidly, "James's child."

"Of course. You surely hardly imagined Gerald's."

"Are you happy? How do you feel?"

"Sick, but wonderful. Father has no choice now but to let me marry James."

"Was that why you did it?"

"Heavens no. I did it because I wanted to. Truly Beatrice, you are not being the support I'd hoped."

"I'm sorry. I'm truly glad for you. How long have you and James...?"

"All year. All spring and summer, until we came here and John would not allow it any more." She leans back amongst the bolsters and closes her eyes. "James bought me some ginger root from the pedlar, for the sickness. Would you pass me a piece, please?"

I pass her a blue ginger jar from the top of the clothes

press. "This must have cost him a fortune. He is truly your slave, I think."

She looks at me sharply. "And I his."

I hesitate. "Is it not a problem... that is, might it not at some time become a problem... that he is uneducated? That he cannot read nor write?"

I feel I am on dangerous ground, but Verity simply replies, "No." After a moment she adds, "Anyway, John is going to teach him."

I am suddenly flooded with optimism, and an unrealistic hope that my father will accept the situation. I ask, "Does John know you're with child?"

"He does now. I told him yesterday. He says he'll speak to Father for me." She smiles. "So, Beatie, is our unfortunate father to have a double shock then, judging from what I saw earlier? Are you finally seeing the point of heavenly John?"

I feel a blush rising past my ears. "Verity, you saw nothing. I'm going to marry Hugh. That's all there is to it."

She smiles, and passes me the ginger jar, and I take a piece and half choke on its savage flavour.

By the time I am ready to set off again the rain has set in, a fine drizzle billowing across the green. "You really ought to get yourself another horse." Verity stands with me on the front step. "I know how sad you are that poor Saint Hilda drowned, but you can't keep on walking everywhere."

"Plenty of other people do."

She rolls her eyes. "Take Meadowsweet. Germaine can bring her back for me later."

John comes up behind us. "I'll take you home on Universe, Beatie."

"I'd truly rather walk," I reply, but he has already gone round the side of the house to catch his horse in the meadow. Verity reaches down my cloak from a peg, and Mother Bain comes out of the kitchen to say goodbye.

"Goodbye, Mistress Bain." I bend to kiss her cheek.

"Goodbye. God bless you, lass. Take care of yourself. I feel there is some darkness hanging over you." Mother Bain tends to make these apocalyptic remarks in such a practical tone of voice that they take a moment to sink in. She has a reputation as a seer, and has issued accurate warnings before.

"What is it, Mistress Bain?" I rub my arms to take the gooseflesh away.

She frowns. Her thin hand trembles on my wrist. Then she shakes her head. "Nay. Nought. I know not." She passes her hand back and forth across her eyes, and returns to the kitchen.

Verity drapes my cloak round my shoulders. "You know, Beatie, I think there's a lot you don't tell me. You know all my secrets now. Tell me some of yours. We've lost touch since I left Barrowbeck."

For a moment I consider it. It would be such a relief to talk about Robert, but there would be no point. It would be an extra burden on Verity, having to keep the terrible secret that her sister sheltered the enemy. Just now she is quite burdened enough, and likely to be more so. I shrug. "I have no secrets," I lie. "Except that before, I did not wish to

16

become betrothed to Hugh, and now I do. It is the sensible thing. It isn't as if I loved anyone else – not in the way that you love James. We'll keep the farm in the family, and I'll see more of you again once you're married to James and living just down the valley." I kiss her cheek. "Now that Cousin Gerald cannot marry you, he can marry whomsoever he likes, and everything will work out just as it should."

Verity gives me a cynical look. "How tidy, dear sister. Why do I feel that life is not like that? Anyway, what about..."

She falls meaningfully silent as John reappears at the front door, leading Universe saddled and ready. "Shall we go?" he asks. "Do you mind riding astride? The sidesaddle won't fit us both."

I hesitate, transfixed at the thought of riding all the way to Barrowbeck in such close proximity to John Becker. He adds, "We could go the long, easy way, or quickly by the Old Corpse Road."

"Oh... quickly by the Old Corpse Road. I have to get back for the milking."

I climb up, using the stone water trough as a mounting block before he can lift me, as he had seemed about to. I am becoming more accustomed to the wobbly experience of riding astride, these past weeks, after a lifetime of riding comfortably seated in my sidesaddle. A life of treason does bring some startling new experiences. John swings up behind me. His left hand grips the reins and his right hand grips my waist. He walks the horse forward and I wave to Verity, who pulls a mad, swooning face at me behind John's back.

On the outskirts of Wraithwaite the woman I saw earlier is pulling her washing off the line and dumping it in a big wicker basket. I call to her, "You were right about the rain, mistress."

She stares at us with her hands full of washing. "Aye, Mistress Garth. Indeed I was." She gives John and me a slow, interested look, then glances skywards. "Mebbe you could put in a word for me up there to get it stopped, eh mistress, if you've got the influence?"

I laugh. John halts his horse and asks her, "Do you want to go and hang all that in the parsonage barn, Mistress Thorpe?"

She scrapes her sodden cap off her forehead and answers, "Aye parson, I'd appreciate it. I'll send Alice over. I thank you." Alice, her maidservant, a ten-year-old orphan from a neighbouring village, comes out of the house with another empty washing basket. I notice she has two black eyes.

John says, "Good morrow, Alice," and regards her for a moment, then adds, "I'll call in on my way back, Mistress Thorpe, and have a word with you."

I can feel the two of them watching us go. I glance over my shoulder at John as Universe quickens into a trot. "You do realise it's going to be all over the district by evening, John, that the parson has been out riding with Beatrice Garth at daybreak in the pouring rain."

He laughs, and rests his chin on the top of my head. "Well then, I daresay we shall both be ruined."

Chapter 2

There are more strangers about now, on the plateau and in the woods, armed men who would have marched on Scotland with my father, emerging from amongst the trees, where they have spent the night.

"They'll all be at the tower later," I tell John, "for a paying-off from Father before they go home." We haven't talked much during the journey. The full realisation of Verity's news has been coming over me, and I am deeply apprehensive about my father's reaction.

When we reach the rim of the rockface we both dismount. John says, "You go first. I'll follow right behind with Universe. He dislikes this path. He's a big baby about it. He may need a little coaxing."

"Truly John, I can go on from here by myself. I don't need you to come any further."

He taps his whip against his thigh. "Not with all these moss-troopers about, heavens no. They may be harmless, but we don't know them."

I set off down the rough steps, holding up my skirts with one hand and supporting myself against the damp stone with the other. I turn to watch John pulling on the reins, and Universe's big head stretching out reluctantly. John talks to his horse softly, asking in seductive tones why the animal is making such a fuss, and I feel like making a fuss myself, just to be spoken to in such a way. Universe's round flanks graze the rock sides; he flicks his tail and snorts. Stones clatter down, hitting me. Finally, we all reach the bottom.

John pats his horse's neck, and waits for the animal to calm down. He looks at me and says, "Well, Beatrice." My heart jolts. I pull my hood further forward over my head, even though the rain is easing. John pushes his whip down his boot and scratches his leg. He asks, "Did you love him... your Scot?"

I shiver as a gust of wind is funnelled down through the rift in the rock. I don't feel capable of talking about Robert out here in the woods, where his ghost shrieks at me from every tree.

"I cared about him," I answer stiffly. "Care about him... But love? I think that is another matter. What are you asking me exactly? Whether Robert and I were lovers?"

"Robert? Ah, I never knew his name."

"There's no reason why you should have."

20

"No, I wasn't asking whether you were lovers. I couldn't care less if you'd had every man in the valley."

I give a snort of laughter, but he is being serious, and instantly I feel childish. I ask him, "How old are you, John?"

"Twenty-five."

"I'm sixteen."

"I know, but older than your years, I think. Look, we don't have to talk about this now. I was going to wait for you to get over the Scot, but since you half-drowned, I'm so afraid of losing you..."

I interrupt him. "John, I shall always be grateful to you for saving me..."

"Don't! I don't want to hear that. I don't want to trade on having fished you out of the ocean. There was something between us before that, wasn't there?"

I look back at the rockface. Dazzling streaks of light are stabbing through the clouds above it. John looks too, and for a moment we are both immobilised by the beauty of it. "Yes," I answer. "Yes, there was."

John takes hold of my hand and kisses the palm. "So, can you just tell me it isn't impossible?"

I touch his hair. It is wet from the rain, and still uncombed. I answer, "No, I can't tell you that. It *is* impossible. Verity will be leaving Barrowbeck to farm with James at Low Back. Who will run the farm if I go too? I have to marry Hugh and stay."

For what seems a long time we stare at one another.

21

When we do speak, it is simultaneously, and reduced to politeness. "I should get back, John."

"Have you started your lessons with Cedric yet?" He releases my hand and steadies the horse so that I can remount.

"Not yet. I'm still busy with the winter planting, and stocking the root cellar. There's time enough." Cedric, also known as the Cockleshell Man, is our local healer, a close friend of my mother, and soon to be my teacher in the arts of healing and herbalism.

John and I ride together in silence down through the woods, across a stream, up a steep bank where ferns and tree roots coil out of the earth. I wish we had not had this conversation. Before, I could imagine all sorts of unspoken impossibilities. Now I have been forced to face reality.

Where the trees thin out, Barrowbeck Tower comes into view in its clearing. I glance back at John. "Now I really do want to go on alone, John. It would be better if you were to see Father about Verity and James when the paying-off is over. Let him calm down a bit after handing out all that money. You must be careful of his temper. It's getting more violent than ever."

"I know." John halts the horse and dismounts, and helps me down. He remains with his hands on my waist. Around us, the woods are quiet. Damp spiderwebs show up on the bushes. A flurry of rainwater splatters down on to our faces. He says, "I'll come over this afternoon to speak to your father about Verity."

"It won't be easy."

"I know. He doesn't like me."

"You're always reprimanding him."

"He deserves it."

I kiss him on the cheek. "Goodbye John."

"Goodbye Beatrice." He kisses me on the mouth. Caught unawares, I put my arms round him and kiss him back.

A twig snaps nearby. We both jump. Universe is pricking his ears and glaring into the undergrowth. The bushes rustle and a voice says, "Good morrow, parson. Greetings, mistress." It is Leo, our cowman.

I step back, speechless. John replies, "Good morrow, Leo. How pleasant to see you." Leo is giving us an astounded look. I can see through his eyes my untidied hair and flushed face. I wonder how much he has seen. I try to imagine the repercussions if it reaches my father that his daughter has been seen kissing the parson.

"I must get back." I pull my cloak round me.

John says calmly, as if we had merely been on a nature walk, "Go carefully, Beatrice. I'll watch you as far as the tower," but I hurry away, taking another path which leads me out of their line of vision.

"I'll walk along with you if you're heading back to the rockface, parson," I can hear Leo saying behind me. "There's a sight too many strangers in t'valley today for my liking. I'm just checking a few little snares I've set..." Their voices fade as I rush as far away from them as possible.

I am almost out into the lea now, thinking wildly about what I can say to Leo to ask for his silence. I dawdle at the edge of the trees, and decide to wait for him to come back this way from emptying his snares. The rain is heavier again now, and the wind is rising. Grey planks of rain come skimming over the Pike from the sea. I can see the watchman on the battlements of the tower pulling his hood up. I decide to shelter here and rehearse what I shall say. Leo will surely understand. Everyone employed at Barrowbeck Tower knows the necessity of avoiding my father's temper. I clutch my own hood under my chin to keep the rain out, and this is how I do not see them coming.

"Ha!"

The voice, hands, body all come at once. A massive lout in dark, dirty clothing leaps from the bushes and knocks me to the ground. Another, shorter man follows him. I see a flash of brown jerkin and blue breeches. As I draw in my breath to scream, a stone is rammed into my mouth, crashing against my teeth. Grit and soil choke my voice. A knife flashes before my eyes.

"Back from seeing your fancy man, eh? Let's have your money, lady." The first man pinions my arms whilst the second grapples at my waist to see if I have a purse. I writhe and try to scream, but my throat is full of gravel, and all I can do is cough. I struggle to reach my knife, but the first man finds it before I can and rips it from my belt in triumph. "She's no gold or silver, but I'll have this pretty bit of ironmongery instead." He hooks it into his own greasy green belt, then mutters, "Now what else can we tek off her, eh?"

I lash out, sick with terror. Then suddenly it is as if the first man has flown away. He is lifted off me bodily by a pair of strong, brown hands. "Get away, lady," snaps Leo. "Run for it."

I run.

Chapter 3

I stand behind Father on the battlements. Below us, assembled in the meadow, are the scores of men who walked to Barrowbeck from all over this corner of England. Whatever one might fear or mislike about my father, one can't help admiring his reputation as a warlord. He is certainly better at this than he is at farming.

He raises his hands for silence, and shouts, in a voice for once unslurred, that they should all return home and thank the Lord for sparing them. There will be purses for all of them at the barmkin gate, he tells them. Then he wishes them Godspeed on their journeys home.

The rain has stopped, but a cold wind is blowing across the battlements. The clouds shift. There is a flash of blue sky, brown trees, memories of blue breeches and brown jerkin. I feel unsteady, and support myself against the beacon turret. The pain in my mouth is making me feel sick. I touch the cuts and swellings, now liberally plastered with Mother's marigold balm.

Mother is standing next to Father, her arms folded in her sleeves, smiling serenely. Strange how we keep up appearances in the face of strangers. She turns to me. "Are you all right, Beatrice? You really did come a cropper in the woods, didn't you."

I attempt a smile. "I'm well enough, thank you Mother."

Germaine, music tutor and wardrobe mistress to the household, is standing next to me. She gives me a critical look. "Was it really a fall?" she enquires disbelievingly. Far below, amongst the shuffling crowd, I catch a glimpse of Leo. His gaze is fixed on me.

"Yes," I mutter, averting my eyes from her, from him, from everyone.

If I had not turned back, after I ran from the men, I should not know what I do know now. After Leo rescued me, I fled along the edge of the woods for quite a little way, unwilling to go into the open in the state I was in, my mouth bleeding and my clothes torn. Then I stopped. There were two of those men against Leo. They both had knives. I seized a hefty branch from the ground, and turned back.

Leo met me. He was striding along in his usual way, his hands full of snared songbirds. His mouth was thirled in a horrifying, animal snarl, though. I stood and gaped at him. He said, "Mistress Beatrice, what are you doing still out here? You should be home, getting Kate to tend

27

to your hurts." When I did not reply, he asked, "Do you want to come back with me and let Sanctity see to you?" I glanced beyond him, back along the path and into the undergrowth, and my knees buckled.

Leo supported me through the woods, clutched against his jerkin full of the smells of the cowshed. I could scarcely bear to be touched, but the alternative would have been to fall down. We tottered our way right round the edge of the clearing and down the tiny, briar-tangled path to the cottage he shares with his wife, Sanctity, and their many children. Sanctity helped me to a straw bed in a corner, where I lay on the counterpane of patchworked rabbitskins whilst she mopped my injuries. Sanctity Wilson is a scent-maker by trade, and because she brews potions, she dresses in the fashion of the religious, in high-necked, dark clothing with her hair scraped severely back, to avoid any possibility of being considered a witch. This is how they say Queen Eliza used to dress when she was a princess, as protection against her half-sister, Mary. Several women across the valley dress so. Fear of being accused of witchcraft grows to unreasonable proportions in some.

"Please don't tell anyone what happened, Sanctity," I asked her.

She stood by the small fire under the roof hole, rocking her latest baby, and frowned at me. "Well, I won't if you don't want me to, dear, but you should certainly tell your mother."

I lay back and inhaled the musty smell of rabbitskin, and wondered how much Leo had told her of what had happened. All I knew was that no one would hear any of it from me. My mouth would heal. I had not lost any teeth. My clothes would mend. I heaved myself up and sat with my back against the wall. Next to me a tree was growing as part of the wall. One of the house beams had taken root, and was calloused all over where branches kept having to be lopped off. The smell of cow dung, sweet and familiar, came from walls newly rendered for winter. From the tripod over the fire, where Sanctity was brewing scent, the fragrance of rosewater competed with the dead-flesh smell of the rush lights. On a shelf by the door stood bottles of sticky, brown fluid, full of the perfumes of summer.

"Take one of these," she said. "Lavender will calm you down."

I can smell it on me now as I stand on the battlements, watching my father move to the parapet and raise his hands in blessing. "Go your ways peacefully," he shouts. "There's ale as well as a shilling for you, down at the barmkin gate. God bless you." I can feel his relief that the opportunity for having a drink himself is drawing nearer. The sunlight brightens, and flashes on something amongst the men below. Leo is polishing his broad-bladed knife. In a moment of light-headedness I imagine it hissing through leather, grating on bone.

My father steps back, hands on hips, face flushed and smiling. He is pleased with his performance. He comes towards us waving his pouncet box to perfume the air, as if to say, that's enough of the stinking masses, back to more delicate matters. He peers at my injured face and demands, "What's the matter with you, girl?"

"Nothing, Father. I fell in the woods." I ponder how strange it is that he can still undermine my antipathy so easily, with just one look of concern.

"Come Germaine, Beatrice, will you help me serve ale to the travellers?" Mother ushers us towards the spiral staircase. "Are you fit to do it, Beatrice, or do you want to lie down? Kate can help with the ale."

"I'm late with the milking, Mother. I'm sorry. I should go down to the cowsheds and see if Tilly Turner has managed on her own."

"I don't suppose she will have. Go on then. We don't want them getting milk fever. Whatever were you doing instead?"

"I went to see Verity."

Suddenly I have all my mother's attention. "How is she?" she demands under her breath, so that my father will not hear.

"She's with child," I whisper.

Mother stops, one foot poised, at the top of the spiral staircase. For a long moment she says nothing, then she murmurs, "In that case, the sooner we get her home the better."

A good milker can do a cow in a few minutes. Tilly Turner takes about an hour. She grumbles and mutters about how sore her fingers are, instead of singing to the animals so that they relax and let the milk down. I have to say that singing to cows is not my idea of the best way to start a day either, but now I sit back-to-back with her on a low stool in the cowshed, and hum a tune under my breath, partly from sheer relief at doing something safe and ordinary. The cow's warm, gurgling side is against my cheek, and the rhythmic stroking of fingers against palms, the slap of milk into the wooden bucket, combine to soothe away the terrors of what happened to me. For once, I am even thankful for the distraction of Tilly's tales of injustice and martyrdom. I sneak a look at my aching knees. They are bruised black where I fell. What happened with John now seems so remote and unreal that I don't feel absolutely sure it took place. It seems more like one of my long-ago daydreams about him.

After the milking, we put on our shawls to soften the drag of the yokes across our shoulders, and toil up the hill with the buckets swinging wide on their ropes, past the crowd, through the barmkin, to the dairy in its rock cave. This is when the screaming starts.

My first thought is that the Scots are attacking us again. Tilly and I look at one another, duck out of our yokes so that the buckets bump to the flagstone floor, and run outside. The screaming goes on and on. We race out of the barmkin. The crowd gathered by the gate is now hurrying up the slope, past the tower, towards the woods.

"What is it?" I ask Germaine, who has remained by the trestle table with a jug of ale in her hand.

She shrugs. "I have no idea." She pours a mug for me, since all her other customers have gone. Now we can see two of Father's henchmen emerging from the woods. They are carrying a wooden hurdle. Two homesteaders from the valley follow them, carrying another. The screaming has stopped, but several women from the valley come rushing past us, sobbing. Germaine shoots out her hand and grabs the arm of the first of them.

"Whatever is happening, Betsy?"

"A murder, madam. Two of the men from away have been killed in the forest. We found them..." She gives a gasping moan. "Their throats were cut. Sliced oppen."

I turn away, hands to my mouth. Germaine lets go of the woman, who hurries away down the hill after her companions. She turns to me. "A murder in these parts – how truly shocking. Your Scotsman did *go*, I presume?"

I take a mouthful of ale, and walk away up the hill, ignoring her. I feel too sickened to be angry. The bodies are at the door of the gatehouse, surrounded by a silent crowd. There is no other way in except past them, unless I were to go by the secret passage under the floor of the dairy, which is out of the question with so many people about. My father steps forward. "Put 'em in t'wood cellar. 'Tis a poor end for those who only wished to serve their country." The crowd nods and mutters. A few of the older people are crossing themselves, and for once my father lets it pass.

A piece of bloodstained bedsheet covers the upper part of the first body. The man's arms have slipped off the edge of the hurdle. As the henchmen lift it by poles at either end, the arms flap, as if alive, and for a moment I wonder if the man really is still alive after all. Then the bedsheet slides off completely, and his lolling head is revealed, his throat open in a frightful turtle smile, his brown jerkin and blue breeches drenched in blood.

The face and shoulders of the second body are covered, but there are drops of congealed blood on the arms, crossed over his greasy green belt.

When the bodies have been taken down the curving slope to the wood cellar, I make my way up the east staircase and along a twisting passage to the east landing. I need above all to be alone. The jakes on the east landing is the nastiest of our several latrines in the outer walls of the tower, a last resort for the desperate when all others are in use. Here I can be reasonably sure of being undisturbed. I wonder if Leo's son, Dickon, our laystow boy among his many other duties, has emptied the privies today from the hatches one floor down. Understandably, he looks for any excuse to avoid this particular work. Kate, our cook, has been known to pursue him round the tower with a meat cleaver, to persuade him to greater diligence.

The stink, and the hum of flies, make this little sanctuary an unlovely place to be, but peaceful. It is dark

33

here, with only a faint luminescence from the jakes itself. I light a candle on the linen chest, and carry it in with me, propping the broken door shut with it.

I have been pushing away the terrible thoughts in my head, but now they are unavoidable. The sight of the two dead men as I saw them in the woods keeps flashing across my mind. Sometimes they are alive again, and coming at me with the unexpectedness of the attack. Sometimes they are dead, lolling and staring. It is my fault, all my fault. I want to escape from it, from all the events of today, to stay for ever in this dark place with my guttering candle, to be walled in like a Papist nun. My mouth hurts. My knees and ribs and arms hurt. I want to slough off my flesh the way that grass snakes shed their skins. Yet it remains, white and sluglike, painful and unsheddable. The thought that I kissed John earlier appals me. Isn't he supposed to be spiritual and remote? Isn't that what I like about him? I want to scream that no, I am not to be touched, not by attackers, not by lovers, not by anyone. The urge to scream, in the way that the women who found the bodies screamed, comes roaring up from my feet, but all that emerges from my mouth is a tiny mew, like a kitten's.

Chapter 4

There is something freakish about today; everything feels abnormal and unfamiliar. I'm beginning to wonder if the bang on my head was worse than I thought. There's Hugh for a start, sweet Hugh, fair-haired and funny, whom I thought I knew, but who now looms at me with a predatory look that is new. He has been fussing over my bruises, and teasing me tenderly about being legless so early in the day. Dear Lord, it is grotesque. Normally he would have joked uncaringly, and suggested a ride in the woods, or target practice, to take my mind off it. I wonder if Uncle Juniper has been advising him on techniques for wooing reluctant females. I look at them now, across the crowded kitchen, drinking and conversing by the gatehouse arch. Uncle Juniper, whose real name everyone has long forgotten, is hunched over and gesturing wildly, clearly describing something deeply bloodthirsty. I wonder for a moment if I am really going to be able to do this – seriously do it – marry Hugh and see my future settled for ever within these confines.

I decide to go and hide in the chimney corner. I seat myself facing the flames, my back against the hot stone, my skirts tucked in under my knees. The kitchen fire is roaring, and a tall blackjack of ale stands near me, on a griddle winched to one side away from the flames. Steam curls along the hot poker which Kate has plunged into it, and there is a smell of singed flesh where the poker leans against the lip of the big leather jug. The men who carried the corpses in appear up the slope from the wood cellar at the far side of the kitchen. Kate looks round from plucking thrushes at the table. "Help yourselves to ale, lads," she calls. "I reckon you'll be needing it."

The smell of newly drawn feathers mingles with the other smells of the kitchen, live flesh sweating and dead flesh singeing, and I realise that my mood is shifting. Instead of feeling shaky and terrified, now I am starting to feel angry. I am angry with the men who attacked me, angry that Leo's saving of me had to take such a terminal form, leaving me as good as a murderer, angry at the droning throb of my bruises, at the loss of my knife, at the confrontation awaiting us all when my father finds out about Verity, and above all, angry that such a good friend and cousin as Hugh has to be turned into a husband for me, by those too old and set in their ways to know what they are talking about.

The four men come over and ladle hot ale into their

tankards. They nod to me but I pretend to be asleep. Leo's son, Dickon, is mending the bellows on the opposite side of the fire from me, pleating new leather into the sides where the old has cracked, and if it were not for the tapping of his hammer I should probably indeed have slept.

My parents have not arrived yet. I find myself practising speeches to calm my father's temper when he finds out about Verity and realises that the family's plans to marry her to Gerald, and keep the two farms within the family, are in ruins. He beat her once for her involvement with James Sorrell, and he tried to kill James. Now, faced with the inevitable fact that they must marry, and quickly, I simply cannot imagine what he will do.

I wonder, too, what Gerald's reaction will be. I watch him, a younger, darker, more angry-looking version of his brother, talking to Germaine in a far corner of the kitchen, stooping over her as she sits in a tall-backed chair putting tiny stitches into a pair of lace sleeves. Somehow, I don't think he is going to be too distressed.

Aunt Juniper appears beside me. She points at Gerald and Germaine. "Just look at that, will you Niece? He spends so much time talking to that skivvy that he scarcely gets to see your sister at all. He should be over at Wraithwaite Parsonage at this very moment. I really don't know what's becoming of this family."

"Germaine's a bit more than a skivvy, Auntie," I reply, wondering why I am defending the person who annoys me more than any other in this household.

"Nonsense! She's a serving woman and she's twice his age, and what Gerald wants to be doing talking to her is a mystery to me."

People near us glance round and grin. I suspect Aunt Juniper is the only person to whom it is a mystery.

Mother comes in, her cheeks pink and her hair escaping from its cap. "That's the last of the strangers on their way!" she declares. "I never thought I'd thank a Scot for anything, but I do thank him for forcing our men to stay at home." She crosses to the hearth. "I'm going to open my elder wine. Give me a hand, Juniper. We have good reason to celebrate."

"Them downstairs don't," mutters Kate.

I peer round the corner of the hearth as my mother and aunt lift out two wooden-stoppered clay flagons from the proving oven. "Give Kate a drink, Beatie, for pity's sake," Mother orders me. "I can't be doing with her endless griping. Get out the silver goblets. I'm not using pewter any more. Cedric says it rots your brain." She thumps the flagons on to the table and stares round her for a moment, hands on hips. "I can still scarce credit that the march on Scotland is stopped."

"For now." Kate slams her rolling pin into a soft mound of dough. "We wouldn't have given up so easily in my day – one Scot and a whole war called off – I never heard the like of it."

I take down the best goblets one by one from the dresser, whilst Mother and Aunt Juniper unstopper the flagons. I remember Father coming home with these goblets one Michaelmas, fifty of them in finest silver, beautifully wrought with patterns of herons and reeds. When I have passed everyone a goblet of wine, I go to sit on the bench at the long table, and as I do so there is a commotion in the gatehouse arch and my father comes crashing in. "What's the merrymaking?" he bellows, and lurches towards the kitchen table. "Are the dead men laid out?" He throws an arm round Kate who is putting the lid on the thrush pie. "What's in t'tart, Kate?"

"Songbirds." Kate peers up into his face and scowls at him. "Cupshotten already, master? You wasted no time."

"Aye well, Katie, you see we don't have any time to waste, do we, as them downstairs will surely warrant."

"You're right there, master." She stabs the pie crust three times with her pastry knife, muttering, "Father, Son, Holy Ghost."

"Amen," intones my father, and the two of them nod gloomily at one another.

I pour myself more wine. The sweet-smelling brew rocks to and fro in the shiny round bowl, red, maroon and purple in the shifting firelight. I see my mother leading my aunt away, arm round her shoulders, heads bent, to seat themselves in my place in the chimney corner. My mother is talking. My aunt is listening. I realise she is being told the news about Verity. With a surge of longing I want my own sister here, back where she belongs. I have no one here now who thinks as I do, who is prepared to laugh with me at the absurdity of our elders, and to defy them with me when necessary.

39

Suddenly Leo is at my side. I jump. I had not seen him arrive. I take a large swallow of wine, and then have to lean my elbows on the table to keep myself steady. He sits down next to me and asks, "How are you, lady?"

"Well enough." I realise how ungracious I sound, and stand up to pour him some wine. "I thank you, Leo, for enquiring."

He rummages at his waist. I catch the flash of a blade. "You'll be wanting this back." He produces my knife from where it was pushed into a sheath with his own. I stare at it, so familiar, with its horn handle and curved blade. "Was this what you used?" I ask him, appalled. Our eyes meet. It is as if we were alone in an empty kitchen. He makes a circle of his finger and thumb, touches it to his own broad-bladed knife, then to his lips.

"Nay," he says. "I used my own. It was a pleasure, lady."

There seems to be nothing more to say. My profuse and incoherent thanks of earlier cannot be repeated, back in this normal world. I try to work out my feelings. I try to work out whether there was anything else he could have done. I feel a strange closeness to Leo, like kinship. We share one another's secrets. Perhaps this is how you do feel towards someone who has saved your life. After a while Leo says, "I'll be saying nowt about the other, neither, mistress."

I have to think for a moment what he means, then I realise he means John, and the kiss. "Oh. Well thank you. And... Leo, you can be sure... I shan't be saying anything to anyone about what happened, either."

He nods. A pact has been sealed.

Germaine comes round with cates, tiny squares of bread fried in goose grease, wafer-thin slices of salty black pudding, candied gooseberries, marchpane comfets. We help ourselves from two big platters. My father, leaning lopsidedly on the chopping block, slips off when he tries to help himself, and bangs his cheek. With a spluttering curse he heaves himself upright and crosses the room to the fireplace as if dancing the galiard, relieves himself into the flames, then pirouettes back. He picks up one of the flagons with both hands and drinks from it. The wine spills down his neck, staining his ruff. "Damnation to the Scots!" he shouts. The assembly raises its goblets. The fire flares brilliant, unfocused, into the room. Germaine goes round lighting the candles, and they shine with rainbow haloes in the smoky air. Leo pats me on the shoulder, and leaves.

As the afternoon draws on, Kate puts on barley broth to stew, for those who might wish to recover their senses later. I grow weary of explaining my injuries to people, and wonder if I would have minded less if my explanations had been the truth.

Tilly Turner, curled on the oak settle by the fire, faints with great drama, smashing her head on the hearth, and has to be revived with a burning feather under her nose. Mother pats her cheeks back and forth with more vigour than is strictly necessary, and William the henchman assists her out into the fresh air. Moments later he returns with a flurry, calling to Father, "Master, parson's come out of t'wood."

"Woodworm's come out of t'wood," my father mutters, staggering to his feet. William comes over and props him up.

"Is he to come in, master? Is the parson to come in?"

Everyone waits for my father's answer. They all know his opinion of John Becker.

I creep across the kitchen and take over Tilly's place on the oak settle, where I can be hidden by its high sides. I had forgotten that John was coming. I'm horrified at the thought of him seeing me hot, sweaty and half-drunk. Germaine comes to sit next to me. "Hiding, Beatrice?" she enquires. I nod carefully, fearful that my head might fly off. Germaine laughs. "He might consign the rest of us to hellfire, but not you, my dear."

To me, the kitchen already seems like Hell – hot and full of people whose misdeeds are about to catch up with them.

My father blunders across the kitchen, stumbling over chairs and benches. "Might as well show him in, William lad," he shouts. "Yon whining preacher could do with a drink, I daresay. Can't do aught but improve him."

Everyone's gaze swings towards the entrance. We hear the front door crash open, then William's voice. "They're in the kitchen, sir." My father prepares himself grandly, feet apart, hands on hips. William comes back into the kitchen and whispers something to him.

"Nay lad," my father replies loudly, "I'll see him in here. Is he too grand for the kitchen? Eh? Eh?" His voice is thick. His nose stands out purple with a slight knob on the end where a vein pulsates. William departs, and returns with John.

It is a shock to see him, all the more so because he looks absurdly pale and sober and clean, in comparison with the rest of us. I see how we must look to him, red-faced and rowdy. It dawns on me how unsuitable a match I would be for John, or indeed for any decent and respectable person outside the family. "Good day." He looks round and addresses everyone, then turns to my father. "May I speak to you privately, Squire Garth?"

He is beautiful, beautiful and solemn. I am starting to remember what it was like this morning. He hasn't seen me yet.

"You can talk to me here, lad. No one's going to be eavesdropping," my father answers. Everyone turns away and pretends to be busy doing something else. "We're all celebrating being alive." Father waves his arms. "Even you can understand that, I daresay. You'll take a cup of elder?"

"Thank you." John smiles at my mother, who is already reaching down another goblet. "It's worth the journey here just for your elder wine, Columbine," he says. Mother nods – she obviously realises why he is here – and his attempt to soothe the atmosphere hangs awkwardly in the air. He turns back to my father. "Sir, it is important that I speak to you alone, upstairs in your rooms please, about a matter of great importance."

Everyone is listening. Germaine stands idly chipping flakes of dried food from the knife marks on the table with her fingernail. Kate studies her pie. The henchmen nod meaninglessly to each other, in a pretence of conversation. Suddenly Aunt Juniper rises from the chimney corner and marches towards John. "Young man, I cannot imagine how you permitted this to happen," she snaps. Silence falls across the kitchen.

"Juniper..." Mother tries to hustle her away. "It's better if we talk about this in private."

"Nonsense. Do you imagine you can keep this disgraceful secret for even a moment, Columbine? My niece was in your care, Parson Becker..." She stands before him, clearly almost speechless with fury, and shakes her finger in his face. Mother hurries round her and takes hold of my father's arm.

"Come, Husband. The parson wishes to speak to us privately."

My father brings his fist down on the table with a terrifying thump. "*What* is this? What brings you here, parson?"

John swings his gaze from my father to Aunt Juniper. "This happened before Verity was in my care, madam, indeed it happened whilst she was supposedly in the care of your two Barrowbeck households. Now please excuse me." He turns back to my father. "I have already said that I wish to speak to you privately, sir." He gestures towards the stairway. "Now, will you kindly accompany me?"

My father is silent for a moment. He releases his arm from Mother's grip, steadies himself and brushes crumbs

44

from the front of his doublet. Then he says, "I had assumed you had come to do the job you're paid for, parson, to bless the dead. There have been murders here today. We shall find the murderer, you can count on it, and then you will have the opportunity to lead that lost soul to repentance, afore we hang him. These are the jobs you're paid to do, sir, and not, I think, to decide where and when your betters should speak to you."

John gives a brief sigh of vexation. "Very well then, Squire Garth, let's go and bless the dead. Perhaps you would be so good as to accompany me?"

My father nods graciously, and leads the way towards the wood cellar, followed by John and my mother. Everyone watches in silence as they go. Aunt Juniper is in tears. I put my arms round her.

"Did you know about this, Beatrice?" she asks. I nod. She sinks on to the bench and covers her face with her hands. Hugh and Gerald hurry over to her, whilst Uncle Juniper watches nervously from a distance, fidgeting from one foot to the other.

"What's happened?" Hugh asks me, and since everyone will soon know anyway, I answer, "Verity and James are expecting a baby."

Kate splutters over her pie. "James Sorrell? Yon farm lad? Nay, never!"

I turn on her. "That's enough, Kate."

She tightens her lips in outrage, marches to the hearth, flings her pie into the baking oven and slams the heavy iron door shut with a clang that echoes round the walls.

Aunt Juniper rises to her feet and sweeps out of the kitchen, saying tersely to William, "Saddle our horses, please." Her husband and sons follow her.

People are starting to take in the news. There is a shocked murmuring across the kitchen, and a growing feeling of apprehension as we wait for my father's reaction. It does not come. Instead, when he returns alone to the kitchen, he seats himself calmly at the head of the table and says, "My friends, we have found our murderer. I want four men to come with me to Low Back Farm at once, to arrest James Sorrell." He points over people's heads to William and three other henchmen standing by the gatehouse arch.

"No!" My mother has followed him up the slope from the wood cellar. "This is madness, Husband. James can't possibly have killed anyone."

"Silence!" my father shouts. "We have a witness." He beckons to Michael, a new henchman who joined us last Lady Day, a tall, sly man who never looks anyone in the eye. "Michael, you witnessed this murder, did you not?"

A look of complete bafflement crosses Michael's stupid face for a moment, then he nods vigorously. "Aye, master."

"Say what you saw."

"It was Master Sorrell as did it, master."

"And you'll bear witness to that, before the magistrate?"

"Aye master."

"Then we shall see Master James Sorrell locked in

46

Lancaster Castle before this week is out, to await the assizes and the hangman's noose."

I feel cold, as if there were no fire, no heat. I stand up and climb on to the oak settle. People look at me. I call out, "Father?"

He scowls. "What are you doing, girl? Get down."

"Father, these injuries... look at them." I hold out my arms, touch my fingers to my swollen mouth. "I didn't fall in the forest, Father. Those two men are dead because they attacked me. They tried to hurt me. I lashed out at them, and I must have accidentally..."

My father gapes. Suddenly all his drunkenness is gone. He moves with startling speed and before I know what is happening, he has pulled me off the settle, pinioned my arms behind me and is half-carrying me out of the room. I scream and struggle. People rush forward. I think to myself, where is John, where is Hugh, where are they when you need them?

My father is very strong. My ankles knock painfully against the edges of the stone stairs as he hauls me up the spiral staircase. I can hear my mother pattering behind, crying out, "Be careful, Francis! You're going to hurt her worse than ever." Voices from the kitchen, raised and incredulous, fade away behind us.

When we reach my room Father drags me inside and slams the door, and both my parents stand with their backs against it. I try to get past them and escape, but my father pushes me away.

47

"Father, this is ridiculous. Let me..."

"You'll stay there until you get this idea out of your head," he interrupts me. His voice is surprisingly mild. "You've had a knock on the head and it's turned you daft, girl."

"Mother..." I appeal.

She comes forward and puts her arms round me. "Sweeting, for once your father is right." She glances at him sternly to neutralise any effect this unusual state of agreement might have. "You've had more ale and wine than is good for you, and a knock on the head too. It's addled your brains. You don't want to be saying anything which people might misinterpret. Now we all know you didn't kill those men. However, I think there are things here that you're not telling us, Beatrice. So do as your father says and stay here for the time being. You can decide in your own time when to tell us the truth. I'll send Kate up with some barley broth." My parents bow to each other politely and walk out of the room.

"No!" I shout. "No, I won't stay here!" My voice cracks humiliatingly.

My mother turns round, the big iron key in her hand. "I'll return shortly, Beatrice. First, I want to have a word with Parson Becker." She closes the door and the key grates in the lock. Their raised voices retreat down the stairwell, growing angrier with every step.

Chapter 5

Occasionally in life there comes a moment when you just have to lie down and say, for now I can do nothing; for now I give up. I do so then. I lie down on my bed with my face to the wall. Then I get up, close the bed-curtains and lie down again in darkness. I feel betrayed. How *could* they? Worst of all, my mother has colluded in my imprisonment. How could *she* who defies convention herself? I thought I knew her. I have never felt more let down.

"Beatrice, it's for your own good," she says when she returns an hour later and whips the bed-curtains open. "People heard what you said. Stupid, stupid girl! Do you want to be hanged for murder? I don't believe for a moment that you did it. You're obviously just trying to protect James. Do you think that great lummox can't look after himself?

We've told everyone you have a brain fever, brought on by the fall, and didn't know what you were saying. Now we have to let it die down, so please be good and stay here in your room for a week or so, while people forget about it."

"And James, Mother?" I enquire. "Is he in the meantime to be hunted down and hanged?"

"Well, presumably not, if you tell us who really committed this murder. It wasn't James, was it? Are you going to tell me what really happened? It may not go so badly for the murderer, if he was indeed saving you from the men. Who was it, Beatrice? You do know, don't you?"

I turn my face away. "No. I don't know."

"*Was* it James?"

"No."

"Then you do know. Come along, child, who was it?"

"I don't know!" I shout.

My mother turns away. "Then I'm afraid your father is set on incriminating James." She crosses to the door. I jump off the bed and follow her.

"Mother, you can't allow it! It's obvious that Father only wants him out of the way because of Verity."

"I can't stop him, Beatrice. I have tried."

"Then I shall tell everyone – the magistrate, everyone – that I did it."

My mother walks out and slams the door behind her, calling through it, "Not from here you won't, Beatrice."

It is ridiculous – ridiculous and humiliating. I cannot quite understand how I managed to get myself into this situation, from which there appears no way out. I have heard of girls being locked away before, but never dreamt it could happen to me.

They manage my imprisonment very well. I almost feel as if they have been waiting to do this, as if there were some unspoken agreement between everyone that I have been getting above myself. By the end of the first week I am beginning to think I truly do have brain fever, the boredom and sense of being trapped are so great. By night I lie awake listening to the shrieks of owls, and by day to the screams of pigs, as autumn slaughter gets under way along the valley. It is necessary work, so that we may all eat through the winter, and make soap and black puddings and leather gloves. Usually on our farm I decide on the pig, and the day it shall be dispatched. This year my mother tells me they are managing the autumn work quite well without me – the barns are well filled and she will be asking Leo to kill one of the pigs in a fortnight. There will be no more Scots this year, so now we can settle down to preparing for winter.

One day I hear sounds of fighting from further down the valley, and I learn later from Germaine that a pitched battle has been fought at Low Back Farm. Verity has, it seems, moved there from the parsonage, and my father and his henchmen have been attempting to retrieve her, and to capture James Sorrell. However, James now has henchmen of his own, and my father's forces were driven off.

I have a few visitors, always with the door locked behind them and a henchman on duty outside. It is mortifying. They come as if to an invalid, all keeping up the ghastly pretence that I am ill with brain fever and must be enclosed for my own good. Mother, to whom I cannot bring myself to speak, looks concerned and tired. Kate brings hot possets and titbits from the kitchen, and the news that John has called every day but has not been allowed in. Germaine comes with her sewing, and books of poetry to read to me. One day I wake from an afternoon doze to find Gerald here with her. From where I lie in the dark recesses of my bed they are framed by a gap in my bed-curtains, clutching each other in a wild embrace. I watch the soft triangle of Germaine's underjaw as they kiss frantically, and am filled with sadness. I think of Robert, and the moment I chose not to go to Scotland with him, and for the first time I believe I made the wrong decision.

The weather turns cold and windy. Kate lights the fire in the chimney hole in my room, and the draught under the door fills the chamber with smoke and half suffocates me. I sit with tears pouring down my cheeks, only partly because of the smoke. Kate jerks her chin at the door which Michael, the sly new henchman, has locked behind her. "I don't hold with this," she says, "shutting you in here when there's work to be done. Farm's going to rack and ruin. Brain fever my arse. You're no dafter than you ever were. Your father gets nobbut gristle from me till he lets you out." She hammers on the door for it to be opened.

"Kate," I whisper, "Kate, please let me out. Please, I beg you."

From outside comes the sound of Michael unlocking the door. Kate turns her short-sighted gaze on me. "Oh lass, we'd all fain let you out if we could, but what would your father do? Our lives wouldn't be worth the living, if we still had them to live."

Michael stands in the doorway, listening. "Best be careful, Goody Kate," he says with a grin.

I could have warned him, had I been so inclined, that it is deeply unwise to antagonise Kate, but I do not, since it will be a pleasure to ponder the frightful things which she will now do to his food.

"I thank you for your advice, lad," she says to him as he pulls the door to. "For certain it will guide my actions." Michael gives a self-satisfied laugh.

Sunday comes, and I am not even allowed to go to church. John comes over again afterwards. I hear his horse, which has a distinctive, petulant whinny, and I catch a glimpse of him arriving as I peer out of the awkward angle of my window. My father, whom I can hear coughing and wheezing upstairs, does not go down, and no one opens the door to the visitor. After a while John gives up hammering on it and instead stands shouting up at the battlements. Eventually he comes round the tower looking for my window. I rap on the glass and finally he sees me. He stands up in his saddle, then ducks, as a stone flies off the battlements at him. I can hear my father shouting above, "Give that bow to me, lad, if you're too lily-livered to use it! What, you've never shot a parson? What have you been doing all your life? Call yourself a henchman?" An arrow hisses past my window, and another, and I recoil in horror, then realise as they land quivering in the grass that they are not intended to hit John – my father's aim is better than that – but merely to cause him to go away. He does not go away, however. He sits there for a long time, arms folded, whilst arrows fly past him, then he turns his horse and moves away to the edge of the woods, a one-man siege.

By Monday I have had enough. I have looked at all ways of escaping. It might well be possible to break my window with the warmingstone from my bed. My bedsheets tied together could possibly reach near enough the ground for me to jump. The problem is that the tower is too well guarded for me to get away. There is always a watchman on the battlements, and they fear my father too much to turn a blind eye. I have considered bribery, and ponder what it would take to bribe somebody to leave the door unlocked. What can you offer someone, to risk their life? Do I indeed ever want anyone to risk their life for me again? In the end, when it happens, it is in an unplanned way. Kate brings my supper on Monday evening, and tells me that my father and his men are to attack Low Back Farm again tonight, under cover of darkness. They believe that today's rough weather, which is rapidly turning into a wild night, will enable them to creep right up to the farmhouse undetected.

"If everyone's going down to Low Back Farm, who'll be on watch?" I ask her.

"Leo, that slitgut, him as should be off tending t'cows."

Before she has finished speaking, I have made up my mind.

As night falls, I can hear them preparing for the attack. Swords scrape and tinderboxes click. The smell of hot tar rises up the tower walls as arrows are wrapped and dipped. I offer up a prayer for Verity and James, then rip the sheets off my bed, drag the clothes press against the door, retrieve the warmingstone and wait for it to become silent outside.

It takes a long time. My stomach churns with nervousness as I wait, straining my ears. Raindrops beat against my window, driven by the wind. I can see nothing beyond the wet glass but a great darkness full of moving shadows.

The gale battering the tower becomes too loud for me to know whether or not all the men have gone. I can only hope it is also loud enough to cover the sounds of my escape. Kate will be asleep in her room behind the kitchen hearth. Germaine, I do not know. I just hope she is off on one of her unexplained absences.

For a moment I cannot do it. I hold the green granite warmingstone, and can think of nothing but how expensive this fragile glass was, and how cold my room used to be before the window was glazed. I listen. Will Leo really be on the battlements in this weather, with no Scots likely and no one to check his vigilance? What will he do if he sees me? It is, after all, for his sake that I am imprisoned here. I swing the stone high above my head, and bring it crashing against the window.

In a second it is gone, precious glass smashing and tinkling away into the night. I am almost knocked back against the bedpost by the wind roaring in. Now I must hurry. I stuff the knotted bedsheet out of the window, but it blows back over and over again. When it is finally out, it will not hang down. I think of Robert climbing the wall on his swaying rope ladder, his face at the window, my hands pushing him and the terrible injuries he sustained when he fell. The height and the precariousness of these walls seem suddenly fearsome and impossible.

There is a lull in the gale. Is this the moment to go? No one appears to have heard me so far. The bedsheet whips round and catches on some shards of glass. I free it, prise the fragments out, check that the other end of the sheet is still firmly knotted round the leg of the bed. There is a sound from above. I must just go, never mind the sheer drop and the frightening fragility of the knotted sheets. I drag my cloak round me and climb backwards on to the deep windowsill. The wind rips at my skirts and I feel as if I am being sucked through the narrow aperture before I am ready. I kneel there, holding on to the sheet and the window-ledge, staring back into the room, and as

I do so, the clothes press which was jammed against the door starts to move. It judders along the floor towards me. I stare at it, paralysed. Someone is coming in, and I hadn't even heard the key.

With the opening door, the gale rushes right through the room. Hangings rattle and ash swirls. "What's the matter with this door?" enquires a voice. "I knocked, mistress; is everything all right?" With a final push, Leo enters. "Sweet Jesu!" He rushes across the room and grabs my arms as I frantically try to lower myself out.

"No!" I hit out at him. "No! Let me go, Leo! Let me go at once!"

Almost effortlessly he drags me back in and sets me on my feet in the chamber.

"Leo, how dare..."

"Shh." He goes to the window, pushes the knotted bedsheet out again and watches it spiral around the window space as the wind catches it. Then he crosses to the door, holds it open for me and bows. "An easier way, mistress. I heard nothing, with this terrible wind blowing."

We look at one another. All manner of things are in that look, acknowledgements of deeds done and faith kept. Leo looks away first, as he unhooks a piece of hessian twine from his belt. "Come on, lady, out with you." I step on to the tiny landing that leads to the spiral staircase, and watch as Leo loops the twine round a leg of the clothes press, then hooks it under the door. "Anything

57

more you wish to take?" he asks. I look back, and shake my head. I have all I intend to take bundled into a large pocket attached at my waist. I watch as Leo closes the door and locks it, then pulls both ends of the twine so that the clothes press scrapes back into position, barricading the door on the inside.

"Thank you." My voice is hoarse. I have to clear my throat. "Thank you, Leo."

"Come lady, we'd best get you moving. I'll saddle a horse. You'll be going to the parsonage?" I nod. Down in the blowy barmkin, whilst Leo puts my sidesaddle on Germaine's little mare, Mattie, I stand and watch my bedsheet high on the tower wall, flailing about in the rising gale.

Chapter 6

*I*f I had not gone to stay at John's, everything would have been different.

For my first few days at the parsonage, I am filled with melancholy. I miss my home, my room, the rhythms of life on the farm. I have to remind myself that I was a prisoner there, and that the past week was intolerable. On the many occasions in those first few days when my father comes beating at the parsonage door, only to be turned away, I feel almost glad to hear him, simply for the familiarity of his rage. From a small, high window I watch him walk back to where his horse is tethered at the trough on the green, and I see that he has a severe limp, presumably from his latest encounter with James and the men of Low Back Farm.

My mother does not visit me, but instead sends such

of my clothes as I might need for a short stay, and a note berating me for supposedly risking breaking my neck by climbing out of the window, and commanding me to mind my tongue and under no circumstances to speak about the deaths of the two strangers.

The day after my arrival John and I sit in the kitchen where Mother Bain is baking bread. Smoke rolls through the late afternoon sunlight as she lifts out trays of flat, black loaves from the bread oven, and tips them on to the wooden rack. The bitter scents of smoke and rye fill the kitchen.

"I'll mull some ale." John looks tired. He has been up half the night with one of his parishioners who is dying of consumption. "Will you have some ale?" he asks Mother Bain.

"Nay lad. The bread's done and I'm off to lie down. I daresay the pair of you are safe to be left?"

This has become a joke between the three of us. John watches her go to her room behind the hearth, which she took over when James left, since stairs have now become too much for her.

"We should get a chaperone for you," John says when she has gone. "It's well enough to joke, but your being here is a very different matter from Verity's being here. I don't think it can be entirely unknown to people that you and I have some fondness for each other." He pushes the poker into the fire to heat. "I want you to stay. I want you to stay as long as you're willing to, and I want there to be no whisper of scandal to spoil it."

I do not distress him by telling him that there is already considerably more than a whisper of scandal surrounding my presence here, amid speculation about my imprisonment and escape. I have seen groups of villagers on the green casting curious glances at the parsonage, and we have had a stream of visitors here these first few days, bringing pies and puddings. They say it is to welcome me to Wraithwaite, but I know it is in fact to see the state I am in, since my father's notorious temper appears to have driven yet another daughter to seek refuge here. On the occasions when my father comes galloping up to the parsonage door, a surprising number of people appear to have business requiring their attendance on the village green. John goes out and talks calmly to him each time, locking the door behind him, and in the presence of so many witnesses there is little my father can do but eventually leave.

"Surely Mother Bain is adequate as a chaperone," I reply. "Unless your designs on me are more drastic and immediate than I anticipated."

John smiles. "The problem is that Mother Bain has failing eyesight and hearing, and is also seen as somewhat unorthodox, with all her soothsaying and predictions. I think we need a woman of narrow views and a reputation for utmost propriety. The widow of one of the strangers who was killed in the woods has journeyed to Wraithwaite, looking for work. She is destitute now that her husband is dead. I spoke to her. She seems exactly the sort of person we need. Her name is Widow Brissenden."

I stare at him. "You spoke to her without consulting me, John? I have heard of this woman. They say she is truly dreadful. They say she is carping and narrow-minded and criticises everyone in her path."

"Oh for heaven's sake, you know what people here are like, particularly about strangers. They'll get used to her. She has relatives in Hagditch who speak very highly of her. She's staying with them but does not wish to be dependent on them, which is admirable. One of her nephews rode over here to recommend her to me. It seems only sensible to take her on, since she needs a position and we have one to offer. Also, I almost feel we owe it to her, since her husband was murdered whilst here at the command of your father."

I pace round the kitchen, feeling angry, yet not in a position to vent my anger. I am John's guest, and also I feel partly responsible for this woman having become a widow. The thought of having her as a constant reminder of the attack appals me though. I stop in front of John. "Please do not employ her, John. I shall not be here for long. It does not generally bother you to flout convention."

He pours ale into a battered silver jug and tosses in some cloves, a cinnamon stick and a nutmeg. "It only bothers me because it concerns you," he says mildly. He takes a moleskin mitten, pulls the red-hot poker from the fire and plunges it into the jug. A hissing billow of steam pours out, searing our cheeks.

"The bishop is coming on Friday," he adds, stirring the mixture with the poker then pouring the ale into our two earthenware mugs. "I want to take him to visit your father – he can hardly refuse the bishop entry – so that we can arrange Verity's betrothal and marriage as quickly as possible. Time's going on. She can't continue like this. The bishop can impose fines on your father, or exclusion from Communion, if he continues to attack Low Back Farm. It has become ridiculous. He can't go on refusing to accept the situation. I'd intended that the bishop should also effect your release, if you hadn't already done so yourself."

I take the warm mug from his hands. "I'll come with you to Barrowbeck, John, when you go there with the bishop."

"Is that wise? Your father could have you seized again, and then you would have to... er... climb out of the window a second time."

"You doubt that I climbed out of the window?"

"Sweet Beatrice, I know you. You do not lie well. I think some brave soul succeeded where I failed, and let you out."

I gaze through the smoky firelight. "You were a brave soul, John. I watched you standing there with arrows flying all about you." I pause, made suddenly miserable by the recollection.

He takes hold of my hand. "Who let you out? Tell me. I shall say nothing to anyone. Was it the gallant Hugh?"

I stand up and pull my hand free, finally giving up the

battle to be gracious and conciliatory. "Oh please, not another of you making gibes about Hugh. I had enough of that from Robert." I hurl the name at him deliberately, wishing to hurt him because he has engaged Widow Brissenden without asking me, and because the recollection of him being shot at makes me sick to my stomach, and because I do not wish to feel this way about anyone just now. It is too inconvenient. It is too demanding. I have had enough of it, and I know suddenly that with John it will be worse, because he lays claim to my mind, as well as to other parts of me. He is too clever. He could know me too well. If I let John into my head, how will I ever have secrets again?

He makes no response.

"How controlled you are, John," I remark.

"It doesn't come naturally, Beatie. Unfortunately it is part of my job. I would vastly prefer to go round shouting and hitting people."

I am forced to smile. "Well, I have known you to do that quite well too. I apologise for my rudeness. Please forgive me."

He stands up. "The fault was mine. I should not have questioned you."

"No." I shake my head. "No, of course you have the right, with my father hammering at your door, and an endless stream of the residents of Barrowbeck begging refuge of you."

"Truly, say no more, Beatrice."

We are silent for a while, sipping the ale, which is too

hot. Eventually I say, "The reason I wish to come to Barrowbeck with you is to visit Verity, John. I haven't seen her since she moved to Low Back Farm, and I'm worried about her, particularly with my father's temper as it is."

John is watching me, sprawled in his chair, flushed from the fire. "I think your presence here is keeping your father occupied and saving Verity and James a deal of trouble. Yes. Come. We'll keep you out of his way. I'll be delighted to have your company, and I'd like the bishop to get to know you better too."

On Friday the bishop arrives. He is a man of charm and humour. "So, I am to brave your father," he says to me as we sit in the kitchen finishing the bottle of claret he brought.

"I hope it will not be too alarming an experience, my lord. I fear he is intolerant of the clergy." I am deeply anxious about tomorrow's expedition to Barrowbeck, and have already lost a night's sleep over it. I excuse myself to go to my room to catch up on some rest. As I am leaving, the bishop says quietly to John in Latin, "So is the lady Beatrice to make an honest man of you, John?" I pause on the threshold. John is looking at me with an expression halfway between laughter and despair.

"Master John was my schoolmaster, my lord of Carlisle," I answer the bishop, also in Latin. The bishop clasps his hand over his eyes.

"My child, please forgive me."

"I fear it is I who will be begging forgiveness after you encounter my father, my lord, so please disregard it entirely."

He stands up, so that from deference I must remain. "And the answer, Beatrice? What is the answer to my question?"

John is shaking his head, trying to silence him. I wish above all else that I were lying down in my room, and not having this conversation. I drop a curtsey and reply that on the contrary, his lordship has made a mistake, and that I am to marry my Cousin Hugh. It is whilst I am saying this, that I realise it is no longer true.

The bishop arrived in a red and gold coach most unsuitable for our country roads, and which was mired several times on his journey here, so we travel to Barrowbeck on horseback the following day. We go first to Low Back Farm, and find that James has begun building a fortified pele tower on to his farmhouse. His henchmen, led by George and Martinus, are moving blocks of limestone with pulleys, ready for the Irish builders to lay the foundations.

I stand in this familiar place, and breathe in the smell of first frost, and let the distress of the past two weeks seep away. The ground is getting colder. I can feel it like a great stone under my feet. Overhead, seagulls scream and head inland, a sign of fierce weather coming.

It is wonderful to see Verity again. John, the bishop and I stay for an hour, eating hot buttered wheaten cakes and drinking more wine. Verity has begun keeping bees, and shows us her trussed straw bee-skeps, and the workroom she will use for producing honey and beeswax candles and furniture polish. She is noticeably increased in size.

"Now madam, you must marry," says the bishop sternly as we are leaving.

"Gladly sir, if you can obtain my father's permission," Verity replies irritably. "It is not of my choosing to live thus."

"If necessary we will dispense with your father's permission." The bishop stares along the valley to where Barrowbeck Tower dominates the horizon. "Nevertheless, we will reason with him first."

"God bless your efforts." Verity's expression does not indicate a great measure of confidence in them, with or without God's blessing.

As we are leaving, James arrives back from chopping trees for winter fuel. He is riding bareback on one of the two carthorses which are dragging the huge pallet of tree trunks. He jumps down when he sees us, and I am struck by the change in him, as he smiles and asks if we cannot stay a little longer. He is clearly overawed by the bishop, yet he makes an effort, and converses with us, instead of retreating into silence as he would have done until recently.

John explains our mission, and we bid them an affectionate farewell and set off up the valley. I have told John that I shall visit my aunt whilst he and the bishop call upon my father. I have not told him the purpose of my visit. Behind us, from all along the valley, comes the dull beat of axes on wood, as logs are chopped for winter, and I find I am worrying about our own farm's winter supplies. Has anyone thought of cutting trees for Barrowbeck's winter fuel yet? My father will not have, since he spends his time roaming the countryside causing grief of one sort or another. Wood needs at least two months to season, before being burnt. Last year we were late with it, and the burning of green wood all but smoked us out of the tower. Then there is the root cellar. When I left, it was already piled high with parsnips and carrots, safely covered with black woollen cloths to keep out the damp, but has anyone thought to lift the first of the turnips yet and bring them in? Anxiety and homesickness overwhelm me. I think with a pang of all my summer's herbs so lovingly cut, dried and hung on their S-shaped metal hooks, filling the root cellar with pungency. This winter I shall be a guest in another house, and it will not be the same.

We part company at the edge of the clearing. "Go carefully," says John. "We'll meet you back at James's farm at sundown."

I guide my horse on to a less-used path towards Mere Point, which will keep me out of sight of Father's watchman on the tower. The path is strewn with bright leaves. Berries like jewels glow on the stripped autumn trees. This is my first time alone in the woods since I was attacked. I duck under the low-hanging branches and ride deep into the forest, and everywhere I go two dead men with their throats cut march behind me.

Chapter 7

At Mere Point they are also chopping wood. Hugh and Gerald, red-faced and sweating, are swinging their axes at a pile of tree trunks near the edge of the clearing.

"I'll be along in a minute," calls Hugh, as I head for the tower.

The sea is far out, distant and innocent-looking under a wide blue sky. Sea birds drop and swoop in the great space below the cliff, turning deftly and rising again on the breeze.

I find Aunt Juniper in the smokehouse at the side of the tower. She is standing on an old stool, hanging black sausages perilously over the glowing embers in the smoke-pit, where several sides of pork already hang. The atmosphere in the smokehouse is thick and greasy. Aunt

Juniper looks round as she hooks the last looped sausage on to the chain, and turns the handle to trundle them along.

"I should be asking you to do this for me, Niece," she comments, "since heights appear not to trouble you." She climbs down and embraces me. Her face is blotched from the heat. "Are you well? Safe and well and in one piece? Welcome, my dear. I'faith, young women today, not willing to be locked in towers any more. I don't know what the world is coming to." She laughs. "Have you come to visit Hugh?"

I avoid replying, and instead wave to Hugh across the clearing as we walk towards the tower. Hugh wipes his face on his sleeve and waves back. Suddenly I feel very fond of him.

"I'm smoking the pork with applewood this year," my aunt continues. "Your mother's was so good last year. What is she using this year? Do you know? I have forgotten to ask her with all this business of Verity going on."

"Rosewood and elder, I think." I am glad to avoid more contentious topics as long as possible, but eventually the moment arrives when I am sitting opposite Aunt Juniper at the kitchen table, waiting for Hugh to come in, and there is no longer any getting away from it.

"Auntie, I am here to tell you something. I must say this to you first. I cannot marry Hugh." I say it as fast as I can, then wait.

70

Aunt Juniper looks at me, then purses her lips and spreads her hands flat on the table. "Is it because of Parson Becker, Beatrice? They are saying you have a fondness for the parson... that you and he have a fondness for one another. Can this be true?"

Hugh comes in. I can see from his face that he has been listening. His hands hang tired and red from hewing the wood. He is unsmiling.

I turn in my seat. "I'm sorry, Hugh. You're like a dear brother to me, and always will be. We're too close to think of marrying. Please forgive me."

Hugh looks hurt and puzzled. He looks as if his pride is wounded, but I wonder if I am imagining that he also looks a little relieved. Aunt Juniper appears distressed and bewildered. "Is this attachment of yours to the priest something of a religious or spiritual nature, Beatrice?" she demands.

I opt for the truth. "I'm not sure."

She shakes her head. "First Verity, now you, going your own ways. What's happening to the world, Beatrice? I warrant the queen started all this, setting her face against good husbands, God bless her. I'm sure I don't know where it will all end."

Uncle Juniper comes in, hurls a log on the kitchen fire and claps me on the shoulder. "They're real killers, my new dogs, Beatrice," he booms. "Canst hear 'em, out in t'barn?" I smile and nod, and he goes to sit in a corner and scratch himself in private places.

Aunt Juniper leans her elbows on the table. "Beatrice, I would like to think you will not make any hasty decisions about this."

Hugh turns away, flushing with anger. "Mother, she has decided. Your plans cannot always go to order." He marches out.

Aunt Juniper watches him in astonishment, then continues as if she had not been interrupted. "You see how much you have upset him, Beatrice? I hope now that you will reconsider. 'Tis no wonder you have been shut up in your room, with such wilfulness on display. Have you and your sister no thought at all for the work and distress your behaviour causes? Marriage is a serious business, not a matter for idle preferences. In heaven's name, what sort of income do you imagine a village priest will have? A lot of thought and planning goes into securing your futures and your fortunes, to give you the best security you can have. I don't mind doing it. It's no more than my duty. But Gerald already has to be found someone else, with Verity gone. I'm considering Mistress Fairweather of Hagditch. She's badly pocked, but has fortune enough to make up for that, and is very young to have been left a widow. Gerald would make her – or anyone – a splendid husband." She pauses, as if struck by an idea. "You wouldn't consider...?"

I bite my lip. "I think I'm unfitted for marriage, Aunt. To anyone. Truly, I am not ready even to think about it."

We sit in silence for a while. Hugh returns and pours

elderflower wine and hands it round. He gives me a brief, rueful look, a glimpse of the old Hugh, which fills me with a strange pang of relief and regret. Aunt Juniper intercepts it. She asks quickly, "Would you care to come and stay here, Niece, rather than at the parsonage? Your uncle and cousins would protect you from your father. You need have no fear of that. You would be closer to Verity and to your mother. It would be a blessing for me to have another woman in the house. You could read Holy Writ to me of an evening, whilst I sew."

There are voices in the gatehouse. We all look round. I have been half aware of someone arriving on horseback. Now Gerald enters, glancing behind him, holding out his hand to an unseen figure. A woman's voice answers him, whispering uncertainly. Gerald steps back, vanishes, then returns with his arm round Germaine, forcing her forward. Aunt Juniper stands up, staring at Gerald's arm. "What in heaven's name are you doing, Gerald?" she exclaims. "What are you doing with that serving woman?"

He moves forward into the kitchen, and Germaine has no choice but to move with him. "I'm glad you welcome the presence of another woman in the house, Mother," Gerald says. He kisses the top of his mother's head. "Germaine is coming to live here. She is coming to stay with us."

One look at Aunt Juniper's face seems to indicate that this is a good moment to leave. I move round the table kissing each of them on the cheek, though hardly noticed by them in their shock-eyed immobility. I stroll out into the bright autumn afternoon, full of relief that my own mission is completed, overwhelmed by startled admiration for Gerald and Germaine, that they have dared to do this.

It is whilst I am mounting my horse outside the stables that I first hear the sound. I hear it, then it is lost again amongst the faint beat of axes that resounds all round the bay. I stop and listen, one foot in the stirrup. The sound comes again. It is different from the woodcutting. It has rhythm and resonance. It grows louder then fades, carried on gusts of wind across the water, two slow beats and three fast, the sound of a drum. I mount up. I cannot imagine what a drum is doing on a clear autumn day with winter coming on and no conflicts threatened, but it seems unimportant, and as my mind returns to the confrontation probably going on behind me in Mere Point Tower, I soon forget about it.

John and the bishop have already returned to Low Back Farm, when I arrive there. They meet me, with Verity and James, at the gate.

"How did you...?" I scarcely need ask how they fared. Their expressions tell me.

"We gained entry," the bishop tells me as he helps me down from my horse. "That much we did achieve, but only to be harangued at great length and ejected again. Your father did not wish to listen to reason."

I see to my horror that he has a red swelling on the side of his face. "And this, sir?"

74

"The doorpost. In his haste to see us on our way, your father deemed some assistance was necessary."

I stand with my hand to my mouth. This is worse, far worse, than I had anticipated. "Oh, I am so sorry. I am so sorry. Please excuse him. He is unused to suggestions from others as to how he should behave."

"I have forgiven him," the bishop declares graciously. "I think it probably does me good to experience life amongst the farther reaches of my wild and scattered flock. It has a most humbling effect."

Verity widens her eyes at me, and I know that despite everything, she feels inclined to side with my father. She leads the bishop indoors, to soothe him with wine and cakes. James hesitates, preferring to stay with us, whom he knows, but when John catches hold of my arm and holds me back, James follows them indoors.

"What?" I respond to John's anxious expression.

"There's something else, Beatie. Your father – I think he is unwell."

I stare at him in alarm. "In what way, John?"

"His colour is bad. It is most unwholesome looking, a very choleric purple in his cheeks and nose, and he seemed short of breath. I suggested to him that he needed a doctor, but the idea seemed to drive him into a further rage. I do think it would be wise for him to consult either a doctor or the Cockleshell Man, before the day is out."

"Was my mother there?"

"No. Was she not at your aunt's?"

"No."

"Then she will be with Cedric."

I glance at him. "Do you disapprove?" When he does not reply, I save him the embarrassment of having to, by adding, "I think I should go and take a look at my father. I will ask James if George and Martinus may accompany me."

"I'll come with you."

"I think not, thank you John."

When I explain my intention to Verity, she also insists on accompanying me. James, John and the bishop escort us up the valley to the edge of the clearing, and watch as Verity, the two henchmen and I go on alone. As we draw near to the barmkin I can see that Michael, the new henchman, is keeping watch on the battlements. We see him calling down to someone. A moment later the door of the pele tower flies open and my father rushes out.

Although there are four of us, we instinctively draw back. I see at once what John referred to. My father's face is dark purple, and as he comes nearer, I hear his breath gurgling in his chest like water from a bottle.

"Daughters!" he shouts, and teeters to a halt. "Oh Daughters, have you come home to me?"

"Is he drunk?" Verity whispers.

I shake my head. "I don't think so." I take a step towards him. He staggers where he stands. "Father, let me help you back into the tower."

Verity takes his other arm. She has not touched him

76

since the day he tried to kill James. He bursts into tears. I feel close to tears myself. Between us we coax him up the slope and through the gatehouse, into the kitchen, closely followed by George and Martinus.

The kitchen is empty, but I can hear Kate singing somewhere in the cellars below. Father is struggling for coherence. The effort is plain on his face. "Daughters," he attempts again, "dear, dear Daughters..."

We help him sit down on the settle. Martinus brings some water.

"Should'st be on watch, lad?" Father asks, peering at him with difficulty.

"You're confused, Father," I tell him. "Martinus doesn't work here any more. Drink the water. Will you let the Cockleshell Man come to see you?"

Father drinks the water quickly. "Nay lass, whatever for?" He wipes a trickle from his chin. His colour is cooling a little. He sounds calmer and more articulate as he enquires, "Beatrice, what are they saying about you, lass? I cannot credit it. You cannot want yon poxy parson! You cannot. You cannot, lass. Come home. There'll be no more locking in. I give you my oath. And we'll forget about the window. I'll not beat you for that." He holds out his cup for more water, and Martinus hurries forward. I reflect how quickly he has fallen back into his old role of serving this familiar master. My father lays his hand on my arm and looks into my face, and I reflect how quickly I, too, have fallen back. He says quietly, "Beatrice, I've cared for you, have I not? It has been my pleasure to provide for you. Many girls in your position would have been married off at twelve. Yet I allowed you to learn. Did I not? Did you not have this privilege which most young women do not?"

I lower my eyes. "Yes, Father."

"Yes. Well then." He sits back. "Now I ask for you to return a little of what I have done for you. Come home. Resume your duties on the farm. All will be forgotten. I shall hold nothing against you." He turns to Verity without giving me a chance to reply. "And you, Verity, naught shall be held against you, neither. Nor against your child. Your babe shall be the apple of my eye. I shall permit no one to call it bastard, and it shall, with your sister's children, inherit all that I have. There'll be no disgrace to you. The yokel violated you. I know that. All who know you know that. There's no disgrace. Come home. Stay with me, Verity."

Verity leans forward and takes his hand. "Father, dearest Father, you know how I love you. Never doubt it."

He nods, and there are tears in his eyes. "Never doubt it," he repeats under his breath.

Verity kisses his brow, which is slick with sweat, and adds, "But I also love James, Father, and you must accept that, and accept James. Please, Father."

She is cut off as he jumps to his feet. The settle crashes over. George and Martinus rush to stand in front of Verity. Father's face is undergoing a horrific change, becoming even more livid at the high points of his cheeks and nose. He pushes George aside. "Must?" he shouts in Verity's face. *"Must?* You dare say *must* to your father? You traitorous harlot! I shall never accept that witless fool. *Never!* You spout what those vile clerics have taught you to say. Well, you shall see, and *they* shall see." He crosses to the door, leaving us all gaping. "They shall see indeed. Yon fair coach I spied on Wraithwaite Green would be a hard job to miss, out on the highway." He goes staggering out of the kitchen, and out of the tower.

I rush after him. I can hear Verity sobbing behind me. The tower door is standing open. Outside, Father is striding unevenly down towards the barmkin. I hear the high-pitched whinny of Caligula, his black stallion, greeting him.

"Oh no..." I run after him. "Father!" He is puffing with the effort, and I catch him up easily. "Father, stop! You're not fit..." I lower my voice. "You're not fit to go out robbing. You'll get caught. I beg you, Father, don't go out now. Please, let us talk some more. If you wish me to come back, then..." but he is not listening. I pray that John, James and the bishop are keeping out of sight as Father proceeds at a lolloping run round the barmkin wall towards the entrance.

Suddenly he stops, and turns back to me, gasping. "He vexes me, your parson, Beatrice. He vexes me greatly. Your babbling bishop vexes me worst of all. Mayhap this night his lordship will learn it is more blessed to give than to

79

receive." He struggles to regain his breath. After a moment he lays his hand on my head and says, "I hope you shall be here when I return, Beatrice. Pig sticking this week, I think? It will never salt down enough, else. Speak to Leo. You know best which of the swine to choose. Fare thee well, Daughter."

I watch him open the barmkin gate and duck into the turf-roofed overhang of the saddlery. Caligula comes trotting up to him. For a moment, faintly on the wind, I hear the sound of the drum again.

Chapter 8

I do my best to persuade the bishop not to leave, but he is expected at Hagditch for Matins early the following morning, and at Kerne Forth for Vespers the following afternoon, and he puts my anxious insistence merely down to good manners.

Verity has given me Meadowsweet, her dimwitted, golden-eyed mare, since she does not wish to endanger her unborn child by riding any longer, and anyway will soon be too big. Mother has given her the carretta from the tower, to be drawn by one of James's slower and less flighty horses. I feel reluctant to replace dead Saint Hilda with any other horse, yet as we ride back to Wraithwaite, taking the long way round the edge of the woods rather than haul the bishop up the rockface, the sound of Meadowsweet's hooves tapping along the rocky bridleway cheers me more than I had expected.

This path, which borders James's land, is hedged along with blackthorn bushes. They have lost most of their leaves now, and only a few slack black sloes remain on the bare branches. Instead, rows of dead moles hang there, upside down like colonies of bats, their tiny, rosy hands outspread. We pass more and more of them, flapping at our passing with a brief mockery of life. James will be wearing new moleskin breeches this winter.

I kick Meadowsweet into a gallop and leave John and the bishop behind. The moles are such an embodiment of mute helplessness that I cannot bear them. They seem to represent all that is inarticulate – James too tongue-tied to be taken seriously by people such as my father, my father himself whose attempts to express affection are nullified by incoherent rage, all of us who are bound to keep Father's own criminal secret, myself locked into the secret I now share with Leo, and worse still, the secret knowledge of everything I shared with Robert, which can never be told. The moles are silent, writhing on their thorn trees. I must outrun them.

My hat ribbons lash my face, and one flicks me in the eye, making it water. My eyes are streaming by the time the bishop catches me up. He says, "Forgive me that I could not help you more, Beatrice." He edges ahead and turns his horse, so that I have to slow down. "Please, do not distress yourself, my dear. I pray that your father will relent, now that he is banished from Communion. John will perform Verity and James's betrothal immediately, without your father's permission, and the first banns will be published this Sunday. All shall be well. I shall visit you again soon."

He repeats his promise later, as he leaves, with just enough time to reach Hagditch before light fades. I look up at the words carved into the lintel as we bid him goodbye at the parsonage gate. *Truth and grace be to this place.* I could tell him the truth. It is clearly wrong to let this man go out on to the highway, conspicuous in his red and gold coach, when I know what probably lies in wait for him. Yet if I were to tell him that my father is a highway robber, not only my father but also my mother would be ruined. Nor, I realise for the first time, would it bode well for John's career in the church if his house guest were revealed to have such scandalous connections. *Take an extra lanthorn; take the coast road not the high road; wait for George and Martinus to join you at the crossroads in case of highway robbers.* Verity and I have done and said all we can. Now we must just pray.

"I love you," says John under his breath, as we watch the bishop's coachman whip up the elegant piebald gelding which pulls his coach. The bishop waves and the coach moves off.

My state of distraction is such that it takes a moment for John's words to sink in. I look up at him. Here is someone who does not have secrets, who says what he thinks, regardless of the consequences, who says it in measured terms, and then listens to a person's reply, whatever it might be. I have a moment of feeling quite overcome by wonder. "I could love you very easily, John," I tell him. "Perhaps I already do."

He holds out his hand to me, and I take it, and we return to the kitchen hand in hand.

"He's left it late. Darkness is barely an hour off." Mother Bain is lighting a taper at the kitchen fire. She goes round the pricket candlesticks on the walls one by one, setting the yellow candles alight. The tallow from which they are made does not smell as sweet as our own beeswax candles, and it drips fast into the wax-pans underneath. The wick next to me drowns and goes out. John brings a stool and sits next to me in the dimness. Mother Bain stirs the rabbit stew in the cauldron over the fire. The seething peace of evening settles on the parsonage, and we all sigh, and smile at one another, and gaze into the fire.

Suddenly there is a loud knocking at the door. We jump, as if caught in some guilty act. "That will be Widow Brissenden," says Mother Bain. "She called earlier, John, whilst you were out. I forgot to tell you."

"Oh God." John bites his lip. Mother Bain clicks her tongue at the blasphemy. "I'm sorry," he says to me, as Mother Bain goes to open the door. "I forgot I'd invited her to come and meet you. There *is* talk, Beatie. I'm sorry. I had to do something. No one else was available at such short notice, and Widow Brissenden's family appear to be

84

able to spare her." As he is speaking, a tall figure clad in black looms in the doorway.

"Widow Brissenden, parson," announces Mother Bain, reduced almost to invisibility in the shadow of this huge newcomer. We stand up and all greet one another, and I feel furious, furious with John that he thinks I will be prepared to live with this stranger for the sake of appearances, furious with Widow Brissenden for the proprietorial glare she is already casting round the parsonage kitchen. Love him? If this is John's idea of love, then I prefer my father's way of showing affection. He wants me home. He shall have me home. I excuse myself, without any attempt at politeness, and go up to my bedchamber.

At once I feel ashamed. This woman is bereaved. I must be patient and kind, and make her welcome. I can hear John showing her round the parsonage. Her voice booms out from the room she will have, next to mine along the landing. When Mother Bain comes and fetches me downstairs for the meal, I find Widow Brissenden already ladling rabbit stew on to her plate from the cauldron. Whilst we eat, dipping our bread in the gravy, a collection of crumbs and fragments of stew builds up on the plateau of Widow Brissenden's bosom. From time to time she refers to her husband, and wipes her eyes dramatically with a large handkerchief, but the rest of the time she regales us with stories of shocking doings in both Hagditch and her home village some miles away. In many cases, it would seem, disaster was only averted by her prompt intervention. John is quiet and gloomy. Mother Bain excuses herself after the meal and retires to bed. The last of the light fades outside, and we wait for Widow Brissenden to go. I want to say to John, I told you so. See, you can't stand her either. Just listen to me next time.

The widow doesn't go. Instead, she starts telling us about her daughters-in-law, one by one, and how none of them is good enough for any of her four sons. It is whilst she is on daughter-in-law number three that I become aware of a commotion outside. I frown at John, and nod towards the door. We get up and go to see what is happening. Widow Brissenden's story trails off, and she comes and joins us.

It is too dark to see much, but people are coming out of their houses with lighted torches and lanthorns. The clamour is quite far off, but growing nearer. We join the crowd and move with them towards the end of the village. I catch the words, "... highway robbers..." and "... murder..." and then someone at the front of the crowd cries out, "I can see his body!"

It is not until I catch a glimpse of red and gold in the distance, illuminated in the flare of a torch, that I realise it is the bishop's coach which is returning. Sick with apprehension, I ask someone coming back through the crowd what has happened, but the woman knows no more than I do. She says, "If there are highway robbers about I'm off home to protect my children," and pushes her way towards the cottages by the tavern.

John and I make our way through the crowd as the coach slowly approaches. The coachman is half slumped on his seat, his face mud-streaked. The piebald gelding is limping. They stop as John reaches them. Silence falls across the crowd as he opens the coach door. For a moment no one is visible inside, then there is movement and the bishop appears. Shakily he takes hold of John's proffered hand and steps down. An old woman near me crosses herself.

"Thank God," I mutter. "I thought they were saying he was dead. Who do they mean, then? Whose body...?"

People around me shake their heads. Everyone is craning forward to see. John directs the coach round towards the back of the parsonage, then makes his way over to me again. "Come inside, Beatie," he says. "I'm afraid something has happened to your father."

Chapter 9

I rush through the house to where the coach has stopped by the stables, and watch John and the coachman lift my father out and carry him through to the kitchen. Mother Bain has just woken. She hurries out of her room behind the hearth, rubbing her eyes, then sweeps mugs and dishes aside to make space for my father's body on the kitchen table. Carefully, they lay him down. At first I think he is dead, then realise that he is breathing.

"He's alive." I move to his side and take his hand. He looks fearsome. His nose and cheeks have a lacework of purple veins standing out on stretched skin. His mouth is slack, curving in glistening grooves down towards his chin. His hands, crossed on his chest, are trembling.

"Aye, he's alive, but there's something sorely wrong."

Mother Bain, still in her nightsmock and nightgown, lifts one of his eyelids and peers in, then holds his wrist to feel the echo of his heartbeat.

"By your *leave*, mistresses!" Widow Brissenden barges past us. "*Kindly* allow me. I have experience in these matters. My own dear uncle is but lately dead of a similar choleric humour." In our astonishment we allow her access to my father's helpless body, and she takes one look at him and announces that he needs to be bled. "*I* am experienced in blood-letting," she booms. "I have my instruments in my bag at the tavern," and she is off through the front door before we can recover enough to answer her. Mother Bain and I look at one another, then she resumes her examination, loosening my father's clothing and placing her ear against his chest. Behind us, the bishop and John are talking in low voices.

"I take it you did not know of Squire Garth's other occupation, my son?"

"What occupation? I do not understand you, my lord. What on earth happened?"

"He was lying in wait for us on horseback, hidden amongst the trees at Haggen Bottom."

"Who? Squire Garth? You cannot mean that Squire Garth was *waylaying* you?"

"That is what I am telling you, John. He was disguised in peasant's clothing and with a black cloth tied over his face. He came out at us with a bullwhip, whipped my coachman to the ground and threatened me at swordpoint. I tried to reason with him, and told him I had very little gold or silver with me, but it was no good. He got off his horse, took my bags from my coach, then set my horse loose and tried to drive it off into the woods. My coachman ran after it."

I look round at them. John is staring at the bishop, open-mouthed. He catches my glance, looks at me for a long moment, then returns his attention to the bishop, who is now telling how Father remounted and rode away into the woods, laughing. It was only as the coachman caught their horse and returned with it, that they heard, some way off, the laughter change to choking, followed by a crashing amongst the bushes. They found my father unconscious in the undergrowth. Between them they carried his body to the coach, and brought him back here.

"We need Cedric." We all turn as Mother Bain speaks. "I do not know if your father needs to be bled, Beatrice. I do not know if it is his heart or his brain affected, so I am going to prepare a poultice of *flos unguentorum* for each. John, will you fetch the Cockleshell Man, and Mistress Columbine too, I think."

"That will take but one journey, from what I hear." The voice in the doorway is sour and disapproving. Widow Brissenden is back, brandishing a selection of knives and a letting cup. Gently we explain to her that her services will not be required, for now. Mother Bain asks her if she would be so kind as to tend the injured coachman, as he is in need of the most compassionate

90

care, for which the widow is renowned. Mollified, Widow Brissenden marches over to where the unfortunate coachman cowers in terror in a corner.

John returns with Cedric and my mother within the hour. By then my father is showing signs of wakening. Cedric administers an infusion of willow bark, hawthorn and motherwort, and asks Mother Bain to mix comfrey and mustard in with the poultices she is applying. My mother holds her husband's hand, and weeps.

"He's not fit to be moved." Cedric stands back and stares critically at his patient. "He'll have to stay here for the time being. Is that all right, John?" Huge, bearded, fish-scented, the Cockleshell Man is lover to my elegant mother, and of late they have stopped bothering to conceal the fact. My mother was married to my father when she was sixteen, as I am now sixteen. Our lives have revolved about this union, and all that stemmed from it, for as long as I have lived. It frightens me that what was a secret liaison between Cedric and my mother is now known even to such people as Widow Brissenden. There is the feeling, this night, as I watch over my father into the small hours of the morning in Mother Bain's hot little room behind the hearth, that certainties of all sorts are crumbling.

Mother comes to relieve me as first light shows through the high window. Her face is puffed from weariness and weeping. She nods to me, and I am too tired to do more than kiss her cheek and leave, whilst behind me my father groans and dribbles in his sleep.

The kitchen feels icy after the heat of the little room. A draught cuts under the ill-fitting door. In the hearth, a large log has burnt away underneath, and now arches in an empty carapace over cold ash. I go to the kindling box and take out tiny wisps of dried moss and chips of bark to coax the fire back to life. I push them into the ash until little by little, smoke rises again. I add bigger sticks, and on top of them a new log angled to fall in once the flames have grown higher. I fill a pot with water from the well outside, hook it on the rackencrock and winch it over the tiny flames. It will boil by the time everyone is up for breakfast.

It scarcely seems worthwhile going to bed, but I do, and sleep uneasily for an hour or so. The sound of many voices wakens me. Crowds of people are converging across the green. It is Sunday, time for church, and I am late. I struggle into my clothes and hurry down. Today was to have been Verity and James's betrothal. I wonder if John will still perform it, after what has happened, but when I arrive in the kitchen I find that the bishop is insisting it should go ahead, and that he now intends to conduct the ceremony himself.

John says only one thing to me before he leaves for church. "Did you know, madam, about your father's activities?"

I gaze at him, so goodly to look at, and so savage of expression, and I answer, "Yes."

He leaves.

I look in on my father. He is propped on bolsters, his eyes closed and his breathing laboured. Mother Bain insists she will stay with him, and that it is more important for me to attend Verity's betrothal.

There is a feeling of winter in the air today, with the sun low on the horizon. I put on my blue, beaver-trimmed winter coat and hat for the first time since early spring. My mother, and Cedric who has also stayed overnight, join me as I step out into the chilly autumn air. I am astonished to find that Cedric will also be attending church. I have never known him to before. He has always preferred to pay fines to the churchwardens rather than attend.

Verity arrives in the carretta with James. George and Martinus ride behind, wrapped in sheepskin jerkins. Verity is shocked when she learns what has happened, and at first declares she would rather stay with Father than go to church to become betrothed. She is briskly persuaded otherwise by my mother.

Word about my father has spread, and villagers and homesteaders, in their wool caps and Sunday best, crowd round, asking how he is. Gerald and Germaine arrive too, riding fast, looking flushed and happy. Aunt and Uncle Juniper come along some distance behind, unsmiling. We all go to stand together in our usual place at the entrance to the lady chapel.

The words of the betrothal are beautiful and solemn. Verity and James stand together in front of the bishop, hand in hand, and are formally blessed and betrothed. At Communion I look at John, to try to judge his mood, but he is always inscrutable when he is here, doing his job.

At the end of the service the first banns of marriage are called between Verity and James, and then we all troop out into the sunshine. Gold leaves lie like reflections under the trees on the green. I shake John's hand at the church door, the contact unsettling. "Are you angry?" I ask him.

"I want to talk to you," he says. "At the parsonage. Now."

"Very well."

I talk to Germaine and Gerald for a while, then after the last parishioner has left, I watch John stride off across the green, his black robes swinging, and after a few minutes, I follow him. Mother Bain meets me in the hall and I ask her, "How is my father?"

"Sleeping. Not in his right senses yet, but his colour is going down. Mistress Verity is with him just now."

"I'll go in and see him."

"Best see John first, I think. He's up in the schoolroom."

I frown. This feels like being summoned. Nevertheless, I gather up my skirts and climb the stairs. John meets me at the top. I stop in my tracks at the look on his face.

"What..."

He throws open the door of the schoolroom. This is the place where I spent many hours of my childhood, first under the tutelage of old Parson Pattinson, later with John. It is strangely comforting to be back here amongst the familiar benches, ink-stained table, shelves of books, tall iron candlesticks and prie-dieu in the corner. I smile, and am about to say this to John, but the door is scarcely closed behind us when he turns on me.

"You knew. You knew about your father and you never told me? This has been going on under my nose, and you didn't think to give me the chance to stop it? What do you imagine my job is supposed to be round here? Just conducting pretty services?"

I cannot answer him.

"Beatrice, I thought we meant something to one another. How long would you have gone on concealing this from me?"

I cross to the small window. The glass is thick and green, and I cannot see through it. I turn back. "For ever, John. I would have concealed it from you for ever. Believe me, I have tried to stop him. We all have. The honest truth is, it never entered my mind to tell you. We have all been so used to keeping it secret. I am sorry, though, and I understand your indignation. It just goes to show how bad a match we would have made." I cross the room to leave, but there is a loud rapping on the door just as I reach it.

"Parson?" It is Widow Brissenden. "Parson? Come along now! The bishop is waiting!"

John steps in front of me and throws open the door.

"Madam, I couldn't care less if the Four Horsemen of the Apocalypse are waiting. Go away."

Widow Brissenden draws herself up in speechless indignation, then she looks past him into the room and sees me. Her mouth drops open. "Mistress *Garth*! Whatever are you doing here? In very truth, this is not proper. Will you kindly accompany me downstairs?"

"I cannot for the moment, Mistress Brissenden," I reply. "Parson Becker wishes to speak to me, and I am obliged to hear him."

Widow Brissenden frowns. "You are young, Mistress Garth," she states, with exaggerated patience. "Let me tell you, it is possible to be *too* obliging to our menfolk. It certainly is. I think you will find that no one has ever accused *me* of being too obliging." She glares at John.

"I don't doubt it." I too give John an experimental glare. "Very well, I think perhaps Parson Becker and I have concluded our discussion." John bites his lip and holds the door open for us.

"Well," says the bishop as the widow and I reach the kitchen, "this has all been quite bracing, but now I must be away. I have two hours before Vespers, and I must not disappoint my Hagditch flock any further. Perhaps I might give you a lift, Mistress Brissenden? I noted that your kinfolk were looking most unhappy without your good advice to guide them." He smiles at her and offers his arm.

"Indeed, I don't doubt you are right, my lord." Widow Brissenden simpers at him. It is a frightening sight. As the bishop guides her towards the door she looks round at me. "Bear in mind what I have said to you, young woman. I can't be everywhere at once, giving guidance to everybody. Would that I could!" She sighs, and beams down at the bishop. "I'm sure you find the same problem, bishop."

As John and I see them off, a mist is rising on the green. A light breeze swirls it like smoke. When he has settled Widow Brissenden in his coach the bishop comes back and says, "Children, go for a ride together. Get away from us busybodies. Take some wine with you. You have a couple of hours before Vespers."

"Do you wish your priests to associate with highway robbers' daughters, my lord?" I enquire. The bishop pats my arm.

"Abduct him, madam. I command you. He needs it." With that he squeezes into the coach next to Widow Brissenden, and with a wave they move off. We stand in silence and watch them until they are out of sight.

In the little room behind the hearth, my father has opened his eyes.

"Father?"

He stares at me, yet does not seem to see me. Then, with a puzzled look, he turns his gaze up to the angled beam of light coming in through the high window.

We go to Little Cove. It is a strange afternoon. We talk as we have never talked. John tells me about his parents,

John and Naomi, who both died of plague whilst he was away studying. I talk about my parents and their loveless marriage, and about Robert. We lie in the florid bracken and drink nettle wine and watch the tide coming in. Waterbirds loop and dive over its white, moving edge, watching for fishes, watching for whatever is not fast enough. Their remote, woodwind voices come to us faintly on the breeze. John is in casual clothes, a blue shirt that matches his eyes, a sheepskin jerkin and old breeches. He tries to break a piece of bracken. It looks brittle, but is in fact tough and stringy and difficult to break. He looks up and says, "Marry me."

I lean on my elbow and gaze at him through the brown stalks. It is turning colder with the coming of the tide. A raw smell is in the air, the smell of nights drawing in, and of frost in the veins of the leaves. Our breath drifts together, part of the mistiness of autumn. "Yes," I answer, "yes, I will."

Chapter 10

"But not yet, John. I have to sort things out at home first. I have to see how my father recovers."

John nods. We get up and walk down the grassy slope to the shore. My cloak is covered in seed-heads and bits of bracken. I take it off and give it a shake, then brush the bits from the back of John's jerkin too. "I'll have to spend a lot of my time at Barrowbeck now, John. The farm was being neglected even before Father was ill. I'll have to divide my time between Barrowbeck and the parsonage, until my father is fit to be moved. When he is, I'll return to the farm full time for a while."

"I'll help you. We can both divide our time. We can manage everything."

We sit down and rest our backs against the base of the cliff. Pink thrift is flowering here in huge drifts, and I consider the irony that thrift grows in such profusion next to the wasteful sea. John removes the bung from the clay wine bottle with his teeth. "Might as well finish it off." He passes me the bottle. The nettle wine is fizzy and light. I pass the bottle back and kiss John's cheek. It tastes salty, like the smell of the sea. A crab's claw, empty and translucent, the same colour as the thrift, is caught in his hair. I pull it loose, and show him. He squints at it, then puts his hand behind my head and kisses me.

Do I want this? I have to think. I have to think now, and know for certain before I commit myself. Out here, with the taste of salt and kisses, this was Robert. This was unfamiliarity and danger, not something to do with someone I've known for years. Yet John is more to me. He brings friendship and security as well as passion.

He draws back and looks at me. "Am I ever going to be able to compete with Robert?"

"It isn't to do with competing. It was just all so recent." I shrug. "I'm recovering. It's like an illness."

He takes the crab's claw from me. "Do you ever wish you'd gone with him?"

"I did once, when I was locked in, but not now."

"Then I believe you will recover." He throws the claw into a nearby pool. "Unlike this crab."

We stand up and walk back to where we tethered our horses. Foxes are barking on the hill as we ride back to Wraithwaite. Evening comes so early at this season. In a short while the congregation will return for Vespers, so I take John's horse and mine round to the stables, whilst he hurries off to get ready. I really miss just being able to hand my horse over to Leo or Dickon when I return from riding, and I start to think about whom I could employ as stable-hand, when I am eventually mistress here. I hang up the saddles on the hooks at the back, and have just begun rubbing down the horses when I realise that I can hear the drum again. It is no longer distant. It is close. I go out into the street. The rain is coming down hard now, but nevertheless a crowd is gathering.

"Ee, I've been hearing yon drum for weeks," says one of John's parishioners, who has clearly spent the afternoon in the tavern. With everyone else, we look along the street towards the north end of the village, the source of the drumbeat. It is as before, two slow beats and three fast. More villagers come out of their houses, some half-in and half-out of their Sunday best, peering along the street. A few Barrowbeck parishioners are just arriving too. Everyone stares and waits.

They come like ghosts down the road from the hills, the long road round the bay, with the last of the day's light behind them. A young drummer in red leads them. Two slow beats and three fast, on and on, never wavering. A captain on horseback with his sword at his side comes next. Four young boys in red and brown uniforms follow him, swords drawn and held in front of their faces. Behind them stumbles a company of spectres, emaciated prisoners in filthy rags, some half naked and some barefoot, most of them a patchwork of festering sores, each man joined to the next at wrist and ankle, by chains. Two more soldiers march behind them, never faltering, never losing the beat of the drum, whilst their charges shuffle, lurch and stagger ahead of them, to no known beat.

The crowd is silenced.

"Who are they?" It is Dickon, Leo's son, newly arrived. Gradually, people are finding their voices.

"Thieves and highway robbers for Lancaster Assizes, I reckon."

"For hanging."

Some of the prisoners are coughing and shivering. One man is bleeding regularly from a wound in his neck as he limps along. The chains look heavy, old and rusty, and the men seem not to be able to co-ordinate the swinging of their arms.

"For trial, anyhow."

"Mebbe for drawing and quartering." Tilly Turner has arrived.

"Nay, they'd hardly all be up for treason, would they. Don't be daft."

As the column of men passes the crowd outside the parsonage, the captain salutes us with his gloved hand, and the boy soldiers salute with their swords. John comes out and stares in horror. He puts his arm round me. "Who are your prisoners, captain?" he calls out. I could have saved him the question. Gently I free myself, and move along behind the crowd, keeping pace with the prisoners.

"Scots, sir." I hear the captain's reply behind me. A shiver runs through the crowd. Scots, here. The enemy in chains, humiliated, without their arrogant woollen draperies and crowbars and scaling ladders. "I can tell you, we've driven off any number of local revenge parties so far." The captain gives a grin and a graceful bow. The crowd starts to move along with the prisoners. I edge between jostling bodies, trying to move faster.

"Aye, but they'll not be such efficient revenge parties as we have round here," calls back a young man with a wild, flickering eye.

People begin to mock and spit at the prisoners. A stone flies past my head and hits one of them. I see Cedric pushing his way to the front. "When will they be tried, captain?" he shouts.

The captain turns slightly in his saddle. "They're for the November Quarter Sessions, sir. Then they'll be up for the March Assizes. The queen wants them tried all open and above board in her Royal Duchy of Lancaster. Set an example to others, you know. At this rate we'll be lucky if we get there by Christmas. It's taken us weeks to march this weak-kneed lot down from the hills."

I reach the edge of the crowd a little further along, and watch the Scots stagger past me. Their chains clank. They sag with exhaustion. Bruises and wounds cover their limbs, and even in this failing light I can see the blood crusted on to their shackles liquefying again in the rain, and pasting itself back on to pale hands and feet.

Robert is last in line. He is wearing the clothes I sent him off in. His guards, little more than children, stamp importantly behind him. He walks steadily with his eyes cast down. He does not look at me again. Once was enough, as I stood outside the parsonage, with John's arm round my shoulders.

The drum can no longer be heard when I return to the parsonage. I know I have been gone too long, and missed the church service, but the wet beechwoods on the outskirts of the village were the only place private enough for the pain.

Church is out. A few people are standing about talking in the damp twilight. A horse goes by, throwing up clods of mud. Light from the cottages glows and flickers. I can hear Universe whinnying in the stables behind the parsonage.

Mother and Cedric are waiting for me in the small courtyard at the front of the house.

"Come in," I say to them, kicking off my muddy shoes on the step.

Mother puts out her hand to me. "Oh, Beatrice."

Cedric steps forward and puts his arm round me. He does not smell so strongly of fish today. "Are you all right, Beatrice?" he asks.

I try to control a feeling of overwhelming physical collapse. "You've told Mother, I gather," I say to him.

"I had to."

I shrug. "Do come in. It's cold out here." I look back across the green. Villagers are still moving about, going to

104

each other's houses, talking about the Scots. "Where's John?" I ask.

"Still in church." I have never seen Mother so lost for words.

We go into the house. Mother Bain comes out of the kitchen, in her nightclothes. "God bless those poor souls and God bless us all. There's pottage keeping warm on the hearth. I'm away to my bed." She kisses my cheek. I cannot tell whether she has guessed anything or not. When she has gone, I turn to Mother and Cedric.

"Pottage then?"

They both shake their heads. My mother puts her arms round me and holds me tightly. "Shall I stay, Beatie? Will you be all right?"

For a moment I am a child again. I try to stop my chin from trembling. "Thank you but you needn't stay. I'm quite all right, Mother."

As I walk with them to where their horses are stabled at the back, she says wonderingly, "I treated you like a child." She mounts up and pats her horse's neck. "I shall come back to sit with Father in the morning, and we shall talk then. Change out of your wet clothes now."

Her words seem meaningless. I am glad when she and Cedric have ridden away into the dark, and I can retreat into numbness.

John comes back whilst I am wandering round the parsonage, room to room, thinking how it can be improved. Distraction and physical occupation are all that will keep me sane, this night. I stand on the landing considering the replacement of warped floorboards. A carved walnut dower chest stands next to the doorway of my bedchamber. I could start filling it with my things. Two intricately carved walnut chairs stand either side of it, and a brass table clock with a design of the four seasons lies on one of them. It was in my father's saddlebag when he was taken ill at Haggen Bottom. Perhaps when we hear news of which other unfortunate traveller was robbed on the highway that night, we might be able to return it to its rightful owner. In the meantime, I have never had a clock in my possession before. It is a most wondrous thing. John says it has an alarum which makes a truly frightening noise, and I am trying to activate this when I hear John's footsteps coming all the way from the back door to the foot of the stairs.

"Beatrice?"

I walk to the top of the staircase and look down.

"You're late back."

At some point he has changed out of his robes and into his wood-chopping clothes. He starts to come upstairs, but half way up he stops. "It's all right, Beatrice. Shh. It's all right."

"What on earth do you mean, shh? What's all right? What are you talking about?" I can hear how shrill my voice sounds. I wipe my perspiring hands down the sides of my rain-drenched skirts, which I have omitted to change. I want to be left alone to sort things out, to sort out what I can sort out, those things over which I have control, setting the clock, filling the dower chest, checking the floorboards.

"Which one was Robert?" John reaches the top of the stairs.

"What?"

"Oh for goodness' sake, Beatie, surely we've talked enough about bloody Robert already, to be able to talk about him now."

"The last one."

"Ah." John walks into my bedroom.

"The one with the light-brown wavy hair." I follow him.

John sits down on the cedar chest. "Yes. I noticed him."

"He noticed you."

John looks down at his hands. "There's nothing you can do, this time. That must feel terrible, but you have to accept it."

I sit on the edge of the bed. I feel cold and hard and lost. "It was all for nothing, John. I mended Robert's arm for nothing. Saint Hilda died for nothing. I was half drowned for nothing. Robert will rot in one of those dungeons under Lancaster Castle until they drag him out and hang him on Gallows Hill."

John comes and sits beside me. He puts his arms round me. I pull away and stand up. "Haven't you been listening to me at all?" I exclaim. "I'm sorry. I'm sorry, but nothing is any good." I stand by the door and hold it open. After a moment, he leaves.

Chapter 11

John was right. We are able to manage everything between us. I ride early each morning to Barrowbeck, travelling fast on Universe, whom I have now trained to the lady's saddle, though he doesn't pretend to like it. My mother runs the dairy and the household, and I run the farm. Some days John comes and helps on the farm, but the gap left by the departure of Verity, Germaine and my father means we are now seriously short of workers, and I wonder how we will manage when spring comes and we once more have to keep watch for raiders.

In the afternoons I ride over to Cedric's cottage at Mere Point for my lessons in medicine. I had looked forward to them, but now my mood is irritable and I cannot be bothered. One golden autumn day, on my way

dispatchings by knife which lie between us, but Leo looks as if he understands perfectly.

"She was born to be pork, mistress. She won't have time to think owt about it."

Veronica Pork is looking at me through the gate. I am overcome by utter bleakness, and an awareness of all such vulnerabilities – Robert's most of all. "I'll send three of the men to help you," I tell Leo, and turn away.

"Aye lady. You go on up and send three of the men down. I've got Tilly Turner and some other women coming to shave the skin later. Best go and lie down a moment, eh?"

"I'll leave it to you, then."

Leo's hand is caressing the knife at his belt. I walk away, up the hill. My legs are trembling. I trip over a tussock, steady myself. I should have stayed with Veronica Pork. There are different sorts of betrayal. I try to think of her as hams, black sausages, brawn, legs of pork, soap, dripping, beautiful leather gloves, but all I can think of is the way she will be – the way they always are – tiny eyes open and watchful, right up to the end, never flinching, even as the knife goes in.

I send William, Jonah and Michael down to help. Michael clearly does not know what to make of me, now that I am running the farm, and his master and protector is no longer here. I feel a shocking temptation to bully him. I ask him awkward questions, and watch him trying to work out what sort of reply I want. This is how he operates – the truth not being a concept with which he is familiar. I try to feel ashamed of giving him all the worst jobs, and fail utterly. I can only remember his complicity in my father's plot against James, and the enjoyment he took in helping imprison me.

The men go off down the hill. I climb the spiral staircase to the beacon turret, and watch for an enemy who will not come.

There is squealing, men's voices, the screech of the pigsty gate. In my mind I see them tying the ropes. Someone shouts, "Heave!" and there is a thud as a pig heavier than a man lands on the low, flat killingstone with its drainage groove. I see it as if it were painted on the insides of my eyelids. Now the little curly tail will be held down hard, immobilising her, and the ropes pulled tight.

I run. I cannot keep vigil for Veronica Pork. I go rushing and slipping down the spiral staircase to the kitchen.

I had hoped to get to the ale cask unimpeded, but Kate is there with a young woman from the village, Tilly Turner's daughter. I slow down and struggle to be calm.

"Greetings, Esther."

"Ah, Mistress Beatie." Kate beams. "Just in time to hold the earlobe for me. Little Esther here wants to be ornamented like her mother." This is a secret joke, as Tilly Turner is known for jewellery of excessive gaudiness and shoddiness. The pedlars find a ready market in her for some of their more outlandish wares. Now her daughter, Esther, is here having her ears pierced by Kate, our local expert.

112

"No Kate, you do it." I cross to the ale cask, hold my mug under the spigot and release the peg. It is last year's ale, almost clear, very strong. I drink a mugful, fast.

Kate wipes Esther's earlobe with vinegar and pulls it until it is thin, white and taut. The girl's frightened mouth is round and open. Then Kate draws back her hand holding the long darning needle, rainbow-ended from the fire, and plunges it straight through. The skin explodes with a pop. Esther screams. Outside, there is an echo of it, primeval and distant. I turn to escape, but it is too late. The walls circle me like birds of prey, and the flagstones come up and hit me in the face.

"She's been doing too much, what with coping with the master's mazed state, and all the extra work to do, and her aunt on at her all the time."

I am lying on the settle and Kate is looking down at me. Esther Turner, with a sliver of willow bark through one ear and a darning needle through the other, is looking at me too. I try to get up. "Stay there," Kate commands me. "I'm sending one of the lads for the Cockleshell Man."

"No no, there's no need for that." I push myself up, leaning against the roll of sheepskin which Kate has placed under my head. "Veronica Pork has just been killed and it upset me. That's all."

Absentmindedly Kate twists the needle from Esther's cringing ear and follows it quickly in with another sliver of willow bark. Copious blood drips down the girl's neck into the cloth which is wrapped round her shoulders. "Keep the willow in for the pain until tonight, then I'll fix the gold rings in," she orders. "You can go over and fetch the Cockleshell Man for me. That'll do as payment." The girl pales even further, and looks as if she would rather pay ten times than visit the Cockleshell Man. I sometimes forget how feared Cedric is amongst those who believe he practises magic, rather than what is simply his own unconventional brand of medicine.

That day is a turning point. It is the day I realise that no amount of work and frenzied activity is going to blot out thoughts of Robert. As the shortening days go by, his journey will have ended at Lancaster. He will have been examined by the visiting magistrates and consigned to the underground dungeons to await the assizes. Perhaps he is ill or going blind in the darkness. Everyone knows about those dungeons at Lancaster Castle, surely the most evil place on earth. I pray that you, my friend, may never have cause to see them.

At the parsonage, John is careful but friendly. I find it intolerable. I would rather he raged at me. He goes about his duties in his parish, preparing sermons, visiting the sick and bereaved, teaching small village boys to read, and at his own insistence, where parents will allow it, small village girls too. I see their parents' bewildered expressions when he explains to them that it is not such an eccentric idea as they might think. Sometimes I remember some of the feelings which made me agree to marry him.

114

My father needs much care. Verity, my mother and I take turns sitting with him, but most of his daily tending falls to me, since I am there at the parsonage. I feed him from a cup with a spout, spoon mashed vegetables into his mouth as if he were a baby, change his clothes and his bedding.

Three weeks after Verity's betrothal, Germaine and Gerald's betrothal takes place in the church. A week after that, Verity and James are married. It is a day of jollity in a miserable month. Verity now has to lace her skirts and bodices looser, and there is no mistaking the condition she is in, but no one comments on it. By now everyone is used to the idea.

It drizzles on their wedding day, fine drops that drift upwards on the breeze as I help her dress in her old room at Barrowbeck Tower. Here, together again, it seems impossible that so much has happened and that our lives have become so different. Mother has attached loveknots of bright ribbon to every item of Verity's clothing on which she can lay hands: russet silk to her chemise-smock and petticoats, yellow satin to her cream bodice and skirt, red and fawn silk to the beautiful and foresightedly vast new kirtle and gown in dull green and autumn colours which Germaine has made for her. Her pearl and garnet earrings pick out the muted reds and creams of the hooped and padded skirts. "Tears and blood," mutters Kate gloomily.

Despite the season, I have managed to find enough flowers to make a garland for Verity's head, with ears of corn woven through it.

"Truly Sister, do I look as if I need corn for fertility?" she enquires, looking at herself in the mirror. "I look bloody ridiculous." Mother clicks her tongue in disapproval and adjusts the complex patterns of plaits and combs in her daughter's hair.

The bride cup, a huge silver goblet, is waiting in the kitchen, and when Verity is ready we all go downstairs and drink from it, then Kate puts a branch of rosemary tied with ribbons into it, for it to be carried ahead of us to Wraithwaite.

The bridecake, an astonishingly beautiful confection studded with coloured shapes of marchpane, is being investigated by my cat, Caesar, when we go up to the living hall to admire it. "I'll kill that cat," Kate declares. I feel suddenly overcome with affection for my home, and everyone in it, and for no reason I can fathom, sit down and burst into tears. Kate assures me she didn't mean it, and that for certain it will be my turn soon to have a beautiful wedding cake and a lot of fuss made over me. I pick up Caesar and hold him close, getting his black hairs all over my red silk gown, which has a history of being ruined, particularly during my adventures with Robert.

Verity and James are married in the morning, so that a long day's festivities can be fitted in before darkness. Relatives and friends from all over the district come, and the mood is extremely merry. Church musicians play their shawms and crumhorns on Wraithwaite Green in the rain, as we arrive. In church, Verity and James stand solemnly by the carved rood screen and make their vows of love and faithfulness. I am overwhelmed. Just words, yet there is no undoing of them.

After the ceremony, we all go in procession back to Barrowbeck Tower. The little-used series of inter-connecting rooms below the living hall, called the Saints' Gallery, has been decorated with flowers and greenery for the occasion. Around the walls are ears of corn plaited with ribbons. The musicians are assembled on a low platform at the end.

Verity and James lead the first pavane, and the formal dance, so much less familiar than our usual country dances, causes a certain amount of confusion and hilarity. The people who do it with most elegance and style are Hugh and his partner for the day, Mistress Anne Fairweather of Hagditch, veiled, as always. It looks as if Aunt Juniper's matchmaking is paying off, even if not quite as she expected. By the time we get to the galiard, with frequent droppings-out for refreshment, most people couldn't care less what the steps are, and simply improvise.

Later, when the rain stops, we dance the old dances in the wet meadow, getting our feet soaked and our shoes ruined. The musicians go up to the battlements and play more and more wildly. A few villagers come up the valley to watch what is going on.

I dance with John. I dance with him all the time. Today I want to be normal, the girl I was. It is easy. It is fun. In the late afternoon we all go in to feast and drink some more. John and I sit side by side, and after a while, I lean against him, and he puts his arm round me. A few people glance at us and smile. Aunt Juniper glances at us and scowls. When the last remove has been cleared away, and the bridecake cut and shared, we all dance back out into the pale evening, and escort Verity and James down the valley to their home at Low Back Farm, where with much ribaldry they are escorted upstairs and the door slammed on them. "'Tis well to keep to the old customs," says Aunt Juniper, "even when they're not strictly necessary."

We have left Widow Brissenden in charge of Father. I feel I should hurry back now, but instead I wander with John along the small paths through the bracken and brambles, hand in hand when the way is wide enough, whilst most of the wedding guests go in a laughing crowd along the main path. A hedgepig, which surely should be asleep for winter now, ambles across our path. The trees are hazy with dusk. At the edge of the clearing, we stop.

"Everyone knows about us now," says John.

"No one seems surprised."

"No one seems to mind, either."

"Only Aunt Juniper. What about Hugh and Anne Fairweather! I'm glad. It makes me feel better for refusing Hugh."

"He looked happy."

"Unflatteringly."

John laughs. "I'm sure you could always change your

118

mind." He puts his arms round me. "For once your red silk gown doesn't seem to have got you into trouble, though I suppose there's still time. Are you cold?" He pulls me into the shelter of an elder tree. I look up at him. He has relaxed today. He has not felt it necessary to be so cautious with me. His blue eyes are humorous and he looks capable of mischief. We stand close, close enough to read minds. I know he wants to say, "It will be all right," but is afraid to, because that refers to things we must not mention, matters which are not in the spirit of the day, horrors that lie beneath. Tomorrow will be soon enough.

Chapter 12

I wake late the next morning. Daylight is already shining through my little window, throwing a pattern of bars across my bed. I turn over and think about the day before, and Verity's wedding. It seems unreal. It was a good day, an easy day. It was easy being with John. This is how it should be. This is what I could have. We have moved closer. People know about us and the sky hasn't fallen in. Aunt Juniper didn't berate me in public. Hugh looks happy, and will be rich, should he wed with Anne Fairweather. The future is there for us all, serene and graspable. So what if a Scottish marauder is rotting in jail? What in heaven's name did he expect, crossing the border and attacking people's homes?

I remember his skin, pale and slightly freckled on lower arms and upper cheekbones. I remember the way his eyelashes – unseemly long for a man – looked reddish in the sun. I remember him, whole and beautiful, and black melancholy comes crashing back down, only partly caused by the after-effects of all the wine I drank the day before.

John is out. I feed Father his morning posset, then put on my cloak and ride over to Barrowbeck as usual. I am out of patience with all the henchmen, and particularly with Michael. I ask him if he has ever considered the startling concept of being absolutely truthful at all times. He is so surprised that he stares me in the face, unusual in itself, and answers, "No, mistress."

By noon I know I have to get away. I have spent much of the morning stocking and checking the root cellar, and bringing Verity's account books up to date. I go down to the kitchen and scoop a spoonful of dark roast barley into a mug and add a ladleful of hot water. Kate comes up from the cellar carrying a leg of mutton wrapped in bloodied muslin.

"I'm brewing some barley. Do you want some?" I ask her, spooning in honey.

"Thanks lass." She brandishes the mutton. "Hardly worth the bother. There's scarce anyone to cook for, these days, with all of you gone. I reckon Verity and yon yokel should come and live here at t'tower. Combine the farms."

I stare at her. The idea is shocking in its simplicity and obviousness.

"Then," she continues, "fifteen years or so on, there's the farmhouse for her eldest. Or yours." She grins.

"Assuming t'parson can get out of the habit of condemning the pleasures of the flesh so heartily."

I have to laugh. It feels unnatural, as if my face would break. It feels so out of keeping with my mood that there is a moment when it verges on tears. Kate peers at me and pats my shoulder. "It will be all right."

I nearly tell her. I so want to talk about Robert that I nearly blurt it all out. Instead I say, "Thank you, Kate. Indeed, it will be all right." I finish my barley broth, kiss her on the cheek and go out into the meadow.

It is only when I am part way through the woods that I realise where I am going. I am walking to the hermit's cottage, the place where Robert hid last spring and summer, whilst his injuries mended. I trod this path sometimes several times a day when he was at his worst. Now it is overgrown with briars. I force my way through. I wonder if Robert is dead yet in that dungeon. I wonder if his ghost has returned here, and is waiting for me.

When I reach the cottage, I see that the roof has blown off in the autumn gales. This seems so distressing that I sit on the crumbling boundary wall and sob. I put my face in my hands and let the tears drip through my fingers. When I cannot cry any more I still sit there, watching a spider in its web systematically killing a few, late, foolish flies. It is in no hurry. It lets each one become thoroughly enmeshed before it wanders over and finishes it off. Likewise us, I think. I know then that I have to go to Lancaster.

Walking back in the late afternoon, I find that the slugs have come out in the meadow in front of the tower. They cover the grass. It is impossible to avoid stepping on them. Some are long, thick and brown, grained like wood or turds. Some are spheres with flattened edges like the flukes in the bay, and they shift underfoot in the same way that a flatfish hidden in the sand does. Some burst when trodden on, turning explosively inside out, bags of sticky juice, bladders of lard. Likewise us, I think, likewise us all.

When I return to the parsonage it is late. The green is one great shadow, full of all the things which shadows contain. I walk Universe round to the stables at the back. We have taken Dickon on to help us here, and he comes forward now, flushed, from the back of the stables. I glance behind him.

"How are your ears, Esther?" I call. There is shuffling, but no reply.

"I'll see to the horse, mistress."

I hand over the reins. "Thank you, Dickon. I notice that Esther's ears appear to be rotting on her head, where Kate pierced them. I don't know what she's been hanging in them. Do get her to go and see my mother for some marigold balm."

He nods warily. I sigh. For the past few weeks Esther and Dickon have been almost permanently spreadeagled in the hayloft.

I go to check the cart at the back of the stables. I shall need it, if I am to go to Lancaster. It is a slightly sturdier version of our carretta at the tower, with big, broad wheels for getting through the mud, and a high seat at the front.

Esther slides down the ladder from the hayloft and rushes past me before I can speak. Doubtless she is under the impression that I am endowed with the same moral certainties as the parson. If only I were.

The cart's axles seem well-greased, and its wheels have no chips in them. The spokes ring firm and true when I clatter a stick round them. It will take me to Lancaster with no trouble. I have never driven so far alone before, and thoughts of highway robbers and footpads cross my mind, but I know that Universe can outstrip almost anything else on legs, and anyway, I am about to go in and give one of our most dangerous local highway robbers his evening bowl of gruel.

My mother arrives just after sunset, bringing more of Cedric's remedies for my father, and something for me too.

"You are suffering from melancholy, Beatrice," she announces severely, as if I had brought it on myself, which perhaps I have. When Mother Bain has struggled up the stairs to the room she now uses next to mine, and John has gone up to the schoolroom to prepare a sermon, Mother seats herself in the chimney corner, next to my place on the settle, and prepares to give me a lecture. I sigh. I need an early night if I am to leave for Lancaster before sun-up, but I realise this has to be endured at some point. Mother has made several attempts to talk to me about Robert, and so far I have made excuses and avoided it. Now she holds out a small bottle. "Borage and milk thistle. Take it morning and night, without fail. I think we also need to cut down on what you're doing. Kate said you fainted." She peers at me. "You're not pregnant by that Scot, are you?"

"Mother, for heaven's sake…"

"That's a relief then. You realise you must never breathe a word of it? It's worse than the other business of those men having their throats cut. As if Widow Brissenden weren't bad enough, we've had the widow of the other one at the tower today, demanding money. She said she was glad to see the back of her husband, but now we owe her a living." Mother shakes her head. "And Leo…" She watches my face. "Oh yes, I know it was him. Leo offered to forfeit a quarter's wages, but that was obvious nonsense with all those children of his to feed and another on the way. Anyway, I gave the woman enough to keep her going for a while."

She stands up. "Good. Well, I must get back. Take the medicine. Get some rest. I shall call again tomorrow." She gets as far as the door, then turns back. The corner of her mouth has a twist to it, and her eyes have become shiny and a little bloodshot. "I'm sorry, Daughter. That wasn't at all what I came to say. Did you love your Scot? Is that why you are so sad? I am truly sorry. I wish I could help you."

It wasn't what I had intended either. I crumple up on the settle, my head on my knees, and weep uncontrollably.

125

John arrives. Mother Bain arrives. I cannot help it. I cannot stop. After a while Mother puts me to bed, and reads me a passage of Scripture on the subject of accepting loss. I cannot listen to her. I feign sleep. Eventually Mother goes, and finally I do sleep.

I dream I am at home, standing in the doorway. The homesteaders are gathered in front of me. "Save us," they say.

I shake my head. "I must save Robert," I explain, then shut the door in their faces and run up the spiral staircase. At the window of the men's common room Robert's face is looking in.

"Save me," he says. I shake my head regretfully, and push.

Chapter 13

When I wake, the house is dark and silent. I push aside the bed-curtains and step cautiously to the floor. The fire in the chimney hole is almost out, and the room very cold. I hear Mother Bain mutter in her sleep, then fall silent again. The house timbers creak as a gust of wind beats round them. I light my candle and stand it in front of the long mirror, so that it illuminates the room, then open the cedar chest in the corner. It is full of bedlinen. I lean in, and feel under the sheets, breathing in the scent of lavender. I am scarcely able to reach the bottom, but at last I locate the rosewood box that I hid there, and pull it to the surface. It is very beautiful, carved with roses and inlaid with mother-of-pearl. It is full of gold pieces. This is my dowry. It will be John's if I marry him. What I am committing is theft. I count out half the

127

gold pieces and put them in my leather drawstring pocket, then pull on my clothes and write a note to John.

The brass clock is still lying on the chair on the landing, but I cannot tell what time it means. One of the markers is between the three and the four, so perhaps that means it is between three and four. That would make sense. I take one look back into my room, the bed draped in grey velvet, the raddled panelling and floorboards, the clothes press with my brushes and hairpins and yesterday's black woollen stockings on it, the long mirror, its frame carved with vine leaves, from which my shadowy form looks back at me. I have come to love this room. For a moment I am afraid to leave it. For a moment I just want to go back to bed.

I tiptoe to John's room. I was going to push the note under his door, but now I lift the latch and creep in. He has gone to sleep sitting up, with a book open on his lap. His candle is still alight, almost burned down. I stand and look at him. His head is turned to one side against the pile of bolsters. He is deeply asleep. I recognise the bedcover, embroidered with blue silk flowers. Verity and I made it between us, in the days when Germaine was still teaching us how to sew, and we fancied ourselves as broderers. It was one of the items of needlework sold on the family stall at the May Fair that year. I hadn't realised that John had bought it.

I look at the flowers' exaggerated design, unsatisfyingly wrong, a triumph of hope over botany. They are the same colour as John's eyes. For a moment I wish he would wake up, see me, stop me. I tuck the note under his candlestick, blow out the candle and go downstairs.

Universe is frisky as I harness him to the cart. I stroke Meadowsweet's nose when she ambles up to me in her stall. "You have to stay and carry the parson for a couple of days," I tell her.

I open all four parts of the stable door and fasten them back. First light is showing now behind the church. The clock must be wrong, or else I have misread it. I lead Universe out, with the cart rattling behind him, unnervingly louder than the birds' dawn chorus. I shut the doors, hitch up my coat and climb aboard.

Universe likes pulling the cart, and now he wants to be away, but I walk him quietly until we are out of the village. Then, despite the twisting track and the mud under our wheels, I snap the long whip over his ears and let him run. His hooves throw up black spray as we gallop with the dawn on our left. When we reach The King's Strete south, I give him his head, and he goes flat out. I don't want to be gone longer than I have to, and controlling the cart will take my mind off what will now be happening back at the parsonage. John will be waking. He will be finding my note. He will be reading it.

When I am well on my way, I slow Universe to a trot. On either side of us the low sun is turning the grass fire-green. I look up and see an arrowhead of grey geese, also flying south. Nearer Lancaster, a merlin plummets into my path, frightening Universe and almost causing us to tip over. In front of my face it seizes a meadow pipit in full flight, then pulls up its long talons and soars, leaving only a fading scream behind. This is fierce country. When I pass the first farms and houses on the edge of the town, I understand what an artificial construct a town is. Below the town lies the land that was once ploughed fields, and below the land that was once ploughed fields lies the wild.

Lancaster is a fair town of many small houses and a few larger ones huddled together below John o' Gaunt's castle. I cross the River Lune by the long, arched bridge, pass the boggy water meadows of Green Ayre with their hustling slap of watermills, gallop along Chiney Lane and stop at the George in Market Street, where Mother, Verity and I always stay when we visit Lancaster. The landlord comes out into the cobbled courtyard and takes the reins as I climb down. I am dismayed. It is a new innkeeper.

"Where is Master Slatter?" I ask.

He shakes his head and inhales through his teeth. "Nasty business that, mistress. He was tekken by the sweating sickness at Michaelmas. Matthew Postlethwaite at your service." He glances at my best coat and hat and ushers me into a private room and fusses about a bit. When I am installed on a cushioned settle in the corner he puts a spill to the fire and then brings me a cup of spiced red wine almost too hot to drink. "Are you travelling far, mistress?" I can see that he is deeply curious that I am travelling alone.

"No, not far, Master Postlethwaite. How go things in Lancaster just now? I hear you have Scots imprisoned in the castle." I look up at the dark building on the hill behind us. Matthew Postlethwaite seats himself, with a raised eyebrow for permission.

"Aye mistress. Twenty or so. Nasty buggers, begging your pardon. The wife and I saw them brought in. They say the queen wants to make an example of them. We serve out good justice here in Lancaster. We haven't forgotten them poxy Scots of Robert the Bruce burning Lancaster down." He pokes the rushes on the floor with his foot. A small mouse runs out. "Little devils. Like Scots they are, right quick and destructive."

"You have good memories in Lancaster, then, considering Robert the Bruce came several centuries ago. Will the Scots get good justice if Lancastrians hate them so?"

"Certainly they will! Our Justices of Assize are even a bit too scrupulous and fair if you ask some folks. They won't even condemn witches to hang no more unless they're proven to have done actual murder by witchcraft. Soft as pie they are these days. Speaking of which, can I get you something to eat?"

"Oh, no thank you. I must be going." I finish my wine, pay him and follow him out to where the stable boy is leading Universe forward for me. I climb up and take the reins. "I'm grateful to you, Master Postlethwaite, and will undoubtedly see you again before too long."

"The pleasure's mine." He bows as I drive out under the arch.

Not many people are about on the hill as I drive over the cobbles, between the small houses. They say that Lancaster hasn't made up its population since the Black Death back in the 1300s. The castle stands on the summit of the hill, alone except for the Church of Blessed Mary of Lancaster, which is behind it. I stop the cart by the castle's great gatehouse with its twin towers. The portcullis is up and two soldiers in the familiar red and brown uniforms are standing guard, their swords out of their scabbards, blades bending slightly as they lean on them.

Two very old women, arm in arm, stop and stare at me sitting there. Their clothes are ragged but neatly patched. They look to be from Gardyner's Almshouses down the hill. "I hear there are Scots in there at the moment," I say to them, in what I hope is a casual, gossipy tone. They nod, move closer and settle their feet comfortably for a chat.

"Aye, we get all sorts of rabble foisted on us here. Folks don't like it, you know. Not Scots. We'll not be safe in our beds."

Her companion frowns ferociously and lowers her basket to the ground. "Sooner they're strung up the better." She jerks her chin in the direction of Gallows Hill on the far side of town.

"They're in there." It's one of the guards speaking, joining in the conversation. He gestures towards a tower visible beyond the gatehouse. "They're under the Well Tower."

"Indeed?" I smile at him encouragingly.

"In the Lancaster Dungeon. You can rest safe, goodwives." He nods to the old women. "They're chained to the walls and half dead by now. They'll not be coming out to hide under your beds." He laughs. "I doubt most of 'em will last until the Lent Assizes anyway. One's dead already. Coughed hisself to death. Them underground walls are running with damp."

"Aye well, God bless his soul and good riddance to bad rubbish." The first old woman looks at me. "Are you looking for aught, mistress?"

"Oh, I, er, have travelled in to visit the church. I thank you." I turn back to the soldier. "These Scots, are they... allowed any food at all from outside? Or are they starving as they deserve?"

The soldier glances round to see if anyone else can hear him. "Well mistress, there's been a number of people tried to send..."

The second old woman interrupts him. "You'd never credit it, lady, but the vicar's sister tried to take in food when she heard they were starving. Just fancy that, sending good food to Scots instead of to honest English folks like us as needs it." She shakes her head in disbelief. "Well, best get on. God grant your prayers in the church, mistress."

"Aye. God bless." They both nod to me and move away.

"And you, mistresses." I watch them go, then move Universe a little closer to the soldiers. The cart jolts over the stones. The two men look at me curiously.

"Are the Scots allowed visitors at all?" I ask lightly. "Suppose a mother or sister of one of them arrived?"

The first soldier frowns. "I can't rightly say, mistress. They'd likely be locked up as well."

His companion steps towards me. "And what would your interest be, lady?"

I ignore him. The first soldier is clearly a better bet. I clank the bag of coins at my waist. "I don't suppose they pay you very well, do they? Would you be interested in doing a few little jobs for me when you're off duty?" I keep my voice cool. "It's just a spot of casual work."

The first soldier shakes his head, though he looks regretful. "Nay madam, it isn't allowed. The captain would have me flogged."

I sigh in irritation, then realise that the second soldier is leaning towards me.

"I'll do it, lady." He tries an experimental leer, then thinks better of it as I give him my coldest stare. "I've a wife back home and kiddies to feed. Captain doesn't scare me."

"Well..." The first soldier seems to be reconsidering.

"Nay, I'm doing it. You had your chance." The second soldier frowns at him. "And I'll kill you if you tell on me."

The first soldier straightens up and stares away righteously into the distance.

"I can use you both." I wonder if I am making a mistake here. The first soldier is clearly not as corruptible as I had hoped, though once corrupted he might prove more reliable than the second. I hold out a silver coin to each of them. "Here's half a crown as a gesture of good faith. There will be ten gold sovereigns each if you prove satisfactory."

Their eyes widen. Ten gold sovereigns is as much as they would normally earn in five years.

"Let's arrange where we can meet when you're off duty, and I'll explain what I need doing."

Chapter 14

$\mathcal{I}$ walk Universe round the side of the castle and stop at the stile to the church. It is peaceful here. The sun warms my back. I loop the reins round a fencepost and leave Universe to crop the grass. So Robert is under the Well Tower – close enough to hear me if it had not been for the walls and solid earth between us. I decide to approach it from the far side, by continuing on round the castle. The soldiers will not see me here. I have no wish for them to suspect my plan before the money is dangling temptingly before their eyes, to silence them.

I take a small piece of paper from my pocket and check the knife at my waist. I walk fast and silently. There is no one about.

The wall below the Well Tower is dark and sheer. I

stand at its base, looking at the place where the stones enter the ground. Somewhere below here is Robert.

"Robert," I say out loud. Around me is silence. There are no birds singing. Robert. I think his name with all the power of my will. I press my palms and forehead to the cold wall, and remember the look and feel of him. I remember his skin and eyes and hands. I remember the spirit of him, imprinted into the stones of Barrowbeck. He will be alive there when he is dead here.

I take out the fold of paper on which I have written the lines of an ancient blessing for those in extremity, copied from a faded inscription on the east wall of the lady chapel in our church at Wraithwaite. I use my knife to dig a crevice next to the wall, then ease the paper into it and press it in deep with the blunt side of the knife, down into the earth which holds Robert. I say the words in my head as they are written:

> *I tell thee thou forespoken toothe and tonge,*
> *hearte and hearte raithe,*
> *three thinges thee boote moste,*
> *the father sonne and holighuoste.*

I remain there for a while with my head against the stones, then stand up and walk back, along by the fence. Beyond it is the church's small sanctuary house. If only Robert and his companions could have reached that. I have heard of them having twenty or more in there at a time, before now.

Universe is fidgeting, but I am unwilling to leave Robert yet, and I have an hour to wait before the soldiers come off duty. I climb the stile and walk past the front of the church, looking down towards the Roman ruins and the river. A fair town indeed, but not so fair from the end of a rope. As I climb back on to the cart I can see Gallows Hill a ghastly mile away across the valley. On it stand five gibbets, twigs on the skyline.

Back at the George I leave Universe to be fed and watered. The landlord greets me like a long-lost friend. It is now mid-afternoon.

"Have you a room, Master Postlethwaite?" I ask when he brings me a small goblet of ypocras.

"We do, mistress, and welcome. Drink's on the house."

"I thank you. I'd like to stay the night then." I start coughing at the strength of the drink. He nods approvingly. "That'll warm your cockles, mistress, and it's a good cure for the melancholic humours too, if you should happen to suffer from them."

I take off my coat and hat. "I wonder, would it be possible to borrow a cloak or shawl, Master Postlethwaite? I want to walk along by your beautiful river for a while, but I would prefer not to be conspicuous."

The landlord nods. "Aye mistress. I daresay the wife'll be glad to oblige."

He leaves me briefly and returns with a knitted black shawl of impressive proportions. I thank him, wrap it round myself and walk out into the cooling afternoon. Once out of sight I draw the shawl up over my head and wind it about me more tightly.

Despite my attempt at invisibility, I realise that, as a stranger, I am being watched as I stride along Chiney Lane, past the Mare Maid where the smell of ale nearly floors me, and down Bridge Lane to the river. The water is sucking at the riverbanks with the turning of the tide.

The men are there already, by Weary Wall. I can feel my hands sweating as I hold on to my pocket of money.

"Good day again, good sirs." I make an attempt at briskness. "The work I have for you requires secrecy. Can I trust you?"

The two men glance at one another. "Let's see the money first, mistress," says the second soldier.

I hesitate, then show them the money briefly before returning it quickly to the folds of my shawl. It seems little enough, suddenly, to ask men to risk their lives for. They nod. "Aye. Right," says the first soldier.

"I need you to get a Scot out of the Lancaster Dungeon." I look at them, and wait.

They draw back from me. Their eyes stay locked on mine for a moment, then the first soldier whispers something to the second, and is gone. I'm shocked at the expression of disgust which I saw on his face. The second soldier gives me what is clearly intended to be a reassuring smile. "He knows I'll kill him if he tells," he says. "Well now, anything can be done. Course, if I'm doing two men's work, I'll be wanting two men's wages. Half of it now." He holds out his hand, moving closer. He stinks of ale.

139

"You'll get it when you've done the job." I hold the money tightly against my stomach. "Tell me how you will do it."

His eyes narrow. "There are ways. At night. It means greasing a few palms. Buying a bit of blindness. Mebbe a heavy drinking session for all the lads afore they go on night duty. Can't be done without money though, lady. When do you want him out?"

When do I want Robert out? Can it be this easy?

"Tonight?"

"Aye, tonight's best. The captain and sergeant are both away tonight." He holds out his hand again. A passer-by gives a whistle. I open my pocket.

"One gold sovereign now, the rest later."

"Two."

"One, take it or leave it."

"Is he your lover, this Scot?"

"One now, the rest later."

"You'll get no one else to do it, lady. Two, or I'm off up the hill to tell on you."

"Look, I don't want to be unreasonable, but if I give you two now, you might be tempted just to pocket them and not risk doing the job." Is this man open to reason?

He thinks for a moment, then holds out his hand again. I place one gold sovereign in his palm.

"Be at the back of the Well Tower, near the sanctuary house, at first light, lady. He'll be there. Failing all else, you can get him into sanctuary. Which one of the evil bastards is it?"

140

"His name's Robert Lacklie. Tell him Beatrice sent you."

"Beatrice." The soldier regards me appraisingly. "Well, Beatrice, there's one more thing. If he's dead already, I still get half the money you promised. I'll still have tekken half the risks."

"Agreed."

Shockingly, then, the soldier kisses me. I can hardly believe what is happening. He presses his mouth to mine, and grabs my backside in both hands, one still bunched with the money. I recoil, gasping in horror, and he strides away, laughing, up the alley away from the river. "Can't be fussy, if you'll have a Scot," he shouts over his shoulder, and vanishes from sight, still laughing.

It seems a long way back to the inn, even running as fast as I can. I expect every moment to hear sounds of pursuit and shouts of "Treason!" The landlord meets me once more in the doorway of the George.

"All well, mistress?" He looks at me more closely and I realise how dishevelled I must look.

"Yes. I thank you." I control my voice and steady my breathing and remove Mistress Postlethwaite's black shawl. The innkeeper leads me through the dim public bar, and I see to my surprise that the young captain who escorted the Scots south is there, drinking alone. A few other drinkers are sitting on benches round the room, talking and laughing. A mangy dog snores by the fire.

"Captain."

The young man looks up sharply and rises to his feet. "Madame?"

"I saw you when you passed through our village with your prisoners."

The landlord looks at me, doubt suddenly in his eyes. He must think I am trying to pick this man up. I need to re-emphasise my respectability. It's vital that I retain his co-operation. "I'm... I'm... er... the parson's wife from a village in the West Moorland." I glance sideways at the landlord to see if this does the trick.

The captain bows. "Enchanted, madame. Captain Foreman."

I see out of the corner of my eye that the landlord has relaxed. Presumably parsons' wives are expected to go round being friendly to everyone. "It must have been a long, difficult journey for you, with your charges, captain," I sympathise.

The captain nods. "Indeed it was. We serve Lord Ravenswyck, and he lends our services to the queen. We'll be glad to go home in April."

"I'm sure of it." I sit on the edge of a table, and the captain resumes his seat. Everyone else in the tavern now appears to be listening to our conversation – two strangers talking about unusual matters. The landlord pours us both a goblet of wine and sits down too. A vast woman with her skirts tucked up to reveal her underskirts, and her head wrapped in a white cloth, comes out of the back room to hear better. I smile at her, and thank her for the loan of her shawl, then turn back to the captain. "I hear the Scots are not to be tried until March. Will they last that long, do you think? They looked in pretty poor case when they were passing through our village."

The captain shrugs. "We lost one on the way, a young lad, and the jailers say another died last week."

"He'd be one of the older ones, would he?"

"No madame, another young lad. There's some choking sickness going round them."

Is Robert a young lad? He's older than I am, though not by much. I suppose to the captain he might seem a young lad. "How did you come by your prisoners, captain?"

The captain leans back expansively in the room's one upholstered chair, and smiles, looking around, sure of his audience. "We rounded them up from all along the border. Most of them were captured when they were on raiding parties."

"Were none just wayfarers? Maybe trying to get back to Scotland? Might some be innocent Scots and not raiders?"

He laughs. "Innocent Scots, madame?" He looks round the room for supporting laughter. There is a ripple of merriment.

I persist. "It's well enough to laugh, captain, but do you not feel we encourage these raids to continue by treating captured Scots so badly? It might be better to use them as a political bargaining tool."

"Political *bargaining* tool..." He says it in a deliberately understated tone, then bursts into even louder laughter.

143

"Well you'd better try telling that to the queen, madame." He shakes his head and raises his eyebrows at his audience.

I rise to my feet and smile tightly at the landlord. "Could we have a word somewhere, please, Master Postlethwaite?"

He looks at me curiously. "Aye. Come with me." He gestures to his wife. "Will you get this lady's room ready, pet?" In a lower voice he adds, "Put a spot of wormwood down." My spirits sink as I wonder what form of infestation this heralds – fleas, lice, bedbugs, or maybe all three. The innkeeper leads me to a room at the back, where casks of ale are stacked. "Come behind the casks, mistress. It's right private there. Now, what can I do for you?" He looks as if strange requests were commonplace for him.

In a whisper, I tell him what he can do for me. It takes some time. "And I shall need my horse and cart ready before first light, sir. I shall pay you now for both my board and for your trouble. Here is the other money to hold for me. Are you willing to do this? Can I trust you? I feel I can. I hope I have not misjudged you."

The landlord holds out his hand. I give him two gold coins and a tightly tied drawstring purse which clinks heavily as it changes hands. He says nothing, but touches the coins to his forehead, and bows. As we return to the public bar he says under his breath, "For my own sake I'll not be seen as favouring you, mistress."

I nod. "I'll take the air in the courtyard until my room is ready."

144

It is a gusty evening. On the hill a bell tolls, the sound loud then soft with the strength of the wind. When I first see Meadowsweet, I cannot at first make sense of it. "Aye sir," the stable boy is saying to someone on the far side of her. "In the tavern, sir. Oh, thank you, sir." I stand motionless just outside the inn doorway, as Meadowsweet is led away, and John and I come face to face across the courtyard.

"Beatrice." His voice is controlled but his face furious.

"Ah! Hubby's arrived then, has he?" It is the captain, reaching a not-too-taxing conclusion, in view of John's attire.

The landlord appears. "Room's ready, mistress. My wife will show you up." He looks surprised when he sees John. "Ah, parson sir, welcome. We didn't realise you'd be joining your wife." He glances at me uncertainly, and I can see he is wondering if my husband knows of the unorthodox duties for which I am paying such large sums of money. "It's a good big room, anyhow," he adds. "You'll both be comfortable."

"Indeed we shall. Thank you, landlord. We'll go up to it now." John takes my arm in a tight grip, nods to the captain and landlord, and leads me indoors. We follow Mistress Postlethwaite upstairs. She barely fits her bulk betwen the leaning wooden walls of the stairwell. At the top a partly open gallery leads to the sleeping chambers, which are ranged along a dark landing. The stables are across the yard below the gallery, and I can hear Universe's

145

distinctive whinny. John glances over the rail towards the stables.

"Will you be wanting food, my loves?" the landlady asks as she shows us into the first room on the corner of the gallery and the landing. It is low-ceilinged, with two truckle beds, a table and bench, two cushioned chairs and a muddy, rush-covered floor. I reply before John can voice an opinion, which I imagine from the look on his face would be negative. I am hungry and tired, and moreover I fear we might need some distraction.

"Yes please, Mistress Postlethwaite. Have you a pie or something like that? Some mulled wine too? Maybe some pickled cabbage?"

"Aye, certainly mistress." She wheezes out and we are left alone.

John takes off his cloak and half sits on the table, one booted foot on the floor and one swinging. I look at how beautiful he is, and I wonder if I am slightly unhinged to be risking losing him, for a Scot.

"Well, Beatrice? What on earth do you think you're doing? I've searched all over Lancaster for you."

I stand with my back against the door. "I left you a letter, John, to explain..."

"So you did. Very well written it was, too. I've taught you well."

I straighten up at his savagely sarcastic tone. "So why are you here? I think it was perfectly clear, wasn't it?"

John takes hold of my shoulders. "How could you,

Beatrice?" he asks in a raised voice. "How could you come here like this?"

"I'm rescuing Robert!" I hiss under my breath. "For God's sake be quiet!"

"Rescuing Robert? *Rescuing Robert?* Have you any idea how sick and tired I am of this sodding Scot?" He is ignoring my plea to lower his voice. "Do you really think I want to talk about him day in and day out, and know how you feel about him? Now you have some mad idea about getting him out of the castle? Beatrice, this desperate foolishness has got to stop."

I look into his flushed, angry face, and am horrified. I see suddenly, and all too clearly, what I am doing to him. I kiss him. "I'm sorry, John. I have to do this for Robert, but I wish it did not upset you."

I think we are both so surprised by my kiss that for a moment neither of us does anything. Then John takes hold of my face and kisses me back. He says, "I am too jealous of this Scot, Beatrice. I truly can't bear it."

I wrap my arms round him. There have always been nine years and a familiar classroom between us. Now, suddenly, we are just two people alone in a strange room in a strange town. John half-lifts me off the floor.

The door opens with a clatter against the wall. "Your pie, sir, madam." The landlady comes in bearing a huge, hot pie. Her husband follows with a dish of buttered parsnips, a plate of pickled cabbage and a steaming jug of mulled wine on a tray. "This'll warm you up all right." She puts the pie down carefully on the splintery table. Hot gravy tips out through the three cuts on top of it, then seeps back again. For a moment I feel a mixture of overwhelming hunger and overwhelming desire. Our hosts leave, with solemn expressions on their faces, but immediately on the landing there is laughter and the landlady's voice exclaiming, "My, but passions run high with yon northerners, and no mistake. I thought earlier as to how he was going to kill her, rather than owt else, judging by that look on his face." I don't think Mistress Postlethwaite realises what a carrying voice she has.

"Nay well, you can't tell with the clergy. Like as not it's all the same to them."

I look over at John who has gone to sit on the bed. He is trying not to laugh. I sit where he had been sitting on the edge of the table, swinging my foot. I can feel the heat of the pie behind me. From the landing comes the sound of a slap and a shriek.

"Get off, Matthew Postlethwaite! Whatever's got into you!"

John and I start laughing. I take my knife from my belt to cut the pie, and as I do so, I see grains of earth still adhering to it. For a moment my knees feel so weak they threaten to pitch me to the floor, but I wipe the black fragments carefully into my handkerchief, tuck it into my bodice and plunge the knife blade deeply into the pie.

John comes up behind me. "Why, exactly, are we pretending to be married, Beatrice?"

I glance over my shoulder. "I need to appear more respectable than I truly am, John." I lift steaming hunks of pie on to the two wooden plates with my knife and the spoon which has been provided.

"So I have my uses."

I hand him a plate. "Occasionally."

"How exactly are you proposing to rescue Robert?" He takes the plate and helps himself to parsnips and cabbage.

"Bribery. Treason."

"I see. And you really think you can get him out of Lancaster Castle? You must love him very much."

I pause, leaning on the table with the serving utensils in my fists. "John... anything I do for Robert does not take away from what you and I have. I nearly killed him when I pushed him off the tower, and I must make up for it. Don't you understand? He's starving and cold and chained to a wall in a dungeon. Surely you must feel some pity for him."

"Of course I do, but there are hundreds of prisoners to pity, and it isn't just pity as far as you're concerned, is it?"

"I don't know the hundreds, John. I only know Robert. I don't deny it isn't just pity. It's... I don't know... I feel responsible for him. I helped Cedric mend his arm. We were friends, and we shared danger. He was going back to Scotland to try to stop the raids. It's a waste, a terrible waste."

I cannot add, he haunts me.

Chapter 15

*B*e at the Well Tower at first light, the soldier said. Despite having slept so little last night, I do not expect to sleep much tonight either. Whilst we eat, I tell John what I have been doing. His expression becomes grim. "You're mad," he says. "I'm feigning marriage to a madwoman."

After the meal we sit by the fire and drink wine. I remove my cap and push my hair back. John throws another log on the fire. He looks exhausted. "I don't expect I shall sleep," I tell him. "Please, you have the bed."

He shakes his head. "No, you'll sleep if you try. I'll wake you before first light."

In the end, we both doze uneasily on the chairs. We keep the candles burning so that we can see the mice, which keep making unpredictable dashes across the floor.

Lancaster is a noisy place at night. There is shouting and banging, and it grows louder as the long hours go by. My courage falters at some point during the dark hours after midnight, and I wonder if I am indeed mad, to be trying to manipulate the power of the law. I watch John sleeping, his head lolling sideways, and if the floor had not been alive with vermin, I would have knelt by him, and rested my head on his knee, for I feel greatly in need of comfort.

The noise in the streets suddenly becomes closer and louder still. It sounds to be just down Market Street. John wakes. "What's happening?" he asks. The fire has reddened one side of his face, and he has kicked off his shoes in his sleep. I feel a painful tenderness towards him.

"I don't know." Despite the vermin, I go and kneel amongst the muddy rushes by his feet. He strokes my hair.

"Mad Mistress Becker, I could live very well like this."

I ignore a mouse that runs lightly over my ankles, and turn my head so that John's hand touches my mouth. "John, I do love you." I turn his hand over and kiss the palm. He leans towards me.

Something is wrong, though. There is the sound of heavy feet on the stairs, and voices coming from the gallery outside our room. At the same moment, loud, rough voices in the street start shouting orders. Fists hammer on doors below us. John and I jump to our feet. As we do so, the door of our chamber crashes open and

151

the innkeeper stands there, holding a candle, barring our way, his nightshirt tucked into his breeches. "'Tis the military," he pants, staring at me. "They're searching for a Scottish spy. A woman."

His wife appears behind him. "You're daft, Matthew. This lady here's a parson's wife."

"This is ridiculous." John steps forward.

The landlord continues, "They're searching all the houses, and soon they'll be here." He never shifts his gaze from me.

John takes hold of my arm. "Really, landlord, whatever is it to do with us? You surely don't imagine that this lady is a Scottish spy?" He gives an airy laugh.

"There, I told you so." Mistress Postlethwaite steps forward into the room, vaster than ever in her nightclothes.

"Nevertheless," John continues, "we are much disturbed by the rowdiness of Lancaster at night, so we shall be on our way, since it has become impossible to sleep."

"Indeed. Very wise." Master Postlethwaite stands back from the doorway and points over the gallery rail towards the stables. "I've put a hayloft ladder down from the gallery, for your convenience. It will save you the trouble of going through the inn. Across the far side of the yard, to the right of the stables, runs a ginnel. It teks you through to Chennell Lane, where I've fastened your horses and cart. The military have searched along there already. Best get on now."

John takes a bag of coins from his belt. "How much do we owe you, Master Postlethwaite?"

The innkeeper puts up his hands in refusal. "Nay sir, I'll tek it out of what your wife gave me. That's more than enough." He turns to me. "I'd not be doing this, mind, if I truly thought you were a Scottish spy. I'll vouchsafe from what you've said to me, and what you said to yon captain, that it weren't treason on your mind, so that's why I'm helping you. There's a fair fever against Scots just now. It clouds folk's sense."

"I thank you for your kindness, sir." I clasp his hand briefly. "My husband was not involved in this matter at all." To emphasise this I say to John, "I'm sorry."

Mistress Postlethwaite gapes at me. "You mean... you *are* the Scottish spy?"

I shake my head impatiently. "Don't be ridiculous, madam. Do I look like a Scottish spy? It's just that some people – mistakenly – might have reason to think me so, because of my desire to avoid a miscarriage of justice." I gather up my possessions and move towards the door. "John, we'd better go."

The landlord holds the door open for us. "I'll help you both on to the ladder."

"There's no need for us to escape down ladders," John answers coldly. "We will leave by the front door. If we meet the soldiers, we will talk to them."

The landlord grimaces in alarm. "You'll not reason with them, sir. They'll tek her in, and it'll mean trouble for the George too. That captain hasn't put two and two together yet. He was well cupshotten when your lady here was talking about releasing Scots, but once he sees her, it'll likely all come back to him. Best get going, sir."

John frowns. "I can assure you, Master Postlethwaite, that this matter is better confronted. It will easily be resolved by a straightforward discussion with this captain you mentioned. The prospect of galloping out of Lancaster at dead of night with the militia after us is not an idea that appeals to me vastly."

I put my hand on John's arm. "John, I am going by the ladder. You may please yourself. It will soon be first light, and I have business to attend to. There is no reason for you to be involved." I turn to the landlady. "Forgive me for my rudeness, madam. I meant no offence."

Mistress Postlethwaite inclines her head, her mouth still hanging open. I step out of the room on to the dark landing, and stop. The narrow space is crowded with soldiers. We are too late.

"Got her!"

"You were right, sarge!"

Hands reach out. In the dimness, more armed figures dressed in red and brown come rushing along the gallery, on heavy feet now, the need for stealth gone. Loud voices burst out all around me. I reel back, crashing into John and the landlord who had emerged behind me. The soldiers all seem to be shouting at once. I cannot tell in the darkness if any of them are the two whom I tried to bribe.

"What's this, madam?"

"Going somewhere at this time of night?"

I find my arms roughly held. There is a scuffle behind me, and John's furious voice. "Let her go *at once!*"

"Steady on there, parson. That's no way for a man of the cloth to behave. *If* that's what you truly are."

"We've got her, sir," an unseen soldier shouts, somewhere along the landing.

So this is it. This is the end. I wonder if they will imprison me with Robert. A brief, ghastly joy blazes amid the terror. Then I hear a high wailing from along the landing where the last soldier shouted, and I find my arms released.

"Here she is, sir. This is the one."

A candle flares. The captain appears at the far end of the gallery. The men's pushing and shouting turn to a hushed shuffling. In the flickering light I see a woman being dragged from a room along the landing. She is thin, her clothes plain, a woman twice my age. Tinderboxes click and more candles blaze. The woman's eyes fix momentarily on mine. Then she is bundled away.

"Who...?"

There is no answer to my question. The woman does not wail again. Slowly the commotion dies away into the street, and only the captain remains.

"Begging your pardon, madame. Sorry to have disturbed you. Our informant said upstairs at the George, and naturally, when my men saw you leaving at this hour of the night, well, it was just a case of mistaken identity. No harm done, I trust? Then I'll say good morrow to you, ladies, sirs." He bows to me and to the landlady who has come to stand next to me, salutes John and the landlord, then strides away along the gallery and down the stairs.

For several seconds none of us speaks, then Master Postlethwaite says in a shaky voice, "I'll get us all some ypocras."

An hour later, in the squelching blackness of the stable yard, I climb on to the cart and John once more mounts Meadowsweet. "The sooner we're home the better," he says in a cool voice. He has been chilly towards me ever since my threat to leave on my own. He turns in the saddle. "I trust you no longer intend to wait at the castle, considering what we have just been through, and the levels of security there will be?"

I gather up the reins. "Do we really have to go all through this again, John? Do I have to keep justifying what I am doing over and over again to you? Truly, I am weary of it. I do not require your assistance or your escort. Please go home." I flick the reins across Universe's back and send us moving out of the yard. I know that John is probably right, and that there is little point in keeping my appointment with the second soldier now. This will not have been a night for freeing Scots. My alternative arrangement with the innkeeper will undoubtedly have to be called into action. Nevertheless, because miracles sometimes do happen, I turn up the hill towards the castle.

Great torches burn at the castle gates and along the battlements, lighting up the walls as if in a masque. Soldiers are patrolling to and fro, but no one pays any attention to us, a respectably clad woman traveller heading towards the church in the darkness before dawn, with a member of the clergy as her escort. John rides behind me in silence as we proceed round the back of the castle to the dark church and sanctuary house. Down the hill to the west are green flickers of iridiscence from the marsh, where the river makes a sharp curve. To the east, beyond the Well Tower, the first lightening of the sky outfaces the false brassiness of the torches. We stop. There is no one waiting for us here.

It is very cold. We wait a long time, not speaking. I gain the impression that John is wordless with fury. I have nothing left to say. It grows colder still. I suddenly notice in amazement that John has brought a small firearm with him. It is hanging next to his saddlebag. It is far smaller than anything of the sort which I have ever seen before, light enough to be fired held in two hands, and beautifully inlaid with bone and ivory. There is a matching decorated horn flask for gunpowder, attached to a strap. I gesture at it. "That is a fine looking thing."

John jumps, as if waking from a dream. "Oh... I thought that if we travelled back late yesterday we might need it. It's a matchlock. It works like that old hagbut you have over at the tower. Unfortunately, I am not very deft at reloading it, so after one shot at a highway robber we should probably both be dead."

157

I laugh. For a moment, just for a brief flash, the desolation lifts. John stares at me. As far as reloading is concerned, I know that I could do it quickly and accurately myself, if the need arose, but now is not the moment to say so. A more immediate concern is the prospect of him shooting his foot off, since the matchlock is hanging barrel downwards beside his leg. Under the pretext of admiring it, I climb down from the cart and move the firearm to the back of his saddlebag. I look up and catch an expression of pity on his face. With a suffocating sense of defeat, I realise then the extent to which I have failed. Dawn is fully up. The morning dew is collapsing in silver rivulets on the harness metal. No one has come and no one is coming. It is time to give up and leave. I climb back on to the cart and gather up the reins.

We set off back the way we came. At the gatehouse the guards have changed, and I realise with a jolt that the first soldier is once again standing by the gates, with a new companion. His expression is prim and dutiful. I stare at him and am swamped with rage. He is standing to attention, and apart from a flicker of the eyelids, shows no sign of recognition when I rein in and climb down from the cart.

"Where is he?" I go and stand in front of him. I can hear John dismounting behind me.

"Whatever are you talking about, madam?" The soldier's eyes slide away from mine. His companion glances across curiously.

"Where is your friend of yesterday? He and I have business to finish."

John takes hold of my arm. "Get back on the cart, Beatrice."

I pull away from him. The first soldier, looking more confident, shrugs. "Can't rightly understand what you're talking about, lady."

I want to grab him by the doublet and shake him. "Answer me, clod-head! I am not here to play riddles with you!"

His companion edges towards us, sensing violence, then stops, and I see to my astonishment that John has come to stand next to me, holding the matchlock, and appears to be innocently polishing its ivory inlay with his sleeve.

"Well?" I demand. "I wish to know what happened."

"He were drunk," the first soldier mutters sulkily. "He got drunk and violent afore the sergeant even went off duty. So were half the night-duty guards. Legless they were. He took 'em for a right poulticing at the Naked Taylor. Sarge locked 'em all up and had him flogged."

"Thank you." I turn away. John holds out his hand and helps me back on to the cart.

We ride out of Lancaster, travelling fast with the day brightening on our right. Half way we stop to eat the bread and cheese which Mistress Postlethwaite packed for us. "I'll speak to the Vicar of Lancaster and see if he can get in to see the Scots," says John. "I'll have a word with the bishop too. But frankly, don't be hopeful, for it is all most unlikely to help."

If we had thought about it, we might have realised it would be more sensible to arrive back separately. We were not to know that the parsonage would be full of people, all aware of our overnight absence, and witnessing our return together. Widow Brissenden, as so often, is our first indication of trouble brewing. She greets us halfway across the green with dramatic shrieks of relief. It seems, having extracted the information from Mother Bain, that she felt it her duty to tell the whole village that both the parson and his lodger were inexplicably absent overnight. She is now organising a search party.

"I tried to stop her," says Mother Bain later, when we have sent the smirking villagers on their way. "I knew there was naught ill, but once she had the idea in her head, she wouldn't be told..."

There is a rapping at the door whilst she is speaking, and without waiting for someone to answer it, my mother strides in.

"Is it true?" she demands furiously, her hair dishevelled from her fast ride over here, and her face scarlet with anger. "Answer me, Beatrice. And you, Master Becker, I do not know when I have ever been more disappointed in someone."

We sit her down and calm her with honey cakes and hot posset. I give a curtailed explanation of why I needed to visit Lancaster – to have an outing, and some respite from nursing my father – and why John was worried and followed me. She shakes her head in disbelief. "Have I taught you nothing in all these years, Beatrice?" she asks. "You are both as good as ruined. John Becker, they will say about you what they said about your predecessor. And with my daughter! I credited you with more sense. I accept your assurance that it was innocent, but who apart from me is going to believe that? Frankly, if things are as they seem to be between you two, then the sooner you are wed, the better."

Chapter 16

So it becomes public that John and I are to be betrothed. The date of the betrothal ceremony is set for the Feast of Saint Stephen, the day after Christmas.

At once a number of things change. My position in the village undergoes a subtle shift. I seem to be regarded as less of an outsider. I hear village confidences, and realise for the first time that there is a running joke in Wraithwaite about the relative wildness and unsophistication of the inhabitants of Barrowbeck and Mere Point.

Village parents assume that at some point in the future I will be happy to teach their small sons reading, writing and Scripture, and their daughters needlework and Scripture. John's wish to teach reading, writing, needlework and Scripture to all small people, regardless of gender, is regarded as an aberration on his part. When I tell them that if I had time to teach anyone anything, I should most assuredly be doing the same, heads are shaken in wonderment. "It's obvious he's filled her full of his foolish ideas," I overhear Widow Brissenden saying to Mother Bain.

Widow Brissenden has now moved permanently into the parsonage as my chaperone, and I am having to find ways of coping with her. Ignoring her works part of the time. Sometimes I remind myself that she is recently bereaved, although she seems remarkably ungriefstricken. Sometimes I simply run out of patience with her.

Our first battle is over a small stray cat which I take in. I miss my own cat, Caesar, left behind to enjoy his old hunting grounds at Barrowbeck Tower. When, one freezing morning, I find a tiny grey kitten half-dead on the parsonage step, it seems like a blessing. I take it in and wrap it in a blanket by the kitchen fire. It is thin and half-bald with disproportionately huge feet and one ear partly chewed off by something. It is too starved to do more than drink a little water and lick at some jelly from the meat, but when I lift it on to my lap it starts purring, and I am lost. I call it Blessing.

"It will have to go," Widow Brissenden tells me. "I can't abide cats."

"No madam, you will have to go," I assure her – it has been a long day – and remove the cushion from her chair for the cat to sit on.

163

"Cannot you at least *try* to get on with her? Do you have to be so aggressive?" John asks me later, when we pass on the landing.

I look at him, and do not reply, and wonder what I am doing here.

In the mornings I still ride over to Barrowbeck to help on the farm. I know that at the betrothal ceremony my dowry will be taken out and counted in public, and I dread the moment when the loss of the gold coins which I stole will be discovered. When I told John what I was doing in Lancaster, this was one aspect I omitted to mention. One morning at Barrowbeck Tower I creep down to my father's secret store under the earth floor of the root cellar, and dig up his box of booty from his highway robberies. With my pocket weighed down by stolen gold, I go up to the chapel over the gatehouse and pray for forgiveness, before riding fast back to the parsonage and replenishing my dowry.

In the afternoons I ride over to Cedric's cottage for my lessons in herbs and healing, and sometimes I accompany him on his visits to patients. One day when he goes out alone, leaving me to mix remedies, I steal some seeds of henbane from a jar on the shelf over his door. Back at Wraithwaite I conceal them in a fold of cloth at the bottom of my dower chest.

Evenings at the parsonage are very bad indeed. John sits upstairs in the schoolroom writing sermons, whilst Mother Bain, Widow Brissenden and I sit by the kitchen fire and sew and weave. I am making tapestries to put on the walls for warmth. Mother Bain is embroidering covers for cushions and footstools, her increasing short-sightedness creating designs of startling originality. John bought her a strong pair of venetians from the pedlar, and sometimes she tries wearing them, but on the whole she prefers the vague, misty world to which she has become accustomed. This would all have been quite companionable, had it not been for Widow Brissenden, sitting there pretending to sew altar cloths, but in truth glowering at me from under her eyebrows whilst Blessing sits on my lap grabbing with his big paws at the coloured tapestry wool.

I take on Esther Turner to help in the kitchen, and it becomes clear that the sooner she and Dickon are married the better. I tell her so one morning in the kitchen, after she has spent her entire time since rising, with her head in the jakes. It is decided that they will be betrothed at once and married at Christmas. It feels strange that it is now appropriate for me to decide such things. For a while that morning Widow Brissenden treats me as a kindred spirit.

As Christmas approaches, we all go out into the woods gathering holly and ivy to drape round the beams. Mother Bain and I bake cakes, pies and puddings, and store them in wax cloths in the church crypt to keep them fresh. I help the village children make a miniature stable and crib from straw and wood. The baby, though we make him early from old linen stockings and sawdust stuffing, must

165

wait until Christmas morning to be put into place. Cedric brings us a star made from mussel shells, full of the shiny luminosity of the sea. I buy John a daring purple silk nightshirt on Kendal Market, and Mother Bain declares in dismay that he will look like the court jester.

John makes two trips away during those weeks. The first is to Lancaster to see Hugh Conway, the vicar. The second is to Carlisle to see the bishop. Both trips are fruitless. It seems the Scots in the castle refuse to be visited by a Protestant priest, and the bishop assures John that he has no influence that could possibly stand up against the will of the queen. He advises John as a matter of policy to take no further interest in the matter, if he values his security, and to discourage this anonymous and misguided parishioner who cares about Scots.

There is no opportunity for John and myself to develop the closeness we experienced during our night at the George. Widow Brissenden takes great delight in watching us, and the atmosphere she creates is one of guilt and furtiveness. For a while we try to make opportunities to talk in private, but soon we give up.

The weather grows colder. My father's condition worsens. He lies hushed and wasting in the little room behind the hearth. I wonder if he will see Christmas. I light two candles in the church each day of Advent, one for my father and one for Robert. Each day, also, I go into the lady chapel and read the blessing on the wall and wonder if Robert is still alive, and if he still has his teeth and tongue and heart. Every day I walk back the length of the church, over the uneven, rush-covered stones which pave the floor, and think of the dead who lie beneath. It has become a daily ritual, a containment of death by awareness of its containment under this floor. The paving stones are uneven because the bones of those long buried sometimes come up when the newly dead are interred. Nowadays more and more parishioners are choosing the churchyard outside as their resting place, to avoid disturbing their ancestors before the Day of Judgement, with who-knows-what consequences. It seems a peaceful thing to sleep so, in the company of one's neighbours. If I could have hoped for such peace for Robert, I should have been content to let him go, but I fear that his end will not have anything of good about it. It certainly will not if my second plan is as dismal a failure as my first.

Robert comes to me at night, his footsteps beneath my window, along the landing, outside my door. By day he stands in dark corners, glimpsed from the corner of my eye. His voice is in the chimney as the logs hiss and burn. Aye, lassie.

I dream one night that his arms are round me. I sink into them, and hold him, and say his name. Then I open my eyes and see that the arms gripping me are broken, scabbed and filthy, the arms of a ghoul. I wake screaming. As I pull myself up against the bolsters I realise that the room is in candlelight, and that John is sitting on the end of my bed, a blanket round his shoulders. He says, "You were dreaming about Robert." For a moment my longing is transferred to him. He has been here whilst I slept, protecting me from the terrors of the night. I hold out my hands to him. His gaze wavers in the candlelight and he looks away, towards the window. "Dawn's breaking," he says, and folds his arms and the blanket more tightly round him.

In the second week of December, travelling players pass through Wraithwaite on their way to overwinter at Carlisle, and we give them lodging for a night in the parsonage. In return, they perform for us. Dickon rides over to Barrowbeck and Mere Point and brings back Mother, Verity, James and Aunt Juniper's household, and we all spend a magic evening in the long-lost world of knights and maidens, courtly love and ancient music. Afterwards, as we sit down to a supper of roast pork, fish pie, Cumberland pancakes, vegetables and preserved fruits, it emerges that the players spent the previous night in Lancaster, at the George. For a while they discuss the relative virtues of the George, the Mare Maid and the Naked Taylor as places of lodging. When John goes out of the room I interrupt their discussion to ask, "Any news of the Scots in the castle?"

The chief mummer, a grey-haired man, clutches his throat and crosses his eyes. "Dying like flies by all accounts." He grins. "Natural justice, eh? Gets a bit parky in those dungeons at this time of year. They say there's a woman in there with them, too."

The company's wardrobe mistress, an ageing beauty with dyed red hair and bleached skin, who is clearly modelling herself on the queen, leans forward so that her bosoms all but fall out of her bodice. "The question is, they say, are they just going to hang them, or are they going to draw and quarter them as well? It's a tricky legal point, the landlord at the George told me. It's not exactly treason since they're not exactly Englishmen. On the other hand, who cares, if it's near enough."

Mother, who is sitting on my right, takes hold of my hand under the table. "Well I certainly enjoyed your play tonight," she says brightly. "Perhaps you can come back at Maytime and perform a masque of Robin and Marion for us."

They nod and smile, and so the subject is changed. I push away my plate and wipe my knife on my napkin, before returning it to its sheath. I am aware of Germaine's stare along the table. She bows her head briefly before turning back to talk to Uncle Juniper again.

Later, when our guests have gone home and the travelling players have ascended the stairs, wiping the paint from their faces with their napkins, I follow them up. In the first of the guest chambers the tall, fair lad who played the Lady Guinevere is helping the chief mummer out of his boots.

"I'm sorry to disturb you." I pause on the threshold. They nod graciously and wait for me to continue. I glance over my shoulder. I can hear the other players talking and laughing in the adjoining bedchamber, and the wardrobe mistress somewhere, complaining at having to cross the stable yard to get to the jakes. I move further into the room. "I have work for you in March, if you are interested." I cross to the low oak chair by the long mirror. The fair lad lifts pots of make-up and goose grease out of my way so that I can sit down.

"Indeed?" The chief mummer looks interested.

"Might you be in the area of Lancaster round about then, good sirs?" I ask, seating myself, less for comfort than to stop my knees from wobbling, for I may in this moment be signing my own death warrant.

The lad Guinevere puts down his armful of pots on the clothes press, and both men move closer. The chief mummer assumes a listening pose, one knee on the floor, one knee bent, elbow on knee, chin on elegant hand. "We might." He glances at his friend. "Tell us about it, lady. We are here to be entertained. Tell us the story."

The fair lad comes and stands beside him, smiling. "Indeed, madam, we love a good story. Pray, do tell us how we can help."

Chapter 17

$\mathcal{I}$n the third week of December we have violent storms. The cockerel weathervane on the church is struck by lightning and falls down.

"Oh well, it's a pagan symbol anyway," says John, holding the blackened and bent object in his hands.

"Nay John!" Mother Bain looks outraged. "It is a reminder to all good Christian folk to be ever wakeful for the coming of the Lord."

John laughs. "Oh well, it had better go back up then, though it looks more like a reminder of Hell at the moment." Sometimes I remember what I love about him. Other times, it quite escapes me.

I sleep increasingly badly now. Fires in all the rooms keep the house warm as the weather grows colder, but I have taken to letting the fire in the chimney hole of my bedchamber burn down and go out. I need to be able to imagine in some small way what Robert is enduring in the dark, bitter cold of the dungeon.

John is sleeping badly too. More than once we meet in the middle of the night on the landing or in the kitchen. These are the times we talk. I say, "Think what it's like in the dungeons." He says, "He may be dead, Beatie. Human beings can only take so much."

Two nights before Christmas I go to bed early. I am weary from all the Christmas preparations, and sick of the sight of Widow Brissenden. The fire in my bedchamber is all but out. I take off my cap and let hairpins come tumbling loose to the floor. I kick them aside. I take off my loose wool mantle and detach my sleeves and collar, then unlace my bodice and take off my kirtle, petticoat and chemise-smock. My black knitted stockings have sagged. I untie the garters and rub the weals they leave behind. When I am naked I lie on the cold wooden floor and close my eyes. It is impossible to sleep. When I am shivering uncontrollably, and ready to weep with cold and misery, I get up and go to bed. I wanted to spend the night there, to know what it was like, but in the end I make excuses – I will be no good to Robert if I am weak and ill; I cannot save him if I am dead of a chill myself. Angrily, I get into bed without my nightsmock or warmingstone, and lie there shivering. How will Robert get through the winter? How will I? How will the festivities of Christmas be bearable?

Inevitably drowsiness comes and the bed grows hot. The feather mattresses are a pit into which I sink. I dream. I am standing in a field full of crows, and the villagers are beating them with sticks to drive them off the crops. After the birds seem all dead or flown, I find one injured crow left, hiding in an alley of the village. I want to nurse it back to health, but do not know how, even if I were able to catch it. I wake, thinking at first that the crows represent the Scots, and the injured crow Robert. Then I understand that in truth the crows are death, beaten off by our midwinter fires and festivities, and that the injured crow is Robert's death, perhaps surviving to do its work, perhaps not.

Lying awake in the darkness, I suddenly realise that the shouts and crashes from my dream are still going on outside.

"I might as well talk to the wall as talk to that lot," says John's voice from the doorway. A candle flares.

I pull the bedclothes hurriedly round me. "What's going on?" The commotion seems to be coming from the front of the house, near the church.

John comes into the room and passes me my thick woollen nightgown and nightsmock from the end of the bed. He is wearing several layers of warm clothing himself, and his outdoor cloak. "You might as well come down and find out something new about your neighbours, Beatie."

From the warmth of the bed I look up at him. From dreams of death to a real, warm person and a real, warm

173

bed. I say, "John…" He comes and sits next to me on the bed. After a moment we lean towards each other and kiss, softly and lightly.

"Paganism! Paganism!" The shriek comes from the landing. "We shall all be damned!" It is Widow Brissenden, roaring along the landing in her night attire, tassels flying. John gives a snort of laughter and stands up.

"I'll meet you in the kitchen, Beatrice. Come and be shocked at how we celebrate winter in Wraithwaite." He bends his head and kisses me again on the lips. "That is not to say I approve of what is going on out there, but oh dear, what the hell." He turns and leaves.

Downstairs in the kitchen I put on my cloak over my nightclothes. Mother Bain and Widow Brissenden are standing in the open doorway. The night outside is knifelike. I wrap my cloak round me with both arms and go to where John is standing outside in the frozen courtyard. He puts his arm round me and leads me out on to the green. My breath floats ahead of me, a wraith. *Hearte and hearte raithe.* From across the universe stars of dazzling beauty light up our village green. The half-moon hangs low in the sky, and the pink berries of the spindleberry tree on the green are lit from behind by white light. Music and dancing continue somewhere unseen. John and I walk over the crunching ground to the church, and the graveyard.

The villagers are dancing under the moon, over the graves, laughing, shouting and singing, drinking from

174

narrow-lipped jugs. They are wearing their best clothes, bright cloths and leathers of red, purple, blue, green and russet. As we watch, they make a formation, a circle, and start to move slowly, with a little skip every four steps. Gradually they speed up as the musicians – church minstrels and others – play faster and faster, stamping and laughing, their breath in clouds about their heads. There are strands of ivy round the dancers' necks. The musicians wear circlets of holly on their heads. The blacksmith, Alan Smith, is wearing ram's horns on his head. Suddenly he climbs on to the churchyard wall and with a chilling scream hurls himself into the centre of the circle, beating with his hands on a small drum which hangs about his neck.

"Paganism..." I whisper, in echo of Widow Brissenden.

"It was either put up with it, or force them to choose," says John. "If they think they can only have one or the other, Christianity or paganism, then I fear what some of them may choose. There would be children going unbaptised and marriages unblessed. This is all they do. It's a folk memory. They're calling back summer, as our forebears did."

"But they're dancing on the *graves*, John."

He hugs me to him, and gazes up at the frozen arch of stars. "Do you suppose the dead mind? They have possibly a long, boring wait until Judgement Day."

I look at him. "You're mocking me." He smiles. I put my arms round him, and he folds me inside his cloak. We kiss again, then walk out of the horned night and back into the parsonage. As we enter the kitchen, my father's stolen clock on the dresser moves one minute past midnight, and into the day before Christmas Eve.

Chapter 18

hristmas Day dawns bright, with a crackle of thaw in the air. All the villagers of Wraithwaite, Barrowbeck and Mere Point were in church at midnight, and the carols we sang in the cold, amid the candles, moved me to tears. There were chairs along the side of the screened-off lady chapel for the lame or pregnant, and Verity was there, now majestically large, with all of us around her.

Without light shining through them, the four stained-glass windows above the white-clothed altar loomed mysteriously. The candlelight on the faces of Matthew, Mark, Luke and John gave them changing expressions. At the stroke of midnight Alan Smith, the blacksmith, minus his ram's horns now, came in bearing the stocking baby and set him in his cradle, and all the village children sang *In Dulci Jubilo* in their high voices. I tried to stem my tears by remembering these same children stoning the ducks on the pond and throwing snails at the squirrels in the forest, but it did not work.

Now, this morning, I can hear Mother Bain singing carols in the kitchen, and I realise with astonishment that I feel riotously glad to be alive. This is the day when witches are powerless, when elves and goblins hide, and when hope of every sort is alive for a while. Moreover, Widow Brissenden has gone home to spend Christmas with her family.

As I make my way downstairs, Mother Bain sweeps into the thumping rhythm of *Personent Hodie*. In the kitchen the fire is roaring high. Esther and Dickon pick out the beat of the carol with wooden spoons on copper pans, and dance round the room. "God be with you!" shouts Mother Bain, and thrusts a large goblet of steaming malmsey at me. I return her greeting and kiss them all. John appears behind me, looking rumpled.

From outside, suddenly, come the sounds of shawms, crumhorns and Flemish bagpipes. We all go to the front door, and see the church lutenist dancing ahead of the band of village musicians, his lute above his head. People come pouring out of their houses in their nightsmocks, gowns and cloaks, to follow the band, and sing the *Corpus Christi Carol*.

Lully lulley, lully lulley
The fawcon hath borne my mak away
He bare hym up, he bare hym down,
He bare hym into an orchard brown.
Yn that orchard ther was an hall
That was hangid with purpill and pall,
And yn that hall ther was a bedde,
Hit was hangid with gold so redde,
And yn that bedde ther lythe a knyght,
His wowndes bledyng day and nyght.
Under that bedde ther runneth a flod
One half runneth watir the othyr half blod.
At that beddes foot ther kneleth a may
And she wepeth both night and day,
And by that beddes side ther stondith a ston
Corpus Christi wretyn theron.

They dance up to the parsonage and Mother Bain passes me the vast tray of spiced cakes which she and Esther have been baking since before dawn. The band and half the village crowd into the kitchen, and the rest fit into the hall, stairs and gallery wherever they can. By the kitchen fire John is opening a kilderkin of best ale.

Richard Battle, our senior churchwarden, dressed as the Lord of Misrule, with bells, ribbons and a stick for hitting people, rushes up and kisses me, then hits John with his brightly painted baton. "Damnation to disbelievers and a merry Christmas to all!" he shouts.

179

The cry is taken up by others. I really don't feel up to this. The lutenist elbows his way through the crowd, refuses a drink and climbs on to the plate dresser. I go to sit in the chimney corner, and say a short prayer for our plates. The lutenist begins to play, very quietly at first. Gradually everyone falls silent. "Put t'wood in t'hole!" someone yells, and the front door is shut. The small gallery round the kitchen, normally used to store barrels of ale, creaks as people shift and settle themselves. Very delicately the lutenist picks out *Puer Nobis Nascitur*, and people begin to sing in the same, unfamiliar, soft way *Unto us a Boy is Born*.

John pulls up a firkin of ale and sits on it next to me in the chimney corner. People sing through mouthfuls of cake, passing along the tankards they have so fortuitously brought, for refilling. A flurry of wind blows down the chimney. Ash flutters on to my skirts.

"I've let the fire go down a bit ready for the Yule log," says Mother Bain, coming to sit opposite us in the other chimney corner. I nod wordlessly. "Nay lass, you do naught but cry these days." She shakes her head at me wonderingly, then turns to look for Dickon. "Come on, Dickon. You too, John. Fetch in the Yule log from the stables. I covered it over with oilcloth to keep the frost out."

As the last verse of the carol begins, Esther takes up her wooden spoon again and taps experimentally on an upended copper pan, rapping out alternate beats of the tune. It is strange music, wild and unsettling.

A cheer goes up when John and Dickon stagger in with the large piece of tree trunk which is the Yule log. I move out of its way, say a short prayer for all the small creatures living in it and watch as it is swung with a mighty crash into the flames. Ash and sparks fly out into the kitchen, and those near it scream and jump back, then they all sing *The Holly and the Ivy*, and march back out into the frosty morning.

We just have time to eat breakfast, and dress, before the morning's church service, which is more an extension of the wassailing than anything else. During the sermon one villager has loud, uncontrollable hiccups, and two more fall over. "I expect it's the cold," says my mother, who is standing next to me. Despite the slight thaw it is still very cold, and there is frost on the lectern and the rood screen. Under our feet the flagstones are thawed by the passage of many feet, but I know that beneath them the ground is still frozen solid. I think of Robert. John includes a prayer for prisoners. I close my eyes and shiver.

After the service Mother, Verity and James come over to the parsonage, and we all sit in the kitchen round the Yule log, drinking and talking and putting the last touches to the food, before moving into the hall to eat it. Father's bed has been brought in, and I sit by him and mash his food for him. Mother Bain, Esther and I have prepared a swan stuffed with quails, pork in claret, spinach and walnut pie, quince and rosehip jelly, pickled cucumbers and cabbage, carrots in butter and cinnamon and a series of tarts and fruit puddings. I think of how Father would once have enjoyed all this. Now he is scarcely aware of it passing his lips.

I am unable to control an absurd tremulousness for the rest of the afternoon. At every carol I have to get out my handkerchief again. "Lord knows what you'll be like when you hear Kate singing," comments my mother as we all go out at dusk to where Dickon has the cart, carretta and horses waiting to transport us all to Barrowbeck. This is the day when my father is to return home for good, transported gently and slowly on a bed made up in the back of the cart, and then carried on a hurdle up the east stairs of Barrowbeck Tower to his old room behind the living hall hearth. It is the day I could return home too, if I chose.

John and I dismount by the barmkin gate in the twilight, and hand our horses over to William who is on guard. He says, "Welcome home, Mistress Beatrice." John takes my hand and draws me to one side.

"Stay," he says. "It's what you want, isn't it."

I put my hands round his face and kiss him. "Yes, it is what I want, sweet John. After the betrothal tomorrow, I want to come back here, and then in a while, be married from here."

He pulls me behind the elder tree by the barmkin gate and kisses me.

"You've got a lot to answer for, lass," comes Kate's voice from the dairy behind us. "Getting that holy man into our

182

loose ways." I laugh, and go to embrace her, and we all go up to the gatehouse together, and into the tower.

The rooms are full of greenery. In the living hall a huge peacock pie decorated with feathers stands in the centre of the table. Christmas Day is the only day of the year on which peacock feathers do not have the power of the evil eye, and Kate always takes advantage of this temporary dispensation.

Aunt and Uncle Juniper, Gerald, Germaine and Hugh arrive, and we all play games for an hour before sitting down to Christmas supper in the living hall, with all the henchmen, and George and Martinus up from Low Back Farm. We change the watch every hour or so, so that no one shall be left out. Afterwards, we open the last big flagon of elder wine, and sprawl, bloated and exhausted, along the table between the two fires, telling ghost stories. Mother tells the story of the Headless Lady of Hagditch, who searches for her lost lover along the highways at dead of night, and I know that her chilling description of the lady's crazed yearnings owes more than a little to the fact that Cedric is not here, excluded from our Christmas festivities for decency's sake. I feel, with her, the slowness of Christmas, the frustratingly measured pace of the rituals which must be gone through, whilst all the time, outside, other more pressing urgencies lay siege to our attention.

Towards midnight Germaine plays her lute and Kate sings *Tomorrow shall be my Dancing Day*.

183

In a manger laid and wrapped I was,
So very poor, this was my chance
Betwixt an ox and a silly poor ass,
To call my true love to my dance.
Sing O my love, O my love,
This have I done for my true love.

I put my head down on the table and sob.

John and I are much teased for choosing a martyr's feast day on which to become betrothed. Our betrothal is to take place straight after Esther and Dickon's marriage tomorrow morning. Then I will pack my things and return here. Tonight I am to sleep in my own bed again. At bedtime John and I go up to the battlements to do an hour's watch. Flurries of icy rain, smelling of the sea, are blown over the battlements, and a crab moon swims through breaks in the clouds. There are no enemies here tonight. We lean against the beacon turret and kiss, and when William comes up to take over the watch, we go downstairs to my bed.

Chapter 19

Immediately after Christmas a terrible tension sets up in me. Esther and Dickon are married in the church porch, and later that same day John and I become betrothed. Lifetime promises made in front of family and friends – what could be more binding than that, I wonder, as we stand in front of the Vicar of Hagditch at the altar rail. Our wedding will take place at Midsummer, and the bishop will officiate.

The twelve days of Christmas pass slowly. After the Feast of Stephen come the Feast of Saint John the Apostle, Childermas and the day we call New Year's Day after some quaint, ancient custom when the year used to start on the first of January instead of the twenty-fifth of March as it does now.

On that day, the first day of January, we all exchange

gifts. John loves his purple nightshirt. Our relationship has changed since Christmas night. I suppose it is quite obvious to everyone. Certainly, now that we are betrothed and living under separate roofs, we are allowed more freedom than before. It is a little unreal to me that my future is now set out before me, with this man, whose body I am quickly coming to like quite as much as I like his mind. Marriage will be a step further. We can wait – though if John had been in any other line of work, I doubt we should have.

Finally it is Twelfth Night and the Feast of the Epiphany. We all go over to Aunt Juniper's for more overeating. I find I am looking forward to Plough Monday, when normal life – not to mention normal eating – can be resumed, whilst simultaneously I am filled with growing terror at the onward progress of time. March will come so soon. Every bare tree looks like a gibbet.

It has become clear, now, that Hugh is seriously courting Anne Fairweather, the rich widow from Hagditch. We know her a little already, from social occasions round the county, but we meet her for the first time in family surroundings at Mere Point on the Feast of the Epiphany. Anne is a good few years older than Hugh, and she owns the large and beautiful manor house at Hagditch.

"Owning all that, she's mad to marry again," comments Verity as we chop the last limp carrots of the year in Aunt Juniper's kitchen.

Anne bears something of an air of mystery, partly

arising from her being so badly pocked that she always wears a veil, and partly from her wealth and family connections to the nobility. I am relieved, if a little insulted, that Hugh has managed to console himself so soon.

Even more interestingly, it becomes clear that Anne is related to one of the Lord Justices of Assize, at Lancaster. I make up my mind to get to know her much better.

After the meal in the long hall at Mere Point, we play games. During a game of Hoodman Blind I notice Gerald taking John to one side. As they go out, Germaine leaves the game and takes my arm. "He's had a messenger from Lord Ravenswyck."

Germaine no longer rouges her cheeks or curls her hair. Instead, she lets her face remain its natural parchment colour, and draws her hair severely back from her forehead. Her posture has become loose and straight and direct.

"A messenger?" I ask.

"All gentlemen of the northern counties are to meet, with their forces, at Newcastle, on Shrove Tuesday."

"Oh no..."

"John won't go, of course, Beatrice. Don't look like that."

"No... no, of course, but Gerald... oh, Germaine." I realise, suddenly, with my father out of action, and bumbling Uncle Juniper not of a military persuasion, that suave, warlike Gerald will now lead the troops, that he, in effect, must now be regarded as lord of the manor. I look at Germaine. "We need the men to work the land then, and... oh... it seems very wrong to fight during Lent..."

is all I can find to say. Hugh rushes past me with a warmingstone bag over his head. Anne Fairweather shrieks and tries to get out of his way.

"Aye. Some will be giving up much for Lent." Germaine clasps her hands until her knuckles whiten. "Yet we'll have no land to work if the Scots keep coming."

I move to the windowseat. "So, Gerald will lead our men?"

Germaine sits down next to me. "He'll have to. Father-in-law would get no further than the nearest dog-pit."

"Will you marry first?"

"We're hoping to wed at Candlemas. There's just enough time for the banns. Gerald is asking John now."

I kiss her on the cheek. "God bless you, Cousin."

I turn to stare into the blackness outside. Despite the noise of revelry here in the long hall, it is possible to hear the sea crashing on the cliffs, and sense all that fearsome world outside, of gaping fishes, predatory seabirds, snapping crabs, unearthly stone creatures in the cliffs – the salamanders which long ago burnt themselves into melted stone – a world of all that is as old as water, and as unreasoning. You could go mad thinking about it. Yet it is in all of us, those of us who stay, and those of us who cross the border.

"Beatrice," Germaine says suddenly, breaking into my thoughts, "your Scot, is he one of those locked in Lancaster Castle?"

"He is." I am surprised at how matter-of-fact I can

sound, in view of the terrifying pointlessness of everything. "I thought we shouldn't have a raid on Scotland now, Germaine. I thought the queen might keep those Scots as hostages. I thought at least that Robert was suffering for some good purpose. Now we are to raid anyway, and Robert is rotting in that dungeon for nothing."

Germaine takes my hand. "Don't forget how he came here, Beatrice. No one forced him to come. The Scottish raids will go on, unless we hit them hard."

I pull my hand away irritably, and walk out of the hall.

A little over three weeks later, Gerald and Germaine are married in Wraithwaite Church, and the woman who was servant to my family becomes my cousin, and to all intents and purposes, lady of the manor.

It is good to be back at Barrowbeck with Mother and all the familiar members of the tower community – Leo, Kate, Tilly Turner and the henchmen – even sly Michael, clearly dismayed because he thought he had got rid of me. I suggest to Aunt Juniper that he might make a good match for Widow Brissenden, who will surely be desolate for company now that her chaperoning duties are at an end. My good aunt looks quite excited at the prospect, and vows to investigate the matter. Esther and Dickon, too, are now back in the valley, their services hired out to Verity for the time being. Germaine, who is getting on better with her mother-in-law than any of us had dared

189

hope, has persuaded Aunt Juniper to take on the widow of the second man who was murdered, as skivvy, and to train her as cook at Mere Point. After initial dubiousness, Aunt Juniper quickly gets to like the idea that she might not always have to do all the cooking herself, and takes to dressing rather grandly in the afternoons, and calling on neighbours all round the district.

On days of clement weather the men get on with hedging and ditching. On days when the milk freezes in the pails and the water in the wells, they chop wood, and mend and sharpen the farm implements.

With John, I learn some very earthly pleasures on icy winter nights in the cow byre and dairy, our breath freezing in the air. John is a most beautiful man. He is dark, where Robert was tawny. It adds to the strangeness, that things should be this way again, with a different man. He calls me his sweeting, his love. He can be outrageous and funny. I see a side of him I never saw before. We laugh a lot. People grin knowingly when they hear us cackling at some foolish jest incomprehensible to others. If it were not for my knowledge of Robert's imprisonment, I should be happy.

As the weeks move on, the men improve the pastures ready for sowing and planting, digging out stones and filling the holes from claybeds and dungheaps. When at last the ground softens enough, we start the ploughing. Verity and I sort the seeds for planting – wheat, barley, rye and beans – and I think of the tiny, black, kidney-shaped

seeds which lie at the bottom of my dower chest –
henbane, a last resort for the desperate. I remember a day
long ago on the rough heathland towards Mistholme
Moss, and Mother saying, "Don't touch this plant,
Beatrice. It's dangerous." I looked at its cream and purple
flowers, little knowing the purpose to which I might one
day put it. I saw the purple-spotted stalks of hemlock too,
and deadly nightshade, and many other subjects of such
warnings. Don't touch this plant, Beatrice. It's dangerous.
I run my fingers now through seeds of barley, wheat and
rye, as if through hair. Don't touch, don't touch. But I
have touched, and it is indeed dangerous.

My afternoons spent learning the art of healing with
Cedric are fewer now, and he more often travels over to
me, teaching me bee-cupping as a remedy for Kate's
swollen joints, the preparation of hawthorn and mulberry
for Father's blood, and the mashing of comfrey poultices
for his bedsores. Sometimes I look at Father with grief
and astonishment, seeing afresh the changes which have
occurred in him. When did all his dark hair drop out?
When did his mouth fall in on his teeth so, and his
cheekbones become wedges? I grasp his dead-wood
fingers, and tell him about Robert. He listens, staring into
my face and nodding.

It is on a day when Verity and I are sitting at her
kitchen table making tooth-soap from ashes of rosemary
and powdered alabaster – the very latest recipe from
London recommended by Anne Fairweather – that Verity

tilts forward in her chair and says, "Sister, I have a pain in my belly, and my boots are full of water."

I had almost forgotten that this was to happen. The lying-in sheets and crib have been ready for months, but Christmas has been so busy, and we have simply become used to Verity being huge. I jump to my feet. "Oh sweet Jesu, Verity! I'll get Mother. Where's James?"

She leans forward and groans. "I think he's working on the fortifications, Beatie. Will you send for Sanctity Wilson and Mother Bain too? Go on. I'm all right."

There is a lot to do all at once. I make up the bed with the lying-in sheets, and help Verity into it. I find George and Martinus in the farm's tool cellar working at the whetstone and woodcarving bench, and send them off to fetch Mother, Sanctity Wilson and Mother Bain. Sanctity arrives with a brew of raspberry leaves. Mother Bain arrives with her tapestry bag of medications. Kate brings a heap of comfortable pillows, and a moleskin blanket in which to wrap the baby.

"She should move about," says Sanctity, putting on her red midwife's apron, and she helps Verity stretch and walk and bend. Mother views them askance, but holds her peace, since Sanctity's many births have been of legendary ease and speed. We eat dinner on our laps in the birthing-room at midday, with French wine brought by Mother, then we stoke the fire with dry logs to last the afternoon.

By the time the cold, wintry sun sets, Verity is no nearer giving birth. Her pains are violent but far apart. By midnight the older women are looking concerned. I go out to where James has been patrolling the landing, but he is no longer there. I find him in the dark lane, lashing at the thorns and briars with his sickle, and weeping.

In the birthing-room, Verity is white with exhaustion. Mother Bain is listening to the baby's heartbeat as I return. Everyone has stopped talking. "Lady." The old woman eases herself upright and gestures to Mother to follow her. I stand in the doorway where I can hear them. Mother Bain says softly, "The child has no water left. It needs to be born now. She will have to have goblin bread."

Mother gasps. "Oh surely… is there no other way, Mistress Bain? Childbirth is bad enough without goblin bread."

"Her contractions are not frequent enough. It has to be done, lady, or the child will die."

I look over at Verity. She is watching us, her expression wary. Mother Bain draws a small package from her tapestry bag and tips a few black morsels of bread from it into her palm. Goblin bread, the evil growth which in a bad year makes the poor see demons and sometimes destroy themselves and others, is here preserved deliberately by Mother Bain for the speeding of childbirth. Thoughts of witchcraft cross my mind, but I push them away, ashamed.

Kate struggles past me, lugging the heavy wooden cradle on rockers. "Goblin bread? God help you, Mistress Verity," she shouts. "Just remember that what you see ain't really there."

"Be quiet, Kate!" Mother snaps.

Kate shrugs. "I've brought a knife to hang over the baby's cradle to keep the snatching fairies away." She brandishes a large carving knife. Mother rolls her eyes and ushers her away.

After Verity has eaten two small pieces of goblin bread, everyone else draws back into the dim candlelight to allow her to rest, but I pull up a stool close to her red-curtained bed, and hold her hands. She closes her eyes and says through scarcely moving lips, "Remember you are to be godmother, Beatrice. Take care of this baby for me."

There is no point in replying. I can see that she is gone away and cannot hear me. I squeeze her hands, by way of a promise.

By dawn, Verity is screaming and lashing out at things we cannot see. By next midnight, she is silent. All of us are on our knees. I fall in and out of sleep, my face on the bed cover. Sometimes I wake because I am face down and suffocating myself, sometimes because my knees have gone to sleep. I wake with a jump as Mother Bain, on the other side of the bed, stands up and straightens her red apron. The muttered prayers, running like an incantation round the room, falter and stop. The old woman cups Verity's cheek in her hand. "She's in right piteous case, mistress," she says to my mother. "You must send for the Cockleshell Man to cut her."

Kate shrieks and falls face down on the floor.

"No." Mother's single word catches the echo which this room sometimes holds. *No, no, no.*

"There's a chance he could save the baby, mistress, though I doubt it."

Verity has been lying very still, her eyes closed, her mind far away, but suddenly a rictus convulses her body, and a groan comes from her.

"Kneel her up!" exclaims Sanctity. "Something's changed!"

Mother Bain rushes to the foot of the bed. "The head's out. Thank the Lord."

Between us we haul Verity to her knees amid the wreckage of the bedclothes. She is back-breakingly heavy and limp. I support her with my shoulder under her armpit, and find myself straining with her. I mutter. "Push, Verity. Don't die. Push, and you'll have everything you wanted, James, the farm, a baby. Don't die. Remember your plan, darling. Just remember your plan."

The only sound she makes is a whisper in the back of her throat. I stagger to hold her weight. People are sobbing. It fills the room. Then, above it all, comes a small cry, a new voice in the world.

Triumphantly Mother Bain lifts the tiny, bloody baby. "It's a boy, mistress." Sanctity ties the cord in two places and cuts it with neat efficiency, then wipes the baby's mouth. My mother holds a linen cloth and the moleskin blanket ready, and swiftly wraps him in them without bothering to wash him. She passes him to me.

"Keep him warm, Beatie. He's half dead. You must take your vows as godmother immediately, and stand in for the other godparents. Plenty of time to wash him later."

John, who is to be one of the godfathers, has been back and forth to the farm over the long hours of Verity's labour, but now he is absent with a dying farmworker at Mere Point, and anyway, men have no place in a birthing-room. Hugh and Gerald are to be the baby's other godfathers, and Germaine his other godmother. I hold my nephew, and listen apprehensively to the fragility of each of his breaths. He is a red-haired boy with dark blue eyes and curled shrimp hands. His weight and solidity feel miraculous.

"If he survives the day he'll survive the week," says Kate.

Like most midwives, Mother Bain and Sanctity Wilson have dispensations from the bishop to baptise the newborn when necessary. Now they approach in their red aprons, a strange aura of holiness about them, amid the meaty physicality of birth. Sanctity pours holy water into a bowl, and Mother Bain enfolds the baby in the family's silk and wool chrisom, then baptises him Thomas Francis, after both his grandfathers.

"Best pass him through the branches of an elder tree as well, just to be on the safe side," pronounces Kate. "You can't be too careful."

Mother wipes the tears from her face with both hands and answers, "Maybe later." Thomas's whimpering stops as I rock him, and he blinks at the first rays of dawn shining in through the window.

Chapter 20

On the day when it becomes clear that Thomas is going to survive, we hold his christening feast. John and I take him a set of silver apostle spoons and a coral teething ring. The pedlar has brought lemons, a rare treat, and Kate cooks hare seethed in lemons for the festive meal. Verity's eyes are black-ringed, and weakness still trembles in her voice, but she is full of elation. "Thank you for bullying me back to life," she says, as we walk outside, viewing the men's latest work on the farm's fortifications. "I heard you from a long way off."

For a while, that February, life seems almost normal again. The ploughing is interrupted by hard frost, but we are glad of it to sear the ground. The necessary work pushes thoughts of the march on Scotland to the backs of people's minds, though some of the young men, who work at hard and tedious labour day after day on the land, are clearly finding the idea of invading Scotland exciting. For me, with February half gone and Robert's trial just weeks away, it is time to move ahead with my own plans. Some nights I scarcely sleep. When I do, I have nightmares. On the farm every innocent piece of chain is a prisoner's shackle, every innocent piece of rope a hangman's noose.

In late February Mother, Aunt Juniper and I visit Hugh's new lady, Anne Fairweather, at her house in Hagditch. She has an Irish wolfhound at her gate, and an elderly manservant at her door. He greets us saying, "I pray you be welcome herein." We are deeply impressed, and I wonder if I could teach one of the henchmen to do this.

We are also impressed by Anne's possessions, silver and gold plate, mother-of-pearl candle shades, brilliantly coloured tapestries. In the library stands a spinet, its lid painted blue, red and gold, its keys intricately carved. Anne plays it for us whilst Mother and Aunt Juniper walk amongst the snowdrops in the garden outside the open library windows. I browse along the bookshelves, and when I find what I am looking for, say hesitantly, "Anne?"

She looks up from her playing, and smiles. "Yes Beatrice?" Her veil is turned back over her cap today. I realise, seeing the exceptional beauty of her smile, how little pockmarks really matter.

"Anne, I believe you have a cousin in the Lancaster judiciary."

She nods. "Yes, my pompous Cousin Edward."

"Oh... pompous?"

"Quite, quite unbearable, my dear. Are you interested in the judiciary? You are very welcome to meet him. He's coming to dinner on Sunday."

This is more than I had hoped. I wrote, necessarily anonymously, to the Lancaster magistrates in the autumn, explaining that Robert Lacklie was committed to stopping the border raids, but I had little hope of altering their minds, and indeed clearly had not done so.

"Thank you... thank you very much. I should like that. Will Hugh be here?"

"Er no. Not this time. Bring John, of course. He will be a fitting counterpoint to loathsome Edward."

"Why do you invite him if he is so loathsome, Anne?"

She turns a page of her music and begins a different tune, fast and intricate. She concentrates for a moment, then looks up again. "Because I want him to get someone out of the castle for me, Beatrice."

I drop the book I am holding.

Anne stops playing. "Are you shocked? I had begun to think you a kindred spirit. Do not tell me I was mistaken."

I sit down carefully on a carved chestnut chair. Anne goes back to her playing. "You may find my Cousin Edward charming, Beatrice, and not loathsome at all. He tries to dazzle ladies. He is very handsome, in a fat sort of way."

I bend, and pick up the book I dropped. It is *The Compleat Herbalyste*.

"Who... whom do you wish to get out of the castle, Anne?"

She sighs. "Oh, it is a tenant woman of my Cousin Elspeth. I have Scottish relatives, for my sins. Needless to say, we have little contact. This foolish woman tried to get herself into the castle disguised as a laundress, with some idea of rescuing her son who is imprisoned for border raiding. She escaped, but they caught up with her again at some inn in Lancaster, and now she is imprisoned herself. It is clearly wrong that she should hang with the rest of them." She closes the lid of the spinet.

I go over to her and rest my hand on the instrument. I can feel the buzz of music still in it. "I also want to get someone out of the castle, Anne," I say. I glance over my shoulder as Mother and Aunt Juniper pass the window.

Anne raises an eyebrow. "Oh. Might one ask...?"

"A Scot. His name is Robert."

"Do you know, Beatrice, I used to think you were boring. Now I think we might truly be friends. Is he your lover?"

Mother and Aunt Juniper re-enter the room.

"May I borrow this book?" I ask, clutching the herbal.

"Of course you may." Anne opens the spinet again, and breaks into something remarkably like a Highland reel.

Later that day I ride over to the parsonage. John is out and Mother Bain is asleep. I go upstairs and burrow down into my dower chest. The seeds of henbane are still safely there, together with a tiny, stoppered flagon. *If time allows, best results will be obtained by steeping the seeds in wine before mashing,* Anne's book tells me. Time does allow, and I hope the usquebaugh which I have been keeping by me will be even more effective than wine. "Whiskybae..." I practise the pronunciation which Robert taught me. It is possible that what I am doing may prove unnecessary, with the advent of loathsome Edward, but I am taking no chances.

I tip the usquebaugh from the flagon into a small, marble mortar, make some calculations, check and recheck, then count out a precise number of seeds into the strong-smelling spirit. They float on the surface, like black commas. Then I put the lid on and push the whole thing away to the furthest corner of the hastening cupboard, above the bread oven. I know Mother Bain cannot reach to the back of it. They will be safe there. In the window I put a pot of rue, dug up from Cedric's garden, as a gesture of apology to the Almighty for my efforts to pervert the course of justice.

On Sunday John and I ride over to Hagditch straight after morning service. Edward is there already. He is indeed handsome. His skin is smooth and flushed, his hair bright chestnut, his expression very confident. We eat a lavish meal during which Anne explains in great detail to Edward why he must arrange at once for the release of their cousin's unfortunate tenant. Edward smiles, nods loftily and assures her it is impossible, but behind his grand manner I can see from the adoring look he gives her that it is not impossible at all.

After the meal Anne takes John's arm. "I am taking your betrothed for a walk in the garden, Beatrice dear. He is far too righteous and I wish to corrupt him."

John smiles and allows himself to be led away, and I am left with Edward. I feel at a terrible disadvantage, unamusing and inarticulate compared with Anne. Edward wanders round the library, sipping his goblet of raisin wine.

"So," he says, after a brief silence, "I gather from my cousin that you also wish someone released. At this rate the castle will be empty. Perhaps you had better explain."

I feel a disbelieving flutter of hope. "Sir, yes, it is so. I also have a Scottish connection, as you and the lady Anne do. I know that the Scot of whom I speak desires only to stop the border raids. His family has the influence to do so. His name is Robert Lacklie. Releasing him could bring peace to parts of the border country. Hanging him would probably just incite more revenge."

"So your motives are noble and altruistic."

"My motives... do include a desire for justice. Robert is not an enemy of England."

"Has he ever raided our country?"

I hesitate. "He repents any raiding he might have done, and wishes all the more urgently, because of it, to make amends."

Edward turns sharply from his perusal of the bookshelves and stares at me. "Madam, if it were not for my gentle cousin's intercession for you, I should have to question you most severely about this matter. It is my duty to uphold the law, and there is little that could ever deflect me from that, save, perhaps rarely, for the love I hold for my Cousin Anne. I despise myself for it. Indeed, she despises me for it, but, you see, we do strange and inadvisable things for love, as you most obviously are aware." He pauses, draws a deep breath and folds his arms across his plump chest. He looks at me angrily, as if I had deliberately persuaded him to say too much, then adds, "You are a member of a family which is threatening to take my cousin away from me for a second time, though I cannot imagine for a moment what she sees in your Cousin Hugh. Well, I still hope to persuade her of her folly. Ladies have these weaknesses, and sometimes need to be guided towards what is best for them. Clearly your Cousin Hugh has aspirations. Well, I can understand that, but I shall do my utmost to see that they remain unfulfilled. As for you, madam, I suggest most fervently that you reconsider your association with this Scot." He turns and strides towards the door. "There is nothing I can do for you. I would not help you even if I could. Now, good day to you."

In late February I take the mortar out of the hastening cupboard and mash the black seeds into the pale spirit. They are bigger and softer now. As the pestle presses each one flat, dark fingers of stain squirt out. I flatten them

203

briskly until all the mixture is black and thick, and the inverted empty skins float on the surface like beetles' wings. Then I sieve the mixture back into the tiny flagon. When I throw the thin muslin full of curled black skins on to the back of the fire, the flames roar dark purple.

In two weeks' time the men will leave, in order to reach Newcastle by Shrove Tuesday. As they assemble there with other men from all over the northern counties, to march on Scotland, so will the Lent Assizes begin in Lancaster.

Chapter 21

*I*t is nearly March. I wish time would move more slowly. I do not feel ready for what I have to do. My mother and I are putting things together for my August wedding. To sit and embroider linen with her and Germaine and Aunt Juniper taxes my patience to its uttermost. Each time I ride over to the parsonage to add an item to my dower chest, I am reminded of the henbane seeds which so lately lay within it. I wake in the night filled with fear and self-doubt.

I comfort myself with visits to Verity and Thomas. They are both recovering well from the ordeal of birth. On the day before the men are to march away, I go to wish James a safe return. Verity is boiling stocking wool with alder bark to shrink it and turn it black. Her face is running with tears and steam. Little Thomas is wheezing gently in his crib. "The steam is good for his breathing," Verity tells me, then, "James may not come back."

I hug her. My tiny nephew's vulnerability undermines me. His father is going to war. Fifteen years from now he may be going to war himself.

Back at the tower, Kate is making an early batch of Lenten cakes. I whip up some almond butter to go with them. We work together in silence in the kitchen. What is there to say, when men are going to war? It is unreal. There is to be no feast this time. No one has the heart for it.

After the noonday meal I ride over to Mere Point to wish my cousins Godspeed and a safe return. Uncle Juniper is not to go this time. "Someone has to tend the land," he tells me uncertainly. Aunt Juniper is sitting by the kitchen fire, trembling. I hold her hands and talk to her for a while, then kiss my cousins goodbye and go out on to the windy clifftop. Germaine is coming up the path, carrying a basket full of driftwood, kindling for the beacon turret. She looks as if she hasn't slept for weeks. She sets down her basket, and we stand together, staring over the bay.

"You are fortunate," she says, "that priests do not have to fight."

"I know it."

It is a bright spring day. The breeze catches our hair and skirts. Beyond the bay the wrinkled layers of lakeland hills look like crouching lizards, row on row to the horizon. In a few days our men will be beyond them. In a few weeks we must start the beacon watches again. Germaine frowns at me. "What are you up to, Beatrice?"

She has caught me unawares. "I don't know what you're talking about," I answer, but I can feel myself blushing.

"Cousin, I cannot imagine what you are planning, but I want to say to you, your duty is to the living. You must remember that. Robert is as good as dead."

"*No!*" I say it under my breath. "No, he is not."

Germaine tightens her lips. "Do you not *know* how lucky you are to have John? Half the women in the district would fall at his feet without a second thought. Whatever are you thinking of, you foolish, foolish woman? We all have pain. We all have burdens to bear, but we move on, despite them. We cannot let them govern us in the way you are letting this Scot govern you."

I turn away so that the wind is blowing in my face, bringing the scents of grass and flowers. I think of Robert lying amongst the scented herbs on the floor of the hermit's cottage, looking at me, half laughing.

"I can't help it, Germaine. I simply want him safe. If he were safe in Scotland, I could let him go." I am overcome by the futility of trying to explain what I do not understand myself. I turn away. "I would change places with him, Germaine."

Germaine stoops and picks up her basket. "Cousin, you are like a spoilt child. You want it all ways." She sounds unutterably weary. From the doorway of the pele tower she says over her shoulder, "You may not get over this, Beatrice. It may always be with you, but keep it for the dark hours. Give up your days to reality. Go and pay a visit to your betrothed, and be thankful."

I watch her go in. I want to go after her and comfort her and tell her that Gerald will come back, but I do not think she is able to be comforted just now.

Next day, when the men leave, some on horseback, some marching, the women of Barrowbeck, Mere Point and Wraithwaite assemble on Wraithwaite Green to watch them go. Some of Wraithwaite's musicians march at the head of the procession, and they go from our sight to the sound of drums and Flemish bagpipes. For a long time the music comes back to us from round the hill.

Three weeks later, on the day after unusually subdued New Year celebrations, I make the final preparations for what I must do. I go down to the barmkin to look at the carretta. No, it will not do. Its wheels are large, but not wide enough to cope with the mud that lies on the highway to Lancaster. It will have to be John's cart. I pray for frost, hard frost, to freeze the ground and give me speed. I have arranged to be at the parsonage for a few days, on the pretext of overseeing repairs to the doors and panelling. The bishop has agreed that we should not start our wedded life in a house that is falling to bits, so the diocese is paying for extensive repairs. I ride over there in the damp, misty morning, and wait for news.

It comes just after noon. A messenger rides into

Wraithwaite, a shabby youth in a grey jerkin and frayed black breeches. John is out visiting parishioners and Mother Bain is resting, when the knock comes at the parsonage door.

"Mistress Garth?" The boy hands me a folded piece of paper. I open it as he stands there, then bring him into the house whilst I write my reply.

"Take this, please, and give it to Master Postlethwaite." I hand him my note, folded and sealed. "This is for you." I give him a shilling. Then I go to the hastening cupboard and take out the small flagon. "Carry this very carefully. Keep it upright in your saddlebag. I have sealed it in oilcloth and there is a note around its neck." I feel a catch of breathlessness in my throat. "It is to be given to one of the players lodged at the George. His name is Master Guinevere, and he will understand perfectly what it is all about." Then I give the youth a large mug of best ale, and send him on his way.

I sit by the kitchen fire for a long time after that, holding the message he brought. It is written in Master Postlethwaite's rough but adequate hand. *All condemned. Robert Lacklie included. Hangings tomorrow at noon. M. Postlethwaite.*

Chapter 22

$\mathcal{I}$ must not sleep. I go over and over the preparations in my mind. I have checked the cart and Meadowsweet's harnessing. I was tempted to use Universe, for speed, but it will not do to be conspicuous on this journey. My hooded cloak and a black Lenten veil are hanging by the kitchen door. A bundle wrapped in black cloth is in the cart already.

John came home late this evening, very tired. There is smallpox in Hagditch. Anne Fairweather is taking charge of care for the victims. John, who seems to get on with her very well, rode over early this morning with some spare red flannel we had at the parsonage, to drape over sufferers' windows and prevent scarring. We discuss the outbreak, over supper, but John does not seem much inclined to talk. I have not written him an explanation for my trip to Lancaster this time. I shall simply leave him the innkeeper's note.

In the dark hour after midnight I get out of bed and dress by the light of one candle. I am clumsy with haste. Let me not be too clumsy to help him. Let me not be too late. The stairs creak as I creep down them. There is a faint glow from under the kitchen door. The fire is still burning. I'm glad. I am very cold. I shall warm myself thoroughly before going out. I shall be cold enough in the plain working clothes I have chosen, but not as cold as some. I tiptoe into the kitchen and move towards the fire. There is a new log on it. Slowly, I come to a halt.

"So you're prepared to risk everything for this man?"

I look over to where John is sitting in the semi-darkness. As I struggle to recover from the shock, I find that I am angry, as angry as he is. I am on my way out. I cannot put up with delays. "I hope you're not going to try to stop me." I cross to the pegs and take down my veil and cloak. "How did you know?"

"You're not the only one who can bribe innkeepers."

"I see."

He has been mulling ale in the hearth, and now he brings me a tankard and puts it on the dresser. "Beatrice, I want you to think before you do this. You've never been to an execution before. I've had to, in the past, to counsel the condemned. You cannot imagine how truly dreadful it is. The sounds... the sights. And when it's someone you care for, and there's nothing, nothing at all that you can do for them..."

I look at the ale and push it away.

"You won't be able to help him, Beatrice. I know you think you can, but there will be armed soldiers round the gallows, and all you'll be doing is putting yourself in terrible danger. You've seen what a crowd is like when it turns against somebody. If they think you are linked to the Scots... well heaven forbid. They used to let close relatives near the gallows in the past, to... to help victims die more quickly, but now that has been stopped. You will not be able to help him. I'm only telling you this because I want you to understand what you're letting yourself in for. I'm certain Robert would not wish you to go."

I put on my hat, hang the veil over it and pull my cloak round my shoulders. "I'm taking the cart and Meadowsweet, John. I'm not taking Universe this time." I move towards the back door. John crosses the kitchen and blocks my path. I stop. "Are you going to force me to go out the front door and all the way round the house to get to the stables, John?"

"Wait. Just wait a moment. I'll come with you."

I stare at him, appalled. I notice now that he, too, is wearing his rough working clothes. He pulls on a heavy kersey jerkin and fetches his boots from where they are warming by the fire.

"No John. I don't want you to come. If I need help I will go to Master Postlethwaite or the vicar."

"You cannot go on your own. I will not allow it."

His manner infuriates me. I have run Barrowbeck

Farm practically unaided for years, and now this man is trying to tell me what I cannot do. I see very clearly why the queen, who runs so much more, declines to marry. I take a deep breath, and go to stand by the fire. I might as well warm myself whilst persuading John to stay behind. I lift the veil back over my hat and look at him as he comes to join me. He makes a very fetching peasant, I have to say, untidy, tired and rather flushed in the face. My anger drains away.

"Just stay. Darling please. Just stay." I take hold of his jerkin and give it a little shake. The material is rough and warm under my hands.

He looks down at me. "You're wasting your breath. Nothing will make me stay." He kisses me, then pulls the veil back down and kisses me through it. I give a spluttering laugh and pull away. The veil has become rather wet. Then we stare at one another, throw the veil away and kiss again. I lean back against the warm slope of the chimney side. The candle goes out and there is just the fireglow. For a moment I am almost shamefully persuaded. He is right. It is madness. Then I push him away again.

"There's no time. I've got to go."

He sighs, and retrieves the veil. "I'll check the cart."

"I've done it."

"Just a moment whilst I leave Mother Bain a note, then."

I wait impatiently whilst he tears a sheet from one of his sermon books, draws two figures, a castle and a crescent moon on it, and leaves it on the kitchen table. Then he takes my hand and we go together into the darkness.

There is a warm, confused feeling between us as we ride in the cart out of Wraithwaite, though we are both in fact shivering with cold. For the first few miles we keep the lanthorns lit on the sides of the cart, then I climb into the back and extinguish them. Watery dawn comes up as we run low and fast past Mistholme Moss. The boggy land shudders to the hoofbeats. We take it in turns to hold the reins, huddling together. "We could still just go home," John says. I look at him, and do not reply. "Do you have any idea how much I love you?" he asks. "Let's get wed sooner than August."

He swerves the cart to avoid running over a sleepy badger which has shambled out of a copse of wild plums, its snout purple from last autumn's fallen fruit.

"If the militia don't throw us into jail first because of our driving, I suppose we could. There will be talk, though."

"Oh, *talk*." He shrugs impatiently.

The mention of jail has had a chilling effect on us, however, and we fall silent for a while. I wonder if I should tell John what I actually intend to do. He clearly thinks this trip is merely to give Robert support and comfort. He is very compassionate, but breaking the law might be another matter. I decide to let things become apparent as the day progresses.

We meet the first crowds on the edge of Lancaster. I have been travelling with my veil up, but now I lower it and raise my hood. "You look like the Intervening Angel," John comments.

There are a few others in carts and on horseback, but most are walking. Some of the women, like myself, are wearing Lenten veils. Overhead, a dark sky is threatening rain. It takes us a long time to cross the bridge into town, and the crowds are even denser on the other side as we move along Bridge Lane, past Weary Wall with its memory of a soldier's kiss, and up towards the castle. People must have come from miles around to see the hangings. There is an air of excitement running through the crowd. Soldiers in their red and brown coats are trying to keep control. Little by little we edge forward. I look up at the dark castle on the hill as Meadowsweet labours up the steep incline, and I try to imagine Robert on the other side of the iron-studded doors. I try to imagine his feelings.

As we pass the vicarage and reach the side of the castle, John is forced to stop the cart. The crowd presses all around. He hands me the reins. "I'll just stand up and see if there's a way through ahead." He steps into the back of the cart and peers over the heads of the crowd. Around us, soldiers have their swords out as they mingle with the people. Next to the cart, a youth tweaks the hat of one soldier so that it falls over his eyes. There is a gasp from the crowd as the soldier wheels with his sword raised.

When he identifies his attacker he presses the sharp edge of the weapon against the boy's neck, lifting vulnerable young skin in a little fold. The boy goes white and still, and the soldier laughs and turns away.

I am afraid, but I have to ask something which has been the source of many of my nightmares. "Sir..." I lean down to the soldier. "Are the Scots just to hang, or are they to be drawn and quartered too?"

He looks up at me, a young but vicious face, and smiles. "What would you like them to do, mistress? Do you enjoy seeing killers strangling slowly then having their bellies cut open and their guts pulled out?" He stresses each word to its full extent, then jumps back as a whip cracks in front of his face. The crowd titters.

"I think you can manage to answer her in a civilised way." The thin, flat leather of the horsewhip swings from John's gloved hand.

"Hanging." The young soldier looks furious. He eyes the whip and adds, "It weren't thought legal to draw and quarter 'em, more's the pity."

An older soldier joins him. "What's going on? Troublemakers, lad? Get on your way, you two. We can do without trouble from country bumpkins. We've got enough from bloody Scots." He wags his finger at John. "We'll be looking out for you, Master Hayseed." I feel their hostile gaze on our backs as John silently takes the reins and the cart moves forward again.

We make some progress round the castle, but cannot

get near the gates. Cake sellers and ale wagons line the path to the twin-towered gatehouse with its slit windows, and those who arrived there first are not giving up their places to anyone. The roar of voices is all around.

"Best pasties! Come and get Fat Lizzy's best pasties!"

"Drink whilst yer can! Grim Reaper's coming this way, and his aim ain't so accurate. Get yerself a mug of Ted's best ale!"

Everyone else is raising their voices to be heard above the din.

"It'll be a reet fine show, I reckon."

"It's allus good to have things where nature intended 'em, leaves hanging from trees, Scots hanging from ropes."

"Are they stopping off at Saint Bridgie's Alehouse as usual?"

"Nay, I heard not. It's not for Scots to be solaced by drinking theirselves senseless. Let 'em choke slowly and know about it."

"Anyway, who'd pay? There'll be no relatives, unless the devil turns up."

Howls of laughter greet this witticism. Someone knows better, though. "Nay Titus, they are stopping. Same as usual. I heard it from t'landlord. Someone's put up money." There are incredulous jeers and shouts of disapproval.

"Who'd put up money for a bunch of Scots, eh? Should be strung up alongside of 'em."

217

John looks at me. I avoid his eyes.

There is an atmosphere of savagery here, the atmosphere of the death hunt. It seems to me that the devil has turned up already.

After a long wait, during which Meadowsweet becomes very nervous and restive at all the loud talk and laughter, there is a drum roll from inside the castle. A cheer goes up. The portcullis, rusty and spider-webbed, rumbles up, and the drum roll continues as the giant doors swing inwards. The drum slows to a regular dead beat. The crowd starts to clap in time with it. I gather the reins into a bunch and thrust them at John. I don't think he realises what I am doing until it is too late. By then I have scrambled down from the cart and am pushing my way to the front of the crowd, muttering, "By your leave. Excuse me."

"Beatrice!" I hear John's furious voice behind me.

"Beatrice!" mocks the crowd, in time with the drumbeat and the clapping. "Bea-trice! Bea-trice!"

I ignore it all and watch the first cart come from the inner compound of the castle. Slowly they come, three primitive rattletraps. They stop because of the crowd, and wait for their escort.

Nothing has prepared me for this. I think others are equally taken aback.

"Nay, just look at them."

"Don't look too bright, do they."

"Course, them dungeons ain't more than six foot high, seven at most."

"It was a starvation diet, right and all."

Some in the crowd are turning away.

"Look at that poor wight."

"I'm going home."

"Well you can go, but I'm off up to t'Moor to get a right good place..."

The whole crowd is shifting. I can still hear, behind the wild talk, John shouting at me to get back in the cart. I know that any moment he will get down and drag me back. I look at the condemned men. After the first shock of their appearance I can see at once that Robert is not here. None of these poor, stooped, shivering skeletons bears the slightest resemblance to him. Hardly any have any hair. Some look half blind, their eyes swollen to slits. All seem too destroyed to stand upright, their lips, cheeks, shoulders all hollow and fallen in. An overwhelming stench comes off them. Some of the older ones' beards seem to have grown huge at some stage, and then to have fallen out in patches.

The woman is not amongst them. Clearly Edward has been persuaded. I look sadly at the condemned men. Their hands are fastened in front of them with short ropes. Their coffins – rough-hewn boxes with the nails not even properly knocked in – are roped on to the carts with them, some on end at the front, some lying flat for the prisoners to sit on.

I lift my veil to see more clearly, standing next to the middle cart and staring in turn at each of the prisoners in each cart, just to be sure. He is not here. No one who looks in the least like my tall, beautiful Robert is here. Thank God, thank God. Clearly he is dead already. His suffering is over and he is safe. What he went through I will never know, but at least it is finished. I can go home and marry John and grieve in peace. I turn to struggle back through the crowd, when one of the skeletons says, "Bea."

I look round. I do not know who has spoken.

"Bea."

It is as if the Angel of Death has spoken.

Chapter 23

No one notices at first. I grip the side of the rattletrap, in order not to pass out. I look at this skeleton which is Robert, and I am ashamed of what our civilisation can do.

His voice is cracked, unrecognisable, as he asks, "Were you here in the autumn?"

I try to see the young man I knew, in this broken form. I cannot. What are any of us then? Just illusions?

"Yes, I was here in the autumn."

"I knew it. I felt it."

The crowd is pushing round the prisoners' carts, pushing at my back, laughing and jeering at the prisoners. I see that one Scot in Robert's cart is smaller and slighter than the others. His bones look unformed and, through a straggle of whiskers, his chin has a babyish bluntness.

Before the dungeon made him old, he was probably a restless lad, out adventuring, drinking, living for girls and loud fiddle music. Now he is weeping and wetting himself. Some in the crowd see this, and roar with delight.

There is some sort of violent commotion going on behind me now. As I become aware of it I realise that it has been going on for some time. A shot explodes close by. The smell of gunpowder drifts over. There is screaming, horrified and close. Part of my mind hears it, but I cannot look away from Robert, for fear he should be gone when I look back. I am knocked against the nearest cart wheel by the turmoil of the mob behind me. The cart in front jerks forward.

"Stand back there! Stand back, ladies and gentlemen!" Two soldiers on horseback have followed the carts out and are using their horses' shoulders to push a way through to the front of the procession. Two more take up position at the rear. There are two horses to pull each cart, grey, black and dun, poor looking creatures in comparison with the soldiers' fine mounts. The smell of horseflesh is all around, usually so comforting, now the scent of death. The cart drivers slap the reins across their beasts' bony backs. The coffins wobble and clatter against each other. Robert lowers himself to sit on one of them. He speaks without looking at me. "Go home now, Bea. I am very glad to have seen you again."

"I'm coming with you." I raise my hand and stroke his arm. He flinches away.

"Don't come. It will be far worse for me if you do. I'm comforted now. Just remember how it was." He looks at me, then away. "I only pray that they will hang me from the north side of the tree, facing home."

Tears come into my eyes. I swallow and blink to keep them back. The north side of the tree, the side the moss grows, the means by which weary travellers find their way home. Suddenly I am aware of growing hostility all around me.

"Eh, what's this?"

"What's he saying? What's she saying?"

"What's going on?"

People start to push at me, deliberately.

"She should be up on t'cart too, if you ask me."

"...spying for them bastard Scots..."

I look round in bewilderment, hardly understanding what is happening. I have to tell Robert about my plan, but people are crowding round me and I cannot see the prisoners' carts any more, beyond a wall of unfriendly faces. An old man pushes me with both hands. "Traitor! Scottish trollop!"

I gasp and look round for John. There is no sign of him. He should have been visible on the cart, but I can see neither him nor Meadowsweet. The surge of the crowd must have separated us, and carried him back down the hill. I realise that the prisoners' carts are picking up speed now. I elbow my way through the crush, back to Robert's side. The crowd shoves and jostles me. Some youths climb

223

briefly on to the backs of the carts to spit at the prisoners. I dare not risk speaking to Robert again. I shall be of no use to him if I am imprisoned myself.

At the edge of the crowd those in carts or on horseback are moving away now, in the direction of Gallows Hill. Where on earth is John? My plan is impossible without transport. I start to ask people if they have seen him, but no one knows what I am talking about. The carts move faster. I run after them, pushing people out of my way. Robert is watching me. Unknowable expressions tremble across his face. As the downward slope grows steeper, the carts jolt along faster. The wheels rattle and the spokes blur. Gradually I am left behind, and the crowd closes in behind the cavalcade. I wrap my arms around myself and let them go.

A young soldier is cleaning his matchlock by the castle gates. He calls to me, "All been a bit much for you, has it, mistress?"

I go to stand near him, looking around now that the crowd has moved on. John is still nowhere to be seen. Can he have been set upon and the cart stolen? Surely I would have heard something, though with my concentration all on Robert, perhaps I would not have. I feel a sort of terror starting in the pit of my stomach. What have I done, leading John into this, into what people might perceive as guilty association with the Scots?

"Did anything happen just now?" I ask the young soldier. "Any incident, or something like that... something concerning a parson on a cart? Though... that is, he wasn't dressed as a parson..." I falter and stop.

"I only just came on duty, lady," the soldier answers quite kindly. "So I wouldn't rightly know."

There is no more time to wait here. I can see across the valley to the Moor, and the row of twig gibbets on Gallows Hill. How powerless we are, insects to be destroyed by twigs.

I nod to the soldier, then lower my veil again and start to walk the mile to the Moor. I must simply hope and pray that John is all right and will turn up in time. Perhaps he lost sight of me and thought I had already moved on towards the hanging ground. If not, if all else fails, at least Robert, like the rest of them, will be without his senses by the time they reach the gallows.

I feel very tired. Lack of sleep has made me light-headed. Even going downhill along Saint Mary Street is an effort. I can still hear the sounds of the crowd in the distance. I start to hurry. It will not do for them to get too far ahead. Faintly I can hear someone playing the pipes as well now, fitting in with the drumbeat. I pray that they will indeed stop at Saint Bridgie's Alehouse. Despite what I heard earlier in the crowd, something might still go amiss. I pray that my little flagon has travelled safely.

At the stone well in the valley I sit down for a moment. Moor Lane lies ahead. I had forgotten how steep it is. I can see the crowd now. They have indeed stopped at the alehouse. I send my fervent blessings to Master Postlethwaite for passing on my gold pieces as I asked.

I look up the long hill to where the trees thin out into wild scrubland beyond. We picked blackberries there once, Mother and I, after visiting Lancaster's Michaelmas Hiring Fair. I was very young then. Was that the year we took Germaine on? I cannot remember. I remember being allowed to turn the blackberries into a dark, sticky sauce to go with the Michaelmas goose.

I set off again. My mouth is dry and my tongue feels swollen and dusty. There is no air here on this hill. I pull at my collar to loosen it. The sound of the crowd's frenzy grows.

"May we give you a lift, mistress?"

I look round, startled. I had not noticed the approach of this neat, modern cart with two soldiers up at the front. The back of the cart is full of matchlocks and powder horns. I recognise the passenger as Captain Foreman from the George, but with my veil down, he does not recognise me. I open my mouth to refuse, then change my mind and accept. The captain steps down and gallantly assists me into the back, amongst the weapons, and kisses my hand with a flourish. I sit awkwardly on an oblong box of metal shot.

"Thank you, sir."

The cart moves forward, drawn by its two black

226

horses. I look at the weapons that surround me — matchlocks like the one carried by John, with the same action as our hagbut at home, though only a quarter the size. Some are half out of their waxed wrappers, and are clearly already loaded, judging by the trickle of gunpowder from their barrels.

It seems we have no sooner started than we stop again. We have reached the alehouse. "Come and I'll buy you a drink, mistress." The captain offers me his hand. "Some fool with more money than sense has paid for the Scots to drink their fear away, just as if they were normal, decent criminals."

"Oh no, how utterly regrettable." I take his hand and step down, looking around for John and the cart. If he lost sight of me by the castle, he might have come here.

There are carts aplenty, but none of them is ours. I hesitate, and glance at the captain. He might know if something happened earlier. Also, he already knows both John and me from our encounter at the George, when we last visited Lancaster. Yet it is important to keep my veil down, and my identity secret, if I am to rescue Robert without becoming a fugitive from the law myself. I wonder if I am being foolish and naive, if my plan is completely hopeless. Oh just start a little riot, kind sirs, and I'll get Robert away amid the chaos, I bade the grey-haired chief mummer and the lad who played Guinevere. It sounded perfectly reasonable at the time, there in the parsonage's guest chamber. I stare at the crowd. It is growing wilder as drinks are handed along from one to the other. I look at the soldiers hefting their weapons. I look at the long hill up to the gallows. It is starting to rain.

I realise that the captain is talking to me. "Do you not have a husband to accompany you, mistress?" He offers me his arm.

"Indeed I do, somewhere, but I cannot find him in the crowd. In fact I am worried about him. Has there been any trouble at all?"

"Nay mistress, none at all, except for a ruffian with a matchlock up by the castle. We soon dealt with him."

People say their blood runs cold. I had thought it just a saying. I realise in that moment that it is true. An icy shiver travels slowly across my shoulders, down through my body, to my legs, so that they start to tremble. The captain is still talking. "...my lads had trouble with him earlier, so they told me it was good riddance..."

I feel sick. I hear once more in my head the shot which exploded behind me at the castle, and the words of the soldier whom John had earlier threatened with the whip. "We'll be looking out for you." Amid the shock of seeing Robert in the state he was, and with the turmoil of the crowd, I failed even to turn to see what was happening.

I throw back my veil. "Sir, do you remember me? We met at the George some months since. I was with my husband. Could it be... could it possibly be that the man with the matchlock was my husband, the parson? And if it is so... can you please tell me what became of him?"

The captain stares at me in amazement. One of his men is trying to attract his attention. "Sir! Sir! There's a bit of trouble over there in t'crowd!"

"Hush!" The captain flaps a hand at him. "I am speaking to the parson's wife."

The soldier reaches us and stares at me. "She don't look like no parson's wife to me, sir," he says.

I am beginning to wonder if I should not have dressed in my old clothes after all. The captain frowns at him. "Nay, she is in truth a parson's wife. I have met her before. Her husband is a man of most severe countenance. Madame, I did not see the prisoner, but is it likely that your husband would have threatened my men with a matchlock?"

"Perfectly likely, since your men had been highly disrespectful to me earlier. Now please, what happened to him?"

The captain hesitates, and in that moment my brain struggles with the unthinkable, that John might be dead. At last the captain says, "Madame, there seems to be something a little odd going on here. You were in Lancaster enquiring about Scots on a previous occasion, and now that they are to be justly hanged, here you are again, together with your husband, who you say is a parson. Well, I can tell you that he is not dead, though he may be a little bruised. When my soldiers tried to move him along, he refused. There was a struggle, I gather, and the matchlock went off. I think your husband is at present imprisoned in the Well Tower of the castle. Perhaps,

229

madame, you had better come along with me, and we will see about reuniting you with him. In the meantime, you can explain to me why he was disguised as a peasant." He takes hold of my arm in a firm grip.

"Sir..." The soldier tries again. "The crowd is trying to get into the alehouse, sir, to get at the Scots. They don't like it that the Scots are drinking in there, whilst they're shut out."

I look over to where a fight has broken out in the doorway of Saint Bridgie's Alehouse. The captain releases my arm. "Madame, please excuse me. I must deal with this. Kindly remain where I can find you. Sergeant!" He pushes his way towards the disturbance, but before he can reach it, a woman sidles up to him and strokes her white hand across his chest. She stands directly in his path, and for the briefest moment, glances in my direction. I smile slightly at the wardrobe mistress.

John is safe, bruised but safe. It is all that matters. By the time I am back at the parsonage, he will be back too. Relief gives me new courage. It will be more difficult to get Robert away without the cart and the bundle it contains, but I shall simply have to find alternative transport. I look at the carts at the edge of the crowd. All of them are occupied. The crowd is becoming very wild now. I am pushed and bumped as others head towards the outbreak of fighting. Titus, the wit from up by the castle, is trying to fight his way into the alehouse. I recognise the chief mummer just before he hits him.

I remember, in the bedchamber of the parsonage, this elegant, grey-haired man who played King Arthur in the masque they performed, asking me, "But exactly how *does* one start a riot, mistress?"

"Oh, I don't know. I suppose you hit someone who has a lot of friends, or you steal something that everyone else will want to start stealing too. Ale, maybe?"

Almost as I think it, I hear the shout go up, "Thief! Thief!"

The air is full of smells of sweat and horse manure. Whiffs of beer and boiled beef come from the alehouse. I start to push my way in the opposite direction from the rest of the crowd, climbing over the mounting block, and then over the rubbish heap, where rotting food releases a vile stink as I stumble over it. I work my way round the side of the alehouse, towards the back. There is a shout behind me. "Out of the way! Out of the way!" The driver of the armaments cart is moving it round towards the back of the alehouse. I watch incredulously. Could this be an astonishing piece of good fortune? I wait for him to pass, and then follow him, my slime-coated boots slipping on the stones of the stableyard.

It is quieter round the back. The cart and horses vanish into one of the stables. I dawdle past a small outbuilding and peer inside. It is full of old saddles and barrels, and there is a dusty workbench. With a jump I realise that there are also two people here, a couple, too involved in kissing one another to notice me. I doubt they would have noticed if the entire riot had gone in one door and out the other. I tiptoe past.

It proves astonishingly easy to walk into the alehouse through the back door. I wonder why the rest of the crowd has not thought of it. I meet Master Guinevere coming out of a side room, rolling a barrel of ale as if he had been doing it all his life.

"Good morrow, mistress. Robert Lacklie is by the back door of the bar. I've tried to cut his ropes, but I don't think I got them right through. There were too many people about to risk sawing away properly. Anyway, he knows something's up, but the stuff you sent me to put in their barrel of ale has fair knocked them out. Do you want the crowd to come in through the front door yet?"

"Perhaps give it a few minutes. It has all gone wrong, Master Guinevere. I have no disguise for Robert. It was with John, in the cart, and he has been arrested."

The fair-haired lad swears, then pauses and thinks for a moment. "Well, there's no time to get more. You'll have to take him as he is. Unless, just a minute, I'll see if the wardrobe mistress has something we can spare." He upends the barrel next to a partly open door, and indicates that I should sit on it.

I raise my voice above the din coming from beyond the door. "I think I've paid you enough to have something you *can't* spare, Master Guinevere." He grins, and strides away towards a dark stairway. I peer through the door, and come face to face with Robert.

It is obvious at once that he is beyond recognising me. He is half lying on the rough bench, propped against the door jamb. A soldier stands next to him. I stare in dismay. I had not expected the contents of my little flagon to render the Scots senseless quite so quickly. All around the tavern they are slumping across the tables or falling to the floor. Their guards drag them upright in agitation, but let them fall again as the uproar from outside takes on a more threatening note. "Best see if the captain needs help out there," says Robert's guard to another soldier. "I'll stay and guard the back here. These lads ain't going nowhere. Reckon as this landlord's going to face a bit of questioning about what he puts in his ale."

I watch as another Scot tips face forward into his tankard, and wonder if perhaps I should not have sent instructions for an additional pint of usquebaugh to be added to the barrel. It had seemed a reasonable precaution at the time, but I had been relying on a slightly slower onset of oblivion for the men, and had assumed that Robert would have at least some use of his legs.

At the far side of the alehouse a window smashes. Under cover of the falling glass I whisper, "Robert!" He does not respond, but the soldier guarding him glances at me. His companions are all heading towards the commotion at the front, but he is resolutely standing his ground. "Oy, you!" he says and seizes my arm. At that moment the mob bursts in.

Chapter 24

*P*eople are fighting all around me. An elbow jabs me in the back. A tankard hits me on the head. When a soldier nearby hauls a rioter off a table, the man's flying legs knock me off my feet. I start to crawl towards the back door. The soldier is no longer on guard there. Robert is lying across the threshold, his eyes wide and glassy.

"Dead and gone." A young man who smells of drink is staring down at him. "Bloody sad, ain't it." He is wearing an apron, and looks like one of the alehouse servants. His voice is filled with drunken sentiment.

"Yes it is. Help me carry his body out."

Unquestioningly, the young man obeys. He takes Robert's shoulders whilst I take his feet. Robert's limbs are light as sticks. It is all the more shocking because my own limbs remember how heavy he was, in the days when I nursed him in the forest.

We carry him out of the back door and across the stableyard. "There." I jerk my head. "Put him in that stable."

The young man backs over the muddy stones, bent double, belching serenely. I walk bent double too, dizzy from the blow to my head. In the stable is the armaments cart. There is no one about.

"Put him in that cart. Yes there, on top of the matchlocks. Thank you so much." I let the young man lift Robert whilst I take out one of my few remaining shillings. "Here, buy yourself something. I'm most grateful to you."

The young man shakes his head. He gives a sedate, tottering bow. "Your servant, mistress," and he pitches forward unconscious into a trough of hay.

Almost at once, Master Guinevere reappears, bearing a red skirt and bodice and a flowing golden cloak. I stare at them in dismay. "Now we shall be truly inconspicuous," I tell him.

"It was all I could find in a hurry. The costume trunk was locked and the wardrobe mistress has the key."

Clumsily we cram Robert into the outfit. I stand back and inspect him. It is impossible. He looks ridiculous. I pull off my own cloak and exchange it for his. I pull the black hood over his head and cover his face with my veil. Then we arrange him so that he is sitting with his head drooping towards his knees in the back of the cart. Now he looks like an old woman, stooped and black-clad. On the other hand I, in the flowing golden cloak, look like a trollop.

I fear that at any moment the driver of the armaments cart may reappear. How long can it be before the captain decides he needs matchlocks against the rioters? I turn to thank Master Guinevere and bid him farewell, but he is already gone.

I overturn the youth who is lying in the hay trough, and seize armfuls of hay to cover the weapons, then lead the two horses towards the stable door, and climb up on to the cart. With what seems an alarming amount of noise, we trundle forward into the rain. I stop. The couple from the outbuilding are standing in the middle of the yard, watching us.

"What are you doing with that cart, mistress?" the man enquires in a suspicious voice. There is a crash and the back door of the alehouse slams open. We all turn, as Master Guinevere staggers out with another limp figure in his arms. It is the young boy who sat opposite Robert in the cart and wept. Like Robert, he is unconscious. His feet trail through the mud and his head flops against the player's shoulder.

"Managed to get another one out," Master Guinevere pants. "Oh." He stops as he sees the couple. The woman is backing away towards the side of the alehouse, as if to summon help.

I look swiftly from one to the other of them. "Please... in the name of mercy..."

They hesitate, and glance at one another, then the woman whispers, "God save them," and the man comes forward to help lift the young Scot into the back of the cart. The boy clatters down amongst the weapons.

"Thank you. Thank you so very much." I climb over into the back and take off my golden cloak. Master Guinevere hurriedly wraps the boy in it, then lays him in a corner of the cart, next to Robert. The rain is beating down now. "I'll get you my own cloak, mistress," he says.

"I thank you, but there is no time." I heap hay over the boy's slight figure. The golden cloak is a similar colour to the hay, and he is barely visible. I grab two matchlocks from the back, and clamber into the driving seat again. "God will bless you, sirs, madam." I hope this will indeed be so. I have little confidence in my standing with the Almighty at this moment. I click my tongue and flick the reins over the horses' backs, and we move off.

It is easier than I had anticipated to push through the screaming, fighting mass of people, with the horses and cart. These horses are more used to barging through crowds than gentle Meadowsweet is. The problem comes when I reach the edge of the crowd, where a barricade of soldiers is trying to contain the now tiring rioters. As I emerge from the mass of people, and speed up slightly, one of the soldiers sees me. Unfortunately it is the cart driver.

"Hey! Hey! You there!" He raises his shortsword and rushes at me. I whip up the horses, grab one of the matchlocks and fumble with my tinderbox in a hand already grappling with the reins. When I try to light the fuse, the reins slide out of my grasp. I aim the weapon above the charging soldier's head, and the gunpowder explodes deafeningly.

Whether I am indeed deafened, or whether the whole scene truly does go silent, I cannot say. What I can say is that a huge woodpigeon plummets out of the sky and thuds to the ground behind me. Feathers drift in the air, and the horses bolt out of control down the hill, with the cart bouncing after them.

I am almost unseated. I hold on to the sides of the cart, and lean forward to catch at the reins as we career round the first sharp bend. On the valley floor people flee from our path, shrieking with fright. I hear an explosion behind me, and risk another glance over my shoulder. Instead of pursuers, I see that the hinged tailflap of the cart has fallen down, and that matchlocks are sliding off the back.

I re-establish control of the horses as we enter Chiney Lane. I grip the reins in my sweating hands, wind them round my fingers, move my backside more securely on to the seat. The horses are still tossing their heads and snorting, and their shoulders jog together uneasily as they weave to and fro, but the frenzy is over.

"Hey!"

"You there!"

I jerk round in my seat. Two elderly men outside the Mare Maid are shouting at me. I stare straight ahead and keep going.

"Stop her!"

Word is being passed along the few people at the side of the street. Two more men step out into my path – young, drunk men. One of them grabs at the harnessing, unsettling the rhythm of the horses again. He swings round, losing his footing, and I am forced to stop the cart or he would have been pole-axed by the shaft.

"Get *off*!" I shout.

"Why'm I stopping her?" asks the drunk plaintively. The two old men arrive at a limping run, panting and gasping.

"The grimalkin's tipped ovver," yells one. "She's well nigh on her back, poor old bugger. Can't yer tek better care of yer granny than that?"

I look round. With the thrashing movement of the cart Robert has fallen sideways and slid down. His thin ankles are sticking out from the bottom of his red gown. The black cloak still envelops the rest of him. Faint groans come from within it. Of the other young Scot there is no sign.

"Oh, sweet Jesu!" I gasp. I wonder how far back along the road he fell out.

"Nay lass, don't tek on so. She'll not have hurt herself." The first old man tries to climb up on to the cart, and fails.

"Would you please hold the horses?" I ask the drunk, and once more climb over into the back of the cart on legs that will scarcely hold me. Straight away I can see what has happened. As the firearms slid out, the hay shifted backwards, and it now covers the boy in a great mound. The mound moves slightly, so I sit on it, and pull Robert back into a sitting position.

From the depths of his hood he says in a slurred voice, "'Tis a right mirksome day, Beatrice."

"Indeed it is..." I pull the hood further down over his face, and jam him into position against the wooden upright of the cart.

"What's she say?" enquires the second old man. He heaves himself up into the back of the cart. I notice that one remaining matchlock is poking out from the hay. I move my feet so that my skirts cover it, and pray that the man who is holding the horses at the front is too drunk to see the two firearms in the footwell.

"Pray don't trouble yourself, good sir," I urge the old man. "My poor grandmother... I fear she is over-tired."

He pats Robert's shoulder. "It's all right, mother. Don't fret. Yer just toppled ovver. Best get her home and give her a cup of broth, eh lady?"

I tuck the black veil firmly into Robert's hood. "I thank you. I shall indeed do that. It's been a long day."

The old man eases himself back to the ground, and fastens up the tailflap at both sides. I turn to step back into the driving seat and instead come to a halt. The

240

drunk, strangely steady now, has raised one of the matchlocks and is pointing it at me.

"Sir..." I stare at the shiny barrel. I can smell the gunpowder.

"'Tis a pity," he says, raising the barrel further and squinting along it. There is a great silence. No one else moves. He rests a foot on the spoke of a wheel to support himself. It has the reverse effect, as the cart shifts slightly. "'Tis a pity," he repeats, giving a little jump to catch up, "when things aren't as they seem."

I clasp my hands together and try to speak calmly. "I'm afraid I don't understand you, sir."

"See these highways?" He makes a wide gesture with one hand in the general direction of the bridge and The King's Strete. "Quiet as anything they seem, don't they?"

I nod.

"But they're not."

"No?"

"No." He shakes his head. "They're full of robbers. You do right to carry these things to defend yourself, lady." He throws the weapon back into the footwell, then staggers as he attempts to remove his foot from the wheel. "You take care." He rights himself. "Good day to you." He hands me the reins and lurches off down the street.

I draw a long, shaky breath, and climb back into the driving seat.

"Goodbye." I wave to the two old men and set the cart moving. I have wasted too much time. Pursuit cannot be far behind, despite the remarkable speed we have made through town. The soldiers will have had to find their horses, mount up, perhaps arm themselves with other matchlocks from elsewhere. They will have done all that by now. They will be setting off. I let the horses trot for a short distance, to steady them, then we speed up as we approach the arched bridge over the river. I look back up the hill at the castle, and think of John imprisoned there. He will be saved, without my help. The bishop, or the vicar, will intervene to have him released. Yet it feels very bad to gallop out of Lancaster leaving him behind. He doesn't need my help in the way that Robert does, but he does need me, as I need him. Feeling distraught at what I am doing, I whip up the horses and let them run.

Chapter 25

They catch up with us at Kerne Forth. It is purely by chance that I have pulled off the highway and into the edge of the woods to light the lanthorns. The darkening sky and overhanging trees have been a cover for us, but as the afternoon draws on, and the cloud and rain come down worse than ever, it has become difficult to see at all.

The two men in the cart have been well out of their senses for most of the journey. The boy has whimpered occasionally, and once a burst of crazed laughter came from Robert, but mostly I have felt cut off from them, up here on the driving seat. The thought that they might be quietly dying back there has been frightening. Now, with the lanthorns flickering, I climb into the rear of the cart again to look at them. They both stink. I peer at Robert.

He is too still and quiet. His skin is warm, and he is breathing, but his inhalations are shallow and hasty, a huffing for breath, as if he dreamt a rope round his neck.

"Robert." I touch his cheek. "Can you hear me?"

The youth next to him is coughing. I remove the hay from over his face. He groans and tries to sit up. "Hush," I whisper. "Hush now." Robert remains motionless. I loosen the laces of his red bodice and put my ear to his chest, to listen for his heartbeat. It is drumming. I wonder in panic if some terrifying and unforeseen effect from the henbane and usquebaugh potion has occurred. Surely his heartbeat should be slower. I say softly into his ear, "You'll be home soon, Robert."

It is puzzling that the pounding of Robert's heart is still in my ears when I climb back into the driving seat. It takes me a moment to realise that the sound is hoofbeats. Frantically I extinguish the lanthorns and ease the cart deeper into the forest, along a path so narrow that branches scrape the sides. The rain rattles in gusts through the leaves and runs down my skin inside my clothes. I circle the cart round a large oak tree which has created its own clearing, and sit shivering, watching the highway, which is just visible from here in the leafy twilight.

Several riders are approaching. The highway is up a slope, and the further trees are outlined against the sky. Also outlined are the riders when they come, eight or ten soldiers travelling at a canter, their angled sword-hilts elegant, threatening silhouettes.

I wait a long time after they have gone. All around me trees creak in the rising wind. I no longer dare look to the sides of me, for I know that things can see me which I cannot see.

It is completely dark by the time we emerge from the trees. I set off slowly. We must not catch the soldiers up. I wait until it is time to turn off the main highway and into the woods that lead towards Hagditch and the sea, before I dare light the lanthorns again. When we have gone some distance down the smaller track, I stop to let the horses drink at a beck. I take out my damp tinderbox to ignite the lamps' greasy wicks in their curve of translucent horn. It takes a while to get them going, with the wind blowing and the rain coming down. Tense with exasperation I tilt the flame to and fro to melt the wax clogging the tiny air holes. I am ready to cry with tiredness and frustration. At last the lanthorns take, and I hook them back on to the sides of the cart. The boy is unconscious again now, and Robert remains so.

As we pass the southern tip of Mistholme Moss, a wind like tempered steel cuts across the flat bogland. I lower my head against the buffeting. I can no longer feel my fingers on the reins, and the lobes of my ears ache as if the blood had frozen in them. Finally we reach the path that runs down through a gap in the cliffs, south of Mere Point, and on to the saltmarsh foreshore. I can hear the roar of the tide retreating somewhere out there in the darkness. I slow the tired horses to a careful walk over the

245

slippery rocks. The cart jolts and slithers. We round the cliff and come to the first of the caves. It gapes black, halfway up the cliff face. This would have been the best cave in which to hide – deep, dry and protected from the wind – but I know I cannot drag Robert and the boy up there on my own. Also, there is nowhere to conceal the cart. We move on, round the pools with their brackish smell, round the winter-bleached thrift and salty grass, phantom shapes in the rocking light of the lanthorns.

The second cave is at shore level, within a cleft that will hide the cart. The horses whinny and toss their heads as I halt them at the cave entrance. I have neither time nor energy to unharness them, and it is scarcely worthwhile anyway, since their work is far from done. I'm thankful for the rain which has fallen in hollows in the rocks, providing fresh water. I release them from the shafts, and they drink, and crop the dried drifts of eelgrass which have washed up. The wind is less fierce here, and the sound of the sea more distant. Now I must get food and drink for the men, and also find out where the soldiers are. One way or another I must get Robert and the boy away, if not to Scotland, then at least to the Augustine monks at Cartmel, though they might no longer be safe even there, if the soldiers are searching this far north. What I cannot think about yet is my own fate. I wonder whether John is safely back at the parsonage, and whether I still have any choices left.

I climb down, unhook a lanthorn and shine it into the back of the cart. Robert's eyes are open. He is staring at me.

"The others will all be dead by now," he says.

At the sound of his voice, the truth crashes over me like the tide. He is here. He is with me. Robert is no longer imprisoned in the castle. The months of terror are over. Fumbling, I let down the tailflap and climb into the back of the cart. I put my arms round him and hold him against me. He is filthy, bent and ill, but this person whom I so injured, and whom my people have now injured so much worse, is back from the grave.

"Oh Robert." I kiss his face and hair, and kneel amongst the hay and rock him. When I look up, the boy is watching us.

I help the two of them into the cave. They both manage to walk haltingly, limping and leaning on me. The cave is deep and dark. Inside, the smell is of dankness and salt and the slow earth. Near the entrance, brown streaks show on white walls in the fitful moonlight, and water trickles down the rockface. At the back, where the ground slopes up to a sandy shelf, it is dry. Here is the tall, narrow crevice which leads to Cedric's cottage, up on the cliffs.

When I was here last week, working out the tides, the cave was warm. Now it is bitter. I help the two of them along to the sandy shelf, listening to the irregularity of Robert's breathing. It echoes in the enclosed space. "You're in no state to travel, Robert," I whisper, "but I'm

afraid we must keep going, once you have rested a while."
I set one of the lanthorns on its stand in a crevice. Images
flash in its unreliable light, worm faces in the darkness.

The youth huddles in a natural corner formed by two
rocks, hugging his gaudy cloak about him. Robert takes
off the black cloak and tries to make me wear it, but I
refuse, so in the end we sit close together with it wrapped
round both of us. "What is your name?" I ask the boy.

"Jonathan." He hesitates. "Do you know what became
of my mother, mistress? She was imprisoned in the castle
with us for a while."

"Come over here." I hold out my arm to him. "Sit with
us and get warm. So it was your mother, was it? I believe
she is probably safe, Jonathan."

Like a child, he comes and sits by me. I put my arm
round his shoulders. "I met her, Jonathan, one night.
When you see her, tell her that the woman on the landing
at the George sends greetings."

After a while they both sleep, Jonathan sucking his
thumb, Robert rasping with each breath, and I leave them
there, blanketed in the smell of the dungeon, waiting for
daybreak.

I take the second lanthorn with me through the crevice at
the back of the cave. I have to squeeze sideways to fit
through. I have never been this way before, though Cedric
has on several occasions said he will show me. As soon as

I am through, the light goes out with a pop. I am in complete darkness. I consider going back and taking the long way round – climbing the cliff path and walking back through the woods to Cedric's cottage – but speed is too important. I continue on in utter blackness, feeling with my feet and hands, listening for sounds, terrified of what I might touch with my fingers. A feeling of unreality comes over me. I am too tired to think. Have I really saved Robert from the gallows, or is this just a dream?

I move and stop, move and stop. I know from Cedric that there are no hidden chasms or traps in this rock passage, but it occurs to me that I do not know the precise mechanism for getting out the other end. I could go back for the other lanthorn, but the need for haste is so great that I decide against it. I cannot stop thinking about how exposed the horses and cart are, outside in the cleft of the rock. Once dawn comes up, anyone passing could see them and go into the cave to investigate.

The ground slopes up sharply. I stumble, strain my eyes, pause, but there is not even a hint of light. Suddenly the walls on either side of me, along which I have been feeling my way, stop. There is nothing. I feel with my foot. The ground continues up, but to the sides of me is space. I find the rock wall at one side again and follow it with my hand. It curves away. The other side is the same. I am in a wide fissure, and I do not know which way to go. If I had a light, it would probably be obvious. I decide that I shall have to go back after all. That is when I hear the sound.

249

I freeze. There was a tiny shift amongst the rocks. I listen with all my concentration. Bats. It could only be bats, a few still here in the dark, not out foraging with the rest. Water drips. The wind and sea roar far off. Then I realise that I can also smell the sea close to. Amongst all the underground smells pressing on me in this lightless place, the smell of the sea is stronger than it should be. Then I hear breathing.

Chapter 26

I am paralysed with fright. Here in the depths of the earth, where I should not be, is something that lives in the earth, perhaps watching me. I edge back into the rock passage. I can hear it moving. It is shockingly close. Then it touches me.

I recoil against the cave wall and lash out, gasping.

"Who's that?" a voice hisses in my ear.

"Oh God! Oh God!" I want to drum my heels, fall down and faint. I want to kill him. "Cedric! Cedric, for God's sake, what are you *doing* here in the dark?" I clench my hands against my pounding heart.

"Shh!" Strong arms close round me, and the smell of the sea, which is Cedric's smell, envelops me. "Don't make a sound. They'll hear us. The soldiers are in my house."

"Oh no!"

A tinderbox clicks and a candle flares. Cedric sets the copper candleholder down on a rock. Now I can see the space we are in. It is a wide, low cave, sloping below head height at the far end, with water dripping down the walls and running away through crevices in the rock. "There's a way up to my house, through a trapdoor." Cedric points to a pile of rocks leading up beyond the low overhang at the far end. "What's been happening, Beatrice?"

"I got Robert out. Another Scot, too."

In the candlelight Cedric's face looks incredulous, disproportionate. "Where are they?" he asks.

"In the cave." I gesture behind me. "But John has been captured. He's imprisoned in the castle. Will you see that he gets out? Speak to the bishop? I have to get away with Robert. Will you guide us over the sands?"

He is silent for a moment, then he answers, "I'll take Robert over the sands, Beatrice. You don't need to come. I'll take him to the Black Brothers at Cartmel. You go back home."

"I can't. The soldiers know me. I stole their cart because ours was taken into the castle with John."

He gapes. "I see. Do they know that you actually rescued Robert? Could you not pretend you stole their cart in a panic to get home?"

"I think they'll have worked it out. The captain was already suspicious that I was taking an interest in the Scots. Anyway, I don't think Robert will be safe even at Cartmel. It will be an obvious place for the soldiers to look. We have to go on north. We have to go to Scotland."

Cedric's lips tighten. Before he can argue further, I take his hand and lead the way back down the rock passage. It is visible now in the light of his candle, and I can move more sure-footedly. Outside the big cave, the sky is still reassuringly dark. Inside, Robert and Jonathan lie sprawled asleep. Jonathan is moaning softly. Cedric kneels down and looks at them. After a moment he shakes his head. "Beatrice, if you try to travel north with these sick men, in a stolen military cart, with an English border raid under way, you will fail. We have to hide them for now. The soldiers have searched Barrowbeck Tower already. They found some of your father's stolen goods in the root cellar, and they're calling it a den of thieves and traitors, but when they saw the state your father was in, they left him alone. I doubt they'll go back. They want to go home too. They're on loan from Lord Ravenswyck, and their tour of duty is almost over. You should go home yourself. If necessary you could hide in the secret passage under the barmkin. I'll look after Robert and the other lad in the inner cave where we were just now. Then in a month or so we'll take them across to Cartmel."

"Cedric, you don't understand. I've got them this far and I can't take any chances. We have to press on immediately. The soldiers won't give up so easily. I assume that stealing a military cart is a hanging offence. I have to get away and I have to get them away too." I touch Robert's sleeping face. "We'll go to the Black Brothers,

253

perhaps stay overnight, then we must continue northwards. If the English raid on Scotland is heading out of Newcastle, we'll go up the west coast. I have no idea where Robert's home is, but presumably he will wake up enough by then to tell me. Cannot you give him something to bring him round, Cedric? I seem to have overdone the henbane and usquebaugh a little."

Cedric raises his eyebrows. "Henbane and usquebaugh?" He gives a short laugh. "You seem to belong to the battering-ram school of healing, Beatrice." He strokes his beard. "Aye, I'll give them mustard and milkthistle and charcoal to get it out of their systems, and sea-belt to liven them up. It's fortunate I keep supplies in the inner cave, for I certainly cannot go back to the cottage just now."

"Why are the soldiers at your cottage anyway, Cedric? Surely they have no business with you?"

"They went to Wraithwaite looking for you, Beatrice, and Widow Brissenden kindly suggested to them that my cottage was a place you might head for."

I feel a surge of fury, and a sense of regret that I shall not be here to make Widow Brissenden pay for this. "I am truly sorry, Cedric. I am truly sorry that you have become so involved."

He smiles. "I have been involved for some time, Beatrice."

I realise suddenly that I can see him better than before. There is a faint lightening of the sky outside.

"Oh God. Cedric, it's nearly dawn. When can you take us across?"

He looks towards the cave mouth. "It's too late now to get you across before the next high tide. I could take you in the morning, when the tide is out again, but it will be broad daylight and there'll be a risk of being seen. Can't you leave it until the following low tide, after dark?"

"We can't wait that long. We'll have to take our chances. I'll go to Barrowbeck and get food and water whilst the men rest some more." Even as I give food as my reason for returning to Barrowbeck, I know the truth is that I must see it one last time. I think of my mother, of Verity and Thomas, Aunt and Uncle Juniper, all the other people whom I may not see again. I think of John.

Cedric is speaking again. "...you'll be less conspicuous in the carretta than in that cart." He goes to the cave mouth where the horses are snorting in their sleep. "We'll leave these beauties somewhere for the soldiers to find. I'll stay with the lads in the inner cave and get them into some sort of state for travelling."

With difficulty we drag and push the two stumbling Scots along the rock passage. When we lay them down in the damp cave they instantly go back to sleep again. Cedric looks up at me. "Beatrice, reconsider. These men are not fit to travel." He stands the lanthorns and candle around them, then pulls out a wooden chest from behind the rock overhang. From it he produces two large, rabbitskin coddling bags of the sort Sanctity Wilson makes and sells. "Help me get them into these," he says. He seems very out of sorts with me suddenly. As we heave

255

the two trembling Scots into the musty bags, and lace up the sides, he adds, "Think of John, Beatrice. Think of your mother. How can you even be considering this?"

We stare at one another, then I blunder away into the rock passage and leave them together in the flickering dimness.

I drive the soldiers' cart as quietly as I can along the shore and up through the woods to Barrowbeck Tower. Dawn is struggling somewhere behind the clouds, but it is a dim, wet morning, and I am thankful for it. I look at these woods, which have occupied so much of my life. I want to seal them in my memory, so that they are with me when I am in a very different place. I have not slept for more than two days. Twice I fall asleep and almost topple off the cart. I drive to the place where the Old Corpse Road begins, and leave the cart by the beck, so that the horses can drink until they are found. Then I walk the rest of the way. At the edge of the woods I pause, and look towards the tower, my home. The watchman comes into view. It is Michael. Clearly fate does not intend to make this easy for me. I wait until his patrol takes him out of view, then dash across the clearing. I am reminded of when I made this same dash with armed men charging at me across the clearing, Robert amongst them.

The door is bolted on the inside. No one else can be up yet. I am dismayed. Dawn is up and the household still asleep. Truly, matters are deteriorating here on the farm. All our minds are so much on other things that normal routines have gone to ruin. Kate's suggestion that Verity, James and little Thomas should move here has never been taken up. I realise now that this is exactly what Barrowbeck Farm needs.

I hear bolts being withdrawn on the inside. My first reaction is to go and hide – what if some of the soldiers are still here? – but it is too late. The door swings open and Michael stands there.

He bows. "Good morrow, mistress." He draws back to let me enter. Cautiously I step past him.

"Good morrow, Michael. The parson and I have been delayed in Lancaster. I trust I find you well?"

His expression is unreadable. How much does he know? "Indeed. And you also, mistress?"

I incline my head. "I thank you. You may return to your watch now."

He bows even lower. It is most unnerving. Here at Barrowbeck we are not so gracious as to be constantly bowing to one another. Michael retreats up the spiral staircase and I step under the low arch into the kitchen.

The kitchen – how can something so ordinary as a kitchen provoke tears? I put it down to extreme tiredness. An unwashed cooking pot stands on the table, with dried flakes of turnip broth curled on its rim. A poker stands in a jug in the hearth where they have been mulling ale. The fire is sunk into ash, but heat comes from within it.

I want to go for one last time to every part of this place – to the dairy to see the churns in silent rows, waiting for my mother to arrive and start shouting at Tilly Turner; to the passage under the barmkin to make sure the wolf-pit is closed so that no one can come to harm; to my bedchamber, where so many of my dearest possessions are stored. I want to stand on the beacon turret and watch the woods for raiders. I tiptoe across the floor, nervously aware of Kate sleeping in her room behind the hearth. My cat Caesar comes butting at my ankles. I push him away, burst into tears, pick him up and cradle him against my chest. For a moment he purrs and pushes his face into my neck, then he becomes tired of so much wetness dripping into his fur, and struggles to get down.

I am being too slow. It is as if I had taken henbane myself. I light a candle and hurry down to the root cellar. I collect bread and cheese, wrap them in oilskin, and fill a leather bottle with water from the copper cistern. Then I hurry back up to the kitchen. It is still empty, but a door is banging somewhere in the tower. People will be waking. I must go.

In the barmkin I hitch my father's second-best horse, Calisto, to the carretta, and stow the oilskin package under the seat. There is no sign of Michael on the battlements. I lead Calisto out under the stone arch and close the gate behind me.

Chapter 27

The sky starts to clear from the east, and the sun shines through holes in the clouds creating a strange light, as I descend the cliff path back to the cave. I feel tense and watchful now, all my tiredness gone. Cedric is waiting. Between us we help the two Scots into the back of the carretta and hide them under piles of fishing nets. The bay is the colour of coral as we race across it, Cedric at the reins. We see no one on the way.

The old monastery is in worse ruins than I expected, destroyed by King Henry's men when they rooted out Papism from the land. Part of the church is still standing. Cedric tells me it is called the Town Choir, and that it survived because King Henry's soldiers regarded it as the villagers' parish church. The monks are not allowed to go there.

We drive on a short distance and come to a wattle and

259

daub longhouse next to a ruined wall. It looks very poor. The tattered reed thatch, and mottled clay-and-lime-daubed walls, are more decrepit than the worst dwelling of any homesteader in our valley. Two men in shabby black habits appear from round the side, carrying straight-sided iron buckets hanging from yokes across their shoulders. They wave. Another who was sitting on a seat cut from a tree trunk, reading a book, comes over to us. Somewhere round the back, a voice sings a chant of delicate descending notes. There is a pause, then the chant is repeated, with ornamentation. Robert sits up in the back of the carretta and asks in an unsteady voice, "Where are we? Who is singing *De Profundis*?"

"Cartmel, Robert. We're at Cartmel." I hold out my hand and he grips it. Cartmel, at last, after so long. "We're stopping for a short rest," I add, finding my own voice unsteady.

"And then?" He kneels up and takes hold of my hands.

"Scotland."

Cedric turns his head away.

"Good morrow, Cedric!" The monk who was reading the book has come to stand by the carretta.

"Father Wolf of the Order of Saint Augustine, Mistress Garth of Barrowbeck Tower, and two refugees who need your help," Cedric introduces us.

Father Wolf inclines his head, and helps me down. "God bless you, madam. I will send two of the brothers to assist your friends."

As he walks away into the longhouse, I look at Cedric. "They know you?" I ask.

"I come here to Mass." He jumps to the ground.

I close my eyes briefly, and laugh. "Oh Cedric."

I wonder why I never guessed it before, but then why should I? Papism is frowned upon. Papists are sometimes still burnt. "Have you always been a Papist, Cedric?" I ask him.

He looks up from where he is letting down the tailgate of the carretta and says, "Aye."

Robert and Jonathan are taken to the infirmary, whilst Cedric and I are led to the longhouse kitchen, where a young monk makes us a hot posset of roasted barley, cream and sweet white wine. "It is most restorative," he assures us, swirling the cream on top with a flourish, and floating a sage leaf on it.

"Beware the sin of pride, Brother Leofric," murmurs Father Wolf, as he escorts us through to a garden at the back. We sit on a worm-eaten bench and sip our steaming drinks. The singer is standing with his back to us, under the remains of a ruined rose arbour, reading music from a battered manuscript and experimenting with a complicated succession of notes. He turns and nods to us, then moves away up the garden. This beautiful place seems to be reclaimed from some long-lost building. Ruined walls are visible amongst the flowering shrubs. A metal cross, buckled as if it had been burnt, leans against a logpile. Early roses run riot along a wattle fence, filling

261

the air with scent. Next to where we sit are medlar trees, mulberry bushes and a crowded herb garden. A robin sings in a willow tree, untroubled by a young monk shaving strips of willow bark into a basket below.

Suddenly Cedric puts down his drink. "Beatrice, don't go. There are places for you to hide. The soldiers needn't find you. Hide in the caves on the shore, or in the hermit's cottage in the woods. The soldiers will eventually go away and forget you."

I did not mean to cry. This is not the moment. I pick up a small, leather-bound book which one of the monks has left lying on the bench. It seems to be poetry by a Scot, William Dunbar. I read where the page has fallen open.

> *Our plesance heir is all vane glory.*
> *This fals warld is bot transitory,*
> *The flesche is brukle, the Fiend is slee:*
> *Timor mortis conturbat me.*

I read the words silently, then aloud. Cedric shakes his head. We are both in tears. Father Wolf appears, takes the book from me, sits down. "There there now," he says severely. "We'll take care of your friends. We'll see them well. Look at this now! Whatever have we here?"

Cedric and I turn. Two apparitions are emerging from the longhouse – Robert and Jonathan in rough, unhooded black habits even shabbier than those of the monks. Robert's is threadbare and far too short for him. His bare feet and ankles stick out below the hem. Both men are washed and shaved and have had their hair trimmed.

Although they are still stooped and trembling, their eyes are brighter and there is colour in their cheeks.

"What do you think of our new novices?" demands Father Wolf. "They've had a good scrub. I think that this on its own will render them unrecognisable."

I have to laugh. I go over and kiss Robert. "My, but you make a wonderful-looking monk."

He smiles. It is like a miracle.

I realise suddenly that I have been hearing a new sound, far off in the distance, for several minutes, without knowing what it was. Now a young monk comes running round the side of the longhouse, his face red and sweating.

"Brother Wolf!" he shouts. We all turn to look at him. Father Wolf goes over and the young monk whispers in his ear. With a feeling of chill I realise what the sound is that I have been hearing. Hoofbeats.

"Oh for heaven's sake, not again." Father Wolf hesitates, rubbing his hands together, then comes quickly back to us. "There are soldiers coming. I assume it is you they are after? Go with Father Oswald at once. He will hide you in the crypt beneath the ruins of the priory. All of you. Go on now, quickly. Brother Leofric! Shift that cart from round the front. Drive it out of town. Anywhere. Quickly!"

The young monk Father Oswald rushes up to us, his robes swinging, and grabs my arm. He is not much older than I am, but he says, "This way, daughter. Come along.

We're used to this sort of thing. We'll get rid of those nasty soldiers for you." He leads us at a run up the garden, stumbling over neat rows of vegetable seedlings, and through a small hurdle gate at the top. The horsemen sound very close now. I can hear jangling harness metal and shouted orders. Beyond the hurdle gate is an area of scrubland, and beyond that the priory ruins. We are halfway across the scrubland when Captain Foreman steps out of the bushes.

Chapter 28

*I*t is degrading and horrible. I try to unsheath my knife, but my arms are grabbed from behind. A few of the soldiers have gone to the front of the longhouse, but the rest have crept round here to lie in wait for us. We all put up a fight, even Father Oswald, who proves remarkably handy with his fists. Robert finds new strength from somewhere, and manages to lay low several soldiers before a blow from a matchlock brings him to his knees, half stunned.

The soldiers tie our wrists behind us, and drag us back to the longhouse. There we find the monks lined up under armed guard.

"Shoot the lot of 'em, captain?" enquires one of the soldiers, a lout with an ale-paunch bulging under his doublet, and his codpiece half undone.

Captain Foreman shakes his head and laughs.

"Heavens no, Victor my man. Where would we come to look for renegades if we were to shoot them all? No no, just keep them quiet whilst we load the traitors and the Scots on to the cart. You won't be driving it this time, madame," he adds to me with a chuckle. "Though we might travel faster if you did."

I look at the armaments cart, come back to haunt me. "Your wit is overwhelming, captain," I mutter. "Cannot you untie our wrists? We will hardly escape, with your men so heavily armed."

"Now now, Mistress Becker, or should I say Mistress Garth, for you do seem to have deceived us on a number of matters? Dear me, the decadence of you West Moorlanders extends even to the clergy, it would appear. I shall be glad when my men and I are back in civilisation." He signals to his soldiers. "Load them up! Gently with the lady now!"

We are herded out to the front. Several villagers have gathered to watch. They point and stare. "Scots," I hear one woman telling her children. "They're Scots, my darlings, but don't worry; they're being taken away."

I see that Father Wolf, Father Oswald and some of the other monks are praying silently. The soldier Victor snorts in disgust and spits at them. Robert is staggering, scarcely able to stand. The side of his head is bleeding. Cedric wrenches himself away from the soldiers' grip. "At least let the brothers tend that man's wound before you take us away," he demands.

Captain Foreman looks as if he is going to agree, but just then Jonathan makes a run for it. Because he is small and slight, he has been temporarily overlooked. He gets as far as the trees on the far side of the track, sending screaming villagers scattering, before two soldiers haul him back. He kicks at them, weeping and shouting, "Kill me, English bastards! Kill me and be done with it!"

"That can be arranged," Captain Foreman tells him wearily. "Indeed, I would shoot you now if it were not that you must be seen to be brought back and dealt with according to the law. Unfortunately, the Lord Justice of Assize was most emphatic on this matter." He turns to the soldier, Victor. "Tie their feet, Victor. This lot are going to be more trouble than they're worth."

The ropes that bind my wrists are tight and already chafing, and my hands are going numb. "Please don't!" I beg, before I can stop myself. There is a frightening, stifling feeling about being tied, which threatens to overcome me.

Victor eyes me up and down, then picks me up and throws me into the back of the cart so that I land on my bound wrists. The pain is excruciating. Then he winds a rope several times round my ankles and ties it in a bow. "Pretty for a lady," he coos. "You want to look your best for this journey, for sure as hell and damnation, no one will see you in them there dungeons."

I am gasping with pain as Cedric, Robert and Jonathan are pushed in after me, also bound at the ankles. Robert is now only half conscious from his head wound.

"Please! Captain Foreman!" I call. "This man is going to die if you do not allow him to be tended."

The captain droops an elegant arm along the side of the cart. For once he is not looking arch or ironic. "Do you not think that dying now would be better for him, considering what lies ahead?" he asks me quietly. "These men have already been tried. There is no further reason to delay their execution when we return to Lancaster." He is very close. I see that his doublet is dusty and grimy, his eyes tired and dull. There is silence as we reassess one another. I am his prisoner, no longer 'a lady' requiring rehearsed notions of gallantry. He is an ordinary man in a stale uniform, exhausted and far from home. I feel something that is almost warmth towards him, until he adds, "Your own fate will take a little longer to implement, but I fear it will also be as inevitable. You are certain to be found guilty of treason and burnt at the stake, Mistress Garth. It would be better for you all if you were to drown in the quicksands. Unfortunately I cannot allow that either, since we shall be going the long way round the bay."

I close my eyes for a long moment. When I open them, he is still there. "How did you find us, captain?" I ask, my voice shamingly tremulous. "How did you know where to search for us?"

He looks now as if he wants to be gone, as if this conversation were undermining him. "Your henchman, Michael I think his name was." He steps back and signals to the cart driver. Over his shoulder he adds, "A patriotic

268

fellow, Michael. He followed you back to the cave, then came to the healer's cottage to tell us. We crossed the bay in your tracks."

The moment of shared humanity is gone. I hate him. I hate him so much. I hate Michael and Widow Brissenden too. I'd have been better off in Scotland. I should have gone with Robert two seasons ago. I should have kept going now, instead of coming here. I feel sick from the pain of my bruises and chafed wrists, sick with fear and fury. The soldiers mount up and form a guard round the cart. I try to sit up so that my arms do not hurt so much and my elbows are not pushed so painfully against the wood. Cedric and Jonathan shift too, trying to ease their positions. There is despair on their faces. Victor checks the fastenings of the tailflap, then mounts up to ride directly behind us. Captain Foreman climbs on to the passenger seat of the cart. The horses ahead move off, and with a jolt, the cart moves too. Robert lies against me and I wish I could put my arm round him. Instead, with every movement, our elbows and shoulders jab each other or bang against the side of the cart.

We go in the opposite direction from the way we came. Once beyond the village the country becomes wild. I want to ask Jonathan about being imprisoned in the castle, about the dungeons, so that I can be prepared, but when I see the lost look on his face, I remain silent.

I wonder if John will still be imprisoned in the castle when Cedric and I arrive there. I wonder whether I will be allowed to contact my family. I wonder what it is like to burn.

The soldiers ahead are slowing down, though we have scarcely gone any distance.

"Halt!" The horses skitter and the cart judders to a stop. A horseman has ridden out of the woods at the crossroads. For a moment of confused disbelief I think it is my father, recovered, and wearing his highway robber's disguise. Then I see that it is merely some stray lordship in fancy furs, mounted on a stocky white horse, probably wishing to gloat at the sight of prisoners. Yet, there is something familiar about the voice which calls out, "Captain Foreman, well done! I congratulate you. I do declare I thought they might be over the border by now."

"Sir Edward!" Captain Foreman jumps down and salutes.

"Oh-oh, you're in right trouble now," chortles Victor. "'Tis the Lord Justice of Assize. As nasty a piece of work as you'll find this side of the border. He tortures prisoners with his own bare hands, they do say."

Edward. It is Anne Fairweather's cousin, Edward. I recognise the voice now, and the chubby profile, visible briefly between milling soldiers on their horses. Edward walks his horse over and stares down at us. "You've done well, captain. I have serious matters on which I intend to interrogate this woman. I've long since suspected her of the most grievous treachery towards queen and country." He addresses me directly. "Did you imagine, madam, that

270

I was deceived for a moment by your foolish pretence of innocence, at my cousin's house? I know your family very well for what they are."

"Edward... Sir Edward..." I search desperately for the right words, for some semblance of the polite, safe formality which we shared in Anne Fairweather's house, for something of her wit and boldness which so clearly captivate him. I can think of nothing. I am dirty, bruised and exhausted. My hair is over my eyes and my clothing torn. I have no resources, no words, to save myself or any of us. Edward is looking at me with a sneer. At last I manage to stammer, "Sir Edward, do you have news of Parson Becker, I beg you? He was taken into Lancaster Castle after an incident with a matchlock."

Edward looks at me incredulously. "I have no interest in parsons with matchlocks, madam." He turns away to speak to Captain Foreman. "I have no fancy to travel all the way to Lancaster just now, captain. Yet I fear there is a plot afoot here, of which these conspirators are only a small part. Kindly follow me to Castle Clough, where we will deal with them."

Captain Foreman hesitates. "Sir, we are due in Lancaster. We must return the Scots for hanging. Your castle is north, and it will delay us if we must wait while you... interrogate the prisoners."

Edward glares. "If you hang these men I cannot interrogate them, can I? Where is your sense, man? There is a conspiracy to be investigated here. Scots are being smuggled to and fro across the border. The queen's security is at stake. Of course you must wait. You will be well housed and fed at Castle Clough. Now, no more nonsense. Follow me!" He wheels his horse. Captain Foreman stands in his path.

"Sir Edward, my men are exhausted. We are on loan from Lord Ravenswyck and due home a week since. Lord Allysson's soldiers have already arrived in Lancaster to relieve us. Sir, kindly understand, this is our last mission, and it is over."

Sir Edward looks down at him in exasperation. "Oh, very well then. You may escort the prisoners to Castle Clough and leave them there. I will send for Lord Allysson's men to take them off my hands when I have questioned them."

Captain Foreman looks relieved. He salutes. "Thank you, sir." He climbs back on to the cart. "Follow on!" he shouts to his men. They re-form into an escort and we move again, following Edward on to a track which leads into dense woodland. I look at Edward, riding ahead straight-backed, and feel a rush of the most terrible fear. He hates us, because of Hugh's involvement with Anne, and now he is in a position to take revenge.

I whisper to Cedric, "Is it true he tortures prisoners?"

Cedric looks grim, and shrugs, but Victor has overheard me. He laughs. "Should've thought of that sooner, shouldn't we, Mistress High-and-Mighty. Good riddance to bad rubbish, I say. It'll save us a few yards of rope."

Jonathan starts sobbing. The horses ahead are slowing as we enter a clearing. Victor dismounts and levels his matchlock at us when the cart stops, as if we might suddenly burst our ropes and take off into the woods. Ahead of us, on a rise, stands a pele tower much like Barrowbeck, though a little larger.

"Welcome to Castle Clough," says Edward, riding once round the cart and looking at us with satisfaction. "Take them into the compound, captain."

I can hear the watchman on the battlements shouting for the gates to be opened. "It seems to me you overstate the matter, calling this a castle, Sir Edward," I mutter. A look of viciousness crosses his face, and I decide that I had better be silent. The cart enters a gatehouse, then veers off into an open compound on the left, and stops. Victor lets down the tailgate and hauls us to our feet, one by one. Robert falls to the ground at once, and the rest of us can scarcely stand, with our feet so tightly tied.

Victor struts round us. "I reckon I'd better say goodbye then," he grins. "You tend not to see folks again once they vanish into Sir Edward's dungeons."

"Your codpiece is undone," I inform him. He makes as if to strike me, but thinks better of it as Captain Foreman approaches.

"Goodbye, madame," says the captain. "You kept bad company, and now I fear you will pay the price. As for you..." He looks at Robert and Jonathan, then shakes his head and turns away.

"Captain," I call after him. "Will you please inform my family, at Barrowbeck Tower, what has happened to me?"

He hesitates. "I regret it, madame, but I cannot, in case they come after you." He turns away quickly before I can implore him further. "Mount up!" he shouts to his men.

They are gone in a moment, the cart clanking behind them. I wonder whether Father Leofric managed to escape with our carretta, and where it is now.

Sir Edward's henchmen come clattering down the stairs into the compound. He hands his horse to one of them and says to the others, "Untie these people and put them in the gatehouse tower. Send Flo up to deal with them." He indicates Robert. "That one needs to be put out of his misery." I give a cry, but Edward is already walking away.

Flo. The name is terrifying. A torturer called Flo.

I cannot feel my feet when the henchmen untie them. It is like walking on hollow blocks of wood. It takes us a long time to totter up the spiral staircase to a tower room over the gatehouse. Robert has to be carried all the way. The henchmen lock us in and leave us.

The tower room is small, with oak settles round the walls and a carved, circular table in the middle. As soon as we are alone, Cedric and I go to look at Robert's head wound. He groans, and tries to sit up. "Bea, I am so sorry for all this," he mumbles. "Are you all right?" He tries to open his eyes.

"Yes, I'm all right." I take hold of his hand.

"Why cannae I open my eyes?" He grips my fingers.

"They're stuck with blood. We'll wash it off. You'll be all right."

"It's just superficial. His skull isn't shattered," Cedric murmurs. "I think the effects of the henbane are still in his system. He'll come out of it."

"Good." The voice comes from the doorway. We turn. It is as if the world has gone away behind glass, behind a wall of sleep and dreams. A small plump woman stands in the doorway, holding a bowl and cloths, and behind her is Anne Fairweather. "Let's sort him out, dear," says the plump woman, who is wearing a nurse's apron. "Dearie me, you all look simply dreadful."

Anne comes into the room. Her veil is folded back over her cap.

I sit down. "Anne, surely you aren't involved in all this?" I notice Jonathan eyeing the door, which she has left unlocked behind her.

"I'm Flo," says the plump woman to Cedric, "and you're the Cockleshell Man. I've heard of you." She hands the basin and cloths to Cedric. "Here you are, Cockleshell Man. I don't want to interfere with your patient. I'll see to these other poor souls."

Anne puts her hand on my arm. "Flo, I'm borrowing this one for a minute. We have matters to discuss." I stare at her, so familiar, someone from home. Her chin trembles, and I wonder for a moment if she does after all have to hand us over to the torturers. "Beatrice, my dear," she whispers, "these are terrible times, and I am sorry for

275

you. Would you come with me? There is someone who wants to talk to you." She leads me a little way back down the spiral staircase, and into a chamber with tapestries on the walls and a long settle with tasselled cushions, by the hearth. A man is standing with his back to me, at one of the slit windows. Anne closes the door behind us. "He rode straight to my house, when they let him out," she says. The man turns. It is John.

Chapter 29

He is white and shocked-looking. He is still dressed in the clothes he wore to travel to Lancaster with me. It seems a long time ago now. He looks exhausted, as exhausted as I am. When was it we both last slept?

I hear Anne go out of the room. John rubs his hand over his face. "How are you?" he asks.

"Well enough. I thank you. How are you?"

He shakes his head and looks away, as if this conversation were ridiculous. I look at my hands, because something is happening to them; they are shaking. I hold them out to him. They are filthy, and my wrists are bruised raw. Now I seem to be shaking from head to foot. "I am glad you are safe," I tell him. "I am sorry for what happened."

He strides across the room, then hesitates. I hold out my arms to him. We are dirty, smelly, weary beyond belief and a mess, but we are the same mess. We wrap our arms round each other. "Oh..." I shake my head, press my face into his neck, bang my fists on his back. "I was so worried about you. I was so worried."

He says into my hair, "You are insane. Why didn't you *tell* me? Why didn't you warn me what you were going to do?"

"I don't exactly know, John. I truly don't. Perhaps because... you see... you are respectable, John. You are not like me and my family, natural lawbreakers. You have a reputation to preserve. I don't think I can marry you, for fear I may always have to do the sort of thing that would bring you disgrace."

He kisses the top of my head. "That is nonsense. I think what you mean is that I would hinder you, that you might not have the freedom to which you are so accustomed, if you were to marry me."

"No. No, that is not the case. It has simply become very clear to me that you will never become bishop if you marry me, and I cannot have that on my conscience. I cannot have another person's future... another person's advancement... on my conscience."

John leads me to the settle and sits me down amongst the tasselled cushions. "I suddenly fear that you might be serious about this, Beatie. Surely you cannot be. Not... not after all we've become to one another."

Sitting down is the undoing of me. I feel sleep rolling over me in great, dizzying waves. "Oh sweetheart, surely it's all beside the point anyway, because I have to run away to Scotland now." I lean my face against his shoulder. His clothing, dusty and grimy from the events of the past few days, suddenly seems to have the whiff of the dungeon about it. I jerk back. "Did they put you in the dungeons?" I ask in horror.

"No! Heavens no, thank God. Though I did go in there. They let me go in there, to speak to the poor souls still imprisoned."

I look up at him. I have a sense of throwing away all that is good in the world. "John, I am so sorry for the ways in which I have wronged you, and I am so glad that I've seen you before I go north. Tell me what happened to you in Lancaster."

He pulls me back against him. "Oh, I had a disagreement with the soldiers we'd argued with earlier. I think they must have followed us up the hill. They were looking for trouble, and they found the matchlock you'd hidden in the bundle of clothing in the back of the cart. When they tried to take it, it went off, and they arrested me."

"I'm sorry. I'm sorry I brought the matchlock, and I'm sorry I didn't see what was happening to you."

"You were busy with Robert. No..." He stops me from speaking. "Of course you were. Anyone with any humanity would have been. *I* would have been if the soldiers hadn't turned up."

279

"I tried to find you afterwards. By the time I found out that they had taken you into the castle, everything was happening too fast to do anything about it."

"Sweet Beatrice..." John gives something between a laugh and a sob. "For heaven's sake, you do not always have to be rescuing people. At least, you do not have to be rescuing me."

I touch the stubble on his chin. "You look like a bandit," I tell him. "I would lock you up, certainly. What happened in the end? How did you get out?"

"They didn't believe who I was, but the Vicar of Lancaster intervened and confirmed my identity. When I got out it was all over Lancaster that two Scots had been rescued."

I interrupt him. "Do you know if the players were all right – Master Guinevere and the others?"

"I didn't hear that they weren't. I don't think anyone knew they'd been involved. I just knew that the military were after you. I drove the cart straight to Anne Fairweather's after they let me out, and told her what had happened, and then she and I rode straight over here. I knew that her Cousin Edward was the only person with the power to take you away from the soldiers and into his own custody. Whether he would do it was another matter, but Anne persuaded him."

I think of Edward as I saw him in Anne Fairweather's house, proud, aloof and pompous, and again as I saw him when he waylaid the soldiers, a man committing treason, with considerable flair and imagination moreover, in the name of love. "He would do anything for her," I reply.

John looks down at me and we examine one another's faces, every grain of grime, every salty eyelash distinct and precious. After a moment he continues, "Anne and I rode the long way round the bay, because of the tide. I was afraid we might not get to Edward in time. We saw your mother in Barrowbeck village and told her what we were doing. She was in the middle of having your henchman Michael, and Widow Brissenden, put into the stocks and pelted with rubbish. I think she would have had them stoned if Germaine had not restrained her."

I have to compose myself for a moment before I can speak. I am too old to be crying for my mother, and anyway, there is no point. Eventually I ask, "So what now, John? Does this mean we are not to be interrogated by Edward?"

"I think he will let you all go. Robert and the other young Scot too. He will say he handed you over to local justice, or something like that, and they will think the worst, and his reputation for brutality will increase. I suspect he may have done this sort of thing before – extended undue mercy – because prisoners have disappeared from Castle Clough in the past, and no one has liked to ask too many questions. The family have a lot of power. They also have a Scottish connection, which might have some bearing."

I take John's face in my hands. "You do know I have to

281

go, don't you. I'm a wanted criminal. I have no choice."

"That's ridiculous. Of course you don't have to go. You can simply hide until it all dies down."

"I'd be a danger to everyone, John. The soldiers think I'm a Scottish spy. I doubt they'll bother Cedric, because he was barely involved, but what I did – well the law doesn't forget that sort of thing, no matter how often the troops might change."

"Is it Robert, Beatrice? Is it simply that you want to go to Scotland with him? If it is, just say so."

I go over to one of the slit windows. A chilly breeze is blowing in. A tiny whirlwind of pink petals spirals about on the deep windowsill. I glance back at John. "Don't make it harder than it is. You saw what Robert was like. You saw the state he was in. I have to make absolutely sure he really does get away this time, so that there's an end to all this. What I do afterwards... well..." I shrug.

Silence falls between us. Outside, sounds of castle life continue, men shouting, pots clanking, wood being chopped in the compound. From below comes a familiar whinny, and the rumble of wheels. I lean along the windowsill in amazement, and peer out. I am just in time to see the carretta disappearing below the angle of the wall. I turn. "It's..." John has come up behind me. I hesitate. "It's the carretta," I inform him softly.

"Oh good. I'm delighted. And I apologise."

"Indeed." I watch his face until it is out of focus and touching mine. His chin is rough. I say against his lips,

"You are not fit to kiss. I am already suffering considerable injury from the day's doings, and do not wish any more. I am going downstairs now, to see what Father Leofric has been doing with my carretta."

John kisses me anyway. I put my arms round his neck, hold his head, kiss him back, letting myself be imprisoned against the windowsill. I tell him gently, "I will come back. One day I shall just be there in the parsonage kitchen, when you walk in."

He lets me go.

When I arrive downstairs in the compound, I find Edward talking to Father Leofric, and Calisto being led away to the stables. The carretta stands by the wall.

"I've been driving around for hours," the monk is explaining plaintively. "Oh daughter, thank goodness you're here. If someone could just give me a lift back to Cartmel..."

It is such a relief to see him safe and well that I quite forget myself and hug him. "I'm glad you're all right, Father Leofric. Yes, I'm sure there are people going back your way, Cedric certainly." The monk beams with quite a saintly glow. I look at Edward, who is regarding me coldly. "Thank you," I murmur. "Thank you so much."

He turns away without answering me.

Back upstairs, John is gone from the chamber where we talked. I find him and Cedric sitting with Robert, who is lying in bed in Castle Clough's infirmarium. The stark, whitewashed room contains three linen-draped beds, shelves of medical instruments and labelled stone bottles, and a large, closed stove instead of an open fire. The other two beds are empty. The three men look round as I enter, and John says, "I'll come with you to the border, Beatrice. Edward has suggested sending a henchman too, but I think it's better if his involvement is kept as secret as possible. The four of us travelling north together will be quite conspicuous enough."

The door opens again, and Anne comes in. She is, as always, beautifully dressed, in startling contrast to the rest of us. She seats herself on a bench and fans herself with a roll of bandage. "Beatrice, what are you going to do after Robert and Jonathan are safely delivered to the border? Have you a plan?"

"Well..." I hesitate. "No, not a definite plan. Obviously I can't go back to Barrowbeck or Wraithwaite for a while. It's possible that even after Captain Foreman and the rest of Lord Ravenswyck's men have gone, Lord Allysson's soldiers who are replacing them might come after me. I can stay in country inns and move about the north for a year or more. I have enough of my dowry left." I cast an apologetic glance at John.

Anne puts down the bandage and sits forward, her elbows on her knees, her long, manicured hands clasped together. "Beatrice, I have a suggestion. Edward and I have a Scottish kinswoman, Elspeth MacCrundle. It was her tenant-woman who was imprisoned in Lancaster Castle, and whom Edward reprieved. From her side of the border she does the same sort of thing that Edward does here. She has saved the lives of several Englishmen, and returned them south. She would put you up."

Flo arrives, bearing cups of hot broth on a tray. She sets it down and leaves. Anne hands them round. "You see, we do not like all these killings." She cradles the steaming cup between her hands. "Not the border killings, nor the judicial killings when they hang or burn people. We have managed to help a number of souls, but it is never enough. We can't... particularly Edward can't... do it for everybody, more's the pity. It would quickly become too obvious, and that would be an end of it. There was nothing we could do for your Scots, without risking wrecking the whole system. We mostly need to catch them before they get into the castle, to have any realistic hope of saving them."

There is a cough from the doorway. Edward is standing there. He picks up the remaining cup of broth. "What my cousin is saying, Mistress Garth, is that we always need more help, and you seem remarkably good at this sort of thing. Cousin MacCrundle would doubtless be glad of your assistance, as well as offering you protection." He drums his fingers on the cup.

"You mean... stay in Scotland?"

"Until it's safe to return home." Edward goes over and peers at Robert's head wound. "You might want to lend a hand as well, Lacklie."

Robert raises his eyebrows. "Aye. I might."

Cedric looks round from his appraisal of the rows of medical instruments. "If you need anyone guiding over the sands... or medical attention... you can always call on me."

Edward nods. I'm not sure he knows how to smile. "I'd assumed as much."

John stands up. "We have a crypt under the church at Wraithwaite. If anyone should need hiding, you can put them in there for a while. The villagers think it's haunted, so they don't go there." He hesitates. "Does it have a name, your organisation?"

Anne and Edward glance at each other. Edward pushes the door shut with his heel. "I wouldn't call it an organisation," he replies, "but the watchword is Salamander, should you ever need to identify yourself to anyone else involved."

"Salamander..." John repeats softly, "... the mythical beast that lives in fire."

"And in doing so, puts it out." Edward strides towards the door. "Time to unstopper some of Flo's ypocras if you ask me. Talking of fire."

Chapter 30

I sleep as if dead, and not just because of the ypocras. John sleeps in the adjoining bedchamber. We are high up in the tower. Towards morning I dream of wolves howling, and wake to hear the wind screaming round the battlements. I light a candle and get up, and find that John is already gone from his bed next door. When I return to my own bedchamber, Robert is there, sitting on my bed in the candlelight.

He stands up. "Bea, I hope ye dinnae mind..."

I stare at him in wonderment. He has not changed back into his monk's robe, but into a rather dashing leather jerkin over a rough wool shirt, with leather breeches and high boots. "Sir Edward's," he says, with a rueful grimace. "He said he'd grown out of them." I realise that he and Edward are the same height, though their difference in girth is very apparent.

"How are you?" I sit down on the bed and he sits down next to me.

"Better. Wonderful. I don't know what I can do to thank you, ever. I hope you will come to let my parents thank you properly."

I gaze at this young man, half destroyed by imprisonment. His face is bruised and bandaged. His eyes are sunken. He is all bones. It seems a miracle that his teeth have survived. They look huge in his skeleton-face. Perhaps in the dungeon, food was so scarce that lack of use preserved them. Yet despite all this, his eyes are watchful and his expression alert.

He touches my hand. He never used to be so diffident to touch me. "I have to tell you something," he says. "I have to be sure you know what you have done, and who I am. You wouldnae let them kill me, but you might wish you had. The truth is, I organised the raids, Bea. I let you think I was just going along with what was expected of me, but the truth is, I was one of the instigators. I loved it. I hated the English." He goes to stand with his back to the dark window. It is cleverly designed so that the wind mostly passes it by, but some of the strongest gusts ruffle Robert's hair now, and in this dim light he is once again the Robert I knew, tawny and wild, a part of the forest. "I know it is my fault that you are a fugitive," he says, "and I know you love the priest more, and will go back in a year's time; but if you should ever change your mind, and want to come home with me, I would spend my life trying to make it up to you."

288

I fold my arms across my chest, suddenly full of vivid physical remembrance of days and nights spent with Robert in the hermit's cottage in the woods, when I nursed him through his injuries. I try to take in this distressing new information about his role in the border incursions, and find that I am scarcely surprised.

"Do you still hate the English?" I ask him. "I suppose you do, after all that we have done to you."

"It's no worse than what we do to our enemies, Bea. I'm no longer sure it has to be like this, though. We're all the same, are we not, inside? I'm going to try to stop the raids. We are only the other side of the mountain from the MacCrundles." He pauses. "I had no idea what they were up to."

"You will keep it secret from your family?"

"Of course." He holds out his hands. "To have you in Scotland for a year... that's wonderful. I'll come and see you. I willnae always be such a wreck."

I smile. "Dear Robert. I have known you a worse wreck than this." I hold his hands in mine. They feel thin and hard, like twigs, kindling for the fire. "I hope you always feel as peaceable as this, my dear. I have to tell you, our men have been raiding your side of the border, and you may feel differently when you see what they have done. They will be on their way home now, travelling towards Newcastle, so we should not encounter them on our journey north."

Robert is silent for a moment. He releases my hands. "I have a cousin, Bea. His name is Duncan. We have always been competitive towards one another. With me gone, he will have taken over the planning of raids. He has a vengeful nature. It may be difficult to stop him if, as you say, the English have raided us again. Someone has to stop first, and as far as Duncan is concerned, it is unlikely to be us. I will do my best, but it may take time to shift people's views." He reaches into his shirt and pulls out a small, leather-bound book. "I wish you to have this. Father Wolf gave it to me."

I turn back the cover. It is the copy of William Dunbar's poetry which I saw in the monks' garden. It is warm from Robert's skin. I hold it against my cheek. Outside, the first birds are singing. It is time to go.

Edward is lending Robert, Jonathan and me three good, strong horses on which to travel north. I have decided to send the carretta and Calisto back with Cedric. I dress quickly in clean clothing donated by Flo, and wave Cedric off in the first light of dawn.

Although Robert and Jonathan are still weak, we have agreed that it is better to go now, before the Scots' presence has a chance to become known outside the castle. We may not be able to travel fast, but with adequate supplies for the journey, we need not risk stopping for food or shelter at farms or villages on the way, and we should reach the Scottish border in two days' ride. If our men can storm the border, I see no reason why we cannot creep up on it gently, without any great fuss.

Anne and Edward see us off. Anne smiles and waves, and Edward glares and waves. So we go quietly from Castle Clough in the early morning, when only one discreet watchman is on duty, and comings and goings are not greatly remarked upon.

My horse, Mirabella, is frisky and young. She and I get used to one another very quickly. As we emerge from the forest she calms down and settles to a steady trot, her ear against the wind. Later in the day the wind drops, and we travel through misty moorland and hazy slate, until the country changes, and new land lies ahead.

Always yours, in this world and the next. Robert has inscribed the flyleaf of the Dunbar book. I read it by firelight on our overnight stop. The men sleep wrapped in blankets amongst the roots of a pine tree, across the fire from me. I watch them, and then drift into sleep myself, my head on my saddlebags, the scent of pine needles in my nose. We keep the fire burning in case any wolves remain this far south, left over from winter. In a very dark hour, when the moon and stars have vanished behind clouds, Robert comes like a ghost through the trees, carrying sticks he has gathered for the fire. "How does it feel to be going home, after so long?" I ask him.

"Frightening. I'm afraid of what might have changed, and of what might have happened to my parents. They

291

will have thought me dead, this past year. I also fear what you English may have done to our homes and land."

"You might hate us again."

He feeds the sticks one by one to the flames, and is silent.

We cross mountain passes, bogland and rivers grey as wolves. We ride bridleways alongside sheer granite drops, in thick mist. We travel north by the sun, and when twilight deepens in the forest, by moss growing on the north sides of the trees. On a bright, open heath, where a few windblown shrubs lean amongst gorse and heather, Robert reins in his horse. "Scotland," he says.

We dismount. Jonathan looks around him, cool and aloof suddenly. "There used to be a stone here, marking the border," he tells me, "until the English took it. There's not much the English wouldnae take."

"Do you also hate us?" I ask him.

Yesterday he would have hesitated. Now he says outright, "Not you, mistress, but aye, the rest."

I say goodbye to John, there at the border. Robert and Jonathan take the horses to the beck to drink, and John and I hold each other for a long time. When the Scots return, John clasps their hands and bids them fare well. I remount. I want this to be over now. I hook my right knee over the leather support of my saddle, and arrange my skirts. John says, "Let me see you ride on to Scottish soil."

Jonathan pauses in the middle of getting on to his horse. "To us it is all Scottish soil," he says seriously. "To us it is all one land, and the monarch of it all is a Scot."

Robert tilts his head, as if to suggest that this is not the moment for a lecture. He mounts up, and he and John nod to one another. "Thank you," says Robert. "We may meet again, since we all live in fire, one way or another."

I wish I still had my Lenten veil, as the three of us cross the Scottish border, for I can no longer keep back the tears. When I look behind, John has set off southwards already. I watch him go, a lone figure heading towards the trees. He does not look back.

Robert, Jonathan and I ride on through hilly country until noon, when we come to a small pele tower in a shallow valley sheltered by pine forest. "This is where the MacCrundles live," Robert tells me.

The watchman on the battlements has already seen us. He turns to shout down to those below. We halt on a rocky outcrop. "I'll go on alone from here, Robert. You get on home to your family. They've waited long enough for you."

He brings his horse alongside mine. "Of course, lovely Beatrice, I could always throw you across my saddle and make off with you."

"Heavens, Robert, you certainly are recovered." I lean over and embrace him. "Fare well, raider."

"Next time you see me I shall be differently clad, sweetheart. I shall be different in many ways. Go on now. We'll wait here and see you in."

I look at Jonathan's disapproving face. "Remember me

to your mother, Jonathan. I hope she is safe and well. I don't suppose we shall meet again, so fare well. God bless you."

I pat Mirabella's neck, and we set off down the valley.

Chapter 31

My first day and night at the MacCrundles are mostly spent in sleeping. I little know, then, that it is the last sleep I shall have for some time.

Elspeth MacCrundle is a woman of about my mother's age. I take to her, yet the thought of spending a year here fills me with homesickness and dismay. Elspeth lives with her crippled brother, Frobisher, who seems very clever and spends his days working out mathematical theories. They are both dressed in woven woollen cloth, green, brown and heather-coloured like the earth, fastened with pins and metal brooches. They look neater than the Scots who raid us, but similar enough for it to be disconcerting. When I have told them my story, a room is prepared for me, and after a meal of oatcakes and herb salad, I sleep through the afternoon.

In the evening we talk again, sitting by the living hall fire. I ask them what they do when the English raid them.

"Kill them, of course," says Frobisher, as if I were mad to ask.

Elspeth smiles. "What else could we do, dearie? My brother does not agree with what Edward, Anne and I do, but just because we help the unfortunate does not mean to say we are traitors. If we are attacked, we fight."

When I go to bed that night, I remember that today has been my birthday. I am seventeen.

I wake before dawn the following morning, and do not know at first what has woken me, though I am filled with nameless terror. Then I hear it again, the shout which burst into my dreams.

"All men to arms! All men to arms! It's the bloody English!"

From within the tower comes the sound of a gong being struck repeatedly. It reverberates in the stones of the walls. I leap out of bed and drag my clothes on. I feel sick to my guts. My first instinct is to do what I would have done at home, rush up to the battlements. This tower, though a quarter the size, is so much like our own that I have no difficulty in finding my way round it. On the spiral staircase I meet Elspeth. She is clutching an armful of arrows. She looks at me severely. "You need not fight, Beatrice, but I shall not expect you to hinder us."

I follow her up to the battlements. Near the beacon turret, two henchmen are settling Frobisher into a wooden seat on an improvised rotating base. "He's the best bowman in Scotland," Elspeth tells me, dumping the arrows at his feet. She turns to one of the watchmen. "Where are they?"

"It's the beacon to the north, mistress. See? There's smoke above the trees."

I turn cold. The *north*? If the English are coming from the north, moving down the west side of Scotland, it can only mean one thing. It is our local men returning. "Elspeth, oh God. I must go out and stop them. They were supposed to be going home by way of Newcastle. I don't know why they're coming this way."

Elspeth and Frobisher look at me. "I daresay they've done as much damage as they can in the east; now it's our turn," says Frobisher. "But do by all means go out and stop them. We should be delighted."

Elspeth puts her hand on my arm. "Will you know them? Will you be safe?"

With a shiver I remember the two moss-troopers who attacked me, all those months ago. There will be no one here to save me. "I don't know." I shake my head. "I truly don't know."

"You will have to explain to them why you are here. That in itself might put you in danger. We had better send a man out with you."

"No, I'll do better on my own. If I do know them, I can probably stop them. If I do not know them, I will come back."

Elspeth nods doubtfully. "Aye well, I'm not so sure, but if it'll save bloodshed, then God go with you."

I go out quietly, watched from the doorway by a henchman. It is just a short walk to where the trees start. The woods immediately become dense and dark. I creep silently from tree to tree, through patches of sucking mud underfoot, round fallen, rotted branches, always watching for movement ahead. The warning beacon looked to be about a mile away, but that might not be any indication of where the raiders are, since it could have been passing on a warning from a beacon further north. I might have a long way to go yet. I dare not move more quickly, for fear of being seen or heard. I know our men can move as silently and invisibly as I can. I wonder again why they are coming home this way. Though this route is certainly quicker for our men, it is more usual for all the troops to demobilise together at Newcastle.

Suddenly I hear sounds ahead, clumsy sounds, voices and coughing. I move out of sight behind a tree, and watch them come.

Gaunt-faced men are moving between the trees, some walking slowly, some riding drooped over their horses, some staggering. They stop in the clearing ahead of me. Green light filters down to the forest floor and illuminates them. They are covered in mud and blood, some bandaged, some half out of ripped and blood-stiffened clothes. There is one young man strapped to a hurdle behind a tall bay horse. Gerald is beside him, bent

298

forward over his own horse's neck, his face ghastly white. I lean forward, disbelieving. I step out from amongst the trees. In a universal reflex, the men reach for their weapons. I know them all, men from Mere Point, Barrowbeck and Wraithwaite. Gerald stares at me blindly. Others move incredulously forward, calling out to me.

I go to the young man on the hurdle. There are no words for this moment. It is Hugh. Hugh, my friend, my cousin, and he is dead.

Gerald dismounts. He says, "Beatie? How can you be here?" and then, as if in a dream, "You have the look of Hugh about you."

I know I do. I always have. How dare I, with the look of Hugh about me, be alive when he is dead? He looks waxy, not visibly injured. I kneel next to him. I talk to him. I think I may go mad, seeing him so. Beside me one of the other men faints, slumping softly to the pine needles amongst the roots of a tree. The front of his jerkin is solid with dried blood from a neck wound.

I say to Gerald, my beautiful, warlike cousin, "This is waste. Just waste." I smack my hand to my forehead. "No no. *No!*"

"I don't know how I shall get them home." He is like a man in a trance.

I get slowly to my feet. "Come with me." I take his hand. "There is someone who will help you."

More than a fortnight has passed since my flight from Lancaster by the time I once more take the long track round the bay, riding escort to my dead cousin. Whether the soldiers will be waiting for me or not seems irrelevant.

Our eventual journey back from the MacCrundles has taken more than two days. We stayed overnight in a tiny, turf-roofed inn at the foot of a pass, sleeping all together on the straw-strewn upper floor reached by a wooden ladder. All the men are now fit to ride, some of them travelling two to a horse. Hugh is wrapped inside a thick blanket, strapped now to something the MacCrundles called a whirlicote, a sort of horse-drawn litter on wheels.

The track down from the hills brings us at last to Wraithwaite. The drummer was killed in battle, but as the villagers gather in groups, gasping and weeping, another of the church minstrels joins us. Alan Smith, the blacksmith, walks ahead of us, beating out the dead beat on his drum. More people come out when they hear the slow, single beats. They follow the procession, helping the wounded to their houses and supporting those who still have further to go. John comes out too, looking distraught. He quickly saddles Universe, and joins us on our way to Aunt and Uncle Juniper's. As we ride side by side to the Old Corpse Road, I tell him what happened.

"Thank God you're safe," he says. "You should go to Barrowbeck and fetch your mother and Verity. I'll go with Gerald to Mere Point."

It takes us all a long time to descend the steps in the rockface of the Old Corpse Road. Some of the Wraithwaite villagers are still helping the more severely wounded along. At the bottom, where the paths divide, I veer off and gallop through the woods, my old familiar woods where I know every path, to Barrowbeck Tower.

William is on watch. He waves, and comes down to let me in. I find my mother and Kate in the wash-house beyond the kitchen, boiling clothes in the two huge cauldrons over the firepit. The room is full of steam. The two women look like ghosts as they move to and fro in it, heaving out dripping linen underwear with tongs, and depositing it with slaps and shoves into wooden buckets, and from there into the stone rinsing tubs. The walls are running with water.

My mother looks at me through the steam, and bursts into tears. "Oh Beatie!" She runs over and folds me in her arms. "Oh Beatie. Stupid girl! Stupid girl to get into such trouble for... for a Scot!" She whispers the last word, and it is drowned out by the noise of boiling. She rocks me to and fro and does not let go of me for a long time.

Kate stands with her hands on her hips. "Well well, whatever have you been up to, young woman, to upset your mother so?" she enquires, and I realise that most people probably have no idea at all what has been going on.

It is hard to tell them about Hugh. My mother sits on the settle with her head in her hands. Jonah is sent to

301

Low Back Farm to bring Verity and James, then we all ride together to Mere Point. When we arrive, Uncle Juniper is shouting and raging and weeping in the smokehouse. Gerald is sitting with his mother in the kitchen, gripping her hands, whilst she stares uncomprehendingly into his face.

Germaine seems affected by a tremor in her hands which she cannot control, as she moves rapidly from one unnecessary task to another, in that well-ordered kitchen.

Later we go upstairs with Aunt Juniper to where Hugh has been laid in the small chapel over the gatehouse. He looks heavy and pale, like a statue. My aunt does not speak. She does not appear to hear what we say. We stay for a while, John talking to her in a low voice, then she gestures that we should leave her alone, and we do so.

In the kitchen Leah, the new skivvy, keeps serving cups of hot posset. The proportions are all wrong – too much wine, too much milk curd or disastrous amounts of cinnamon and nutmeg – but Germaine leaves her to get on with it and does not intervene. John brings Uncle Juniper in from the smokehouse and makes him quieten down. Later, Cedric arrives, then goes straight out again to Hagditch to inform Anne Fairweather.

Aunt Juniper remains in the chapel as noon comes and goes, and the tide marches up and down the bay. I join her again for a while. Afterwards I go outside, and stand amongst the screaming seabirds on the clifftop.

Friends and neighbours arrive in the afternoon. Aunt Juniper neither weeps nor speaks to them. She never does speak again. Instead, as evening approaches, and in a moment when our vigilance must have faltered, she walks down the spiral staircase, out of the tower and over the cliff.

Chapter 32

After the funerals of Hugh and Aunt Juniper, it takes us a long time to return to anything like normality. Little by little life settles down again, but nothing is the same. All the family is grieving. Going back into hiding is not an option now. I am too much needed here. We continue the year's work on the farm, but our hearts are not in it. Unremarkable, everyday events – family meals, churchgoing, visits by the pedlar – are made terrible by the absence of Hugh and Aunt Juniper. Mother enters a state of deep melancholy. I find her one morning in the dairy, turning the handle of the churn, tears pouring down her face. The slap of cream inside the churn thickens to a dull beat. "The butter's coming," she says, raising her face to mine, and then walks out, leaving it half done. I start to follow her, but realise she needs to go alone to Mere Point, as she so often does, to stand on the cliff at the place where Aunt Juniper fell. I turn back and finish the churning.

Our mourning seems to bring out other sorrows too. One evening I find Kate sitting at the end of my father's bed, weeping. He lies half propped up, staring blankly at a heap of child's coloured counters, which she has been trying to persuade him to arrange into patterns. "He won't look at them," she sobs. "I thought he'd like to play with them. Where's he gone, Beatie? Where's he gone?"

Midsummer comes and goes. We do not hold the usual Midsummer Revels, though we can hear the homesteaders celebrating somewhere down the valley. All the things that mattered so much to me before – music, reading, preparing for a good harvest – now seem meaningless. Music I simply cannot bear. Germaine grinding away on her lute drives me to distraction.

Then there is John. I simply cannot be bothered with him. I cannot summon up the emotion required. He understands. I know he does, because he tells me so, but the fact that he needs to remark on it feels like a reproach. As for his church work, his talk of holiness and everlasting life, I cannot listen to it. It becomes a regular occurrence for the churchwardens to call round and collect fines from me, for not attending church.

By August it is clear that both John and Cedric have become involved in the Salamander project. Two witches are mysteriously rescued from hanging at Kerne Forth. A crippled and poverty-stricken beggar, condemned by local magistrates to be flogged for stealing half a barley loaf, vanishes before sentence can be implemented.

"The beggar is in John's church crypt," Anne tells me, joining me one day on watch on the Pike. "He's being sent to Castle Clough, to recuperate and work on the farm. Would you like to help Cedric take him there? I know Edward would be happy to see you again."

I look at her, and wonder about her motives. Has John asked her to find me something to take my mind off Hugh and Aunt Juniper? Anne herself was deeply affected by Hugh's death, I know, and there has been a brittleness in her ever since. Yet she is managing to appear as elegant and composed as ever, whereas I have stopped bothering what clothes I put on, and whether or not I brush my hair. I feel ashamed of myself. I go home and change into a good blue gown and cream kirtle. I brush my hair, smelling the salt in it as I wind it back round my head. I lace up my bodice with a lilac ribbon, and put on a cream lace cap with matching lilac ribbons. When I look in the mirror I hardly recognise myself.

I ride over to the parsonage on Meadowsweet. In the kitchen Mother Bain looks round from stirring a pot of pea soup in the hearth and says, "Greetings, stranger." She tries to straighten up, and I realise how long it is since I have seen her, and how much more bent she has become. She peers at me. "I'm glad to see you, lass, and I'm sorry for how you've been. John's over at Mile Cottages. Old Tarver is dying."

"Oh, I'm sorry to hear that."

"Go and meet the lad. He'll be right glad to see you." She starts to add cream to the soup, and it curdles. She throws down the spoon. "A pox on this pottage!" She backs out of the hearth, and I see that there are tears in her eyes. "Will you fetch some pies from the alehouse, lass?" she asks. "This soup is ruined, and I haven't the heart to start again."

I put my arm round her, and pick up the spoon. "You shouldn't be doing this. It's too much for you." I winch the soup off the heat and stir it vigorously. It remains scummy, but improves a little.

When I ride over towards Mile Cottages later, leaving Mother Bain lying down and resting, I realise that I need to make up my mind about a number of things, amongst them whether I am indeed going to marry John and move into the parsonage.

Mile Cottages lie outside the village. My mind is far away, and I do not hear the hoofbeats until Universe appears round the bend of the track. John and I both rein in. I feel suddenly happy to see him. It is like meeting an exciting stranger by accident. After greeting each other we are both strangely lost for words for a moment, then I ask, "How is old Tarver?"

"Dead."

"I'm sorry to hear that. I shall visit his family."

"Tomorrow would be better. They're glad to see the back of him, and they're all drunk."

We both smile. "I thought I should do something towards the Salamander project," I tell him, and instantly

307

feel hopeless and pointless again, and suddenly deeply irritated by the pretentiousness of the watchword. I wish I could talk to John as I used to, but I feel too numb, and too sure that words will not help. All I can care about, and concentrate on, are Hugh and Aunt Juniper. If I stop thinking about them, then they will be truly gone. I dream about Hugh every night. I am five, playing in the woods with him; ten, riding our first full-sized horses; twelve, sitting with him on watch discussing the problem of our wayward parents. I look for him everywhere in my dreams, sure that I have only mislaid him.

Suddenly John dismounts, and comes over and lifts me off my horse. Dozy, patient Meadowsweet wanders away and starts eating brambles. "You *will* feel better," says John fiercely into my face. "Don't think about anything else. Bugger Salamander. It's all right. You did your bit rescuing Robert." He gives me a little shake. "Truly Beatrice, I should like to drag you off into the woods and comfort you properly, but you are looking too fragile and delicate, and I can see that it would not do."

Meadowsweet comes up and butts my shoulder. Universe blows loudly through his nostrils. "You're frightening the horses," I tell John, unexpectedly wanting to laugh – such an unfamiliar feeling – and I know then, that one day, I shall feel better.

We go to the alehouse, buy some pies and drink some ale, though not as much as the Tarvers. We talk as friends, and I go home feeling peaceful.

I restart my lessons in healing, with Cedric. He has begun keeping bees, for their curative powers, and I spend afternoons swathed in muslin, tending bee skeps, smoking the bees into compliant drowsiness while I steal their honey and pollen to mix into cures for burns, the ague and the bloody flux.

One sweltering forenoon, at the end of summer, after the bees have not been very happy with me and I have been stung twice, I give up for the afternoon and go to visit Germaine at Mere Point. I find her upstairs in the weaving room, hanging wet woollen fabric on the tenter-hooks in the tenter-frame, to stretch and dry it. "It's too hot for this, Cousin," she exclaims, wiping her brow. "Let's go outside and drink elderflower cordial and do nothing."

We go and sit under a tree by the smokehouse, our bodices unlaced and our stockings off. The tide is coming in. Far below, along the pool-pocked shoreline, curls of clay with grassy edges are peeling away into the sea, part of the disintegration of this world of time and tide. Overhead, curved-beaked curlews utter their own name, in long, mournful whistles. Germaine still has some ice left in her ice cellar after the winter, and we drink the elderflower cordial through huge chunks of it.

After we have sat in silence for a while, Germaine says, "Beatrice, what are you going to do about John?"

"What?" I sit up, prepared to be angry, for this is not her business.

"There is gossip, Cousin. Are you aware of the amount of time he spends visiting Anne Fairweather at Hagditch, these days?"

I stare at her. Before I can retort she continues, "Beatrice, you are either betrothed, or not betrothed. You cannot neglect him like this."

"For heaven's sake, I expect he is offering Anne religious counsel. Don't forget she was also very upset about Hugh. I expect John is comforting her."

"Indeed. And it will result in a scandal." She reaches for the jug and tops up my drink. "We all feel terrible, my dear. I have to listen to Gerald's nightmares night after night. Could you not find comfort in John? I'd have thought he was the best person in the world to comfort you."

I wrap my arms round my knees and look out to sea, at the heat-hover on the rocks of the cliff, at the gulls squalling along the tide-line and savaging to death little fishes as they wash into the bay. The world seems a very dangerous place. I glance at my cousin, and wonder if she could possibly understand. "John has such certainty," I tell her. "Too much certainty sometimes. I can only bear so much of it."

"My dear..." She tilts her head suddenly. There is a horse approaching at a gallop along the clifftop path through the woods. She shrugs. "Father-in-law will deal with it. Beatrice, the point is..." She stops as Cedric appears, riding the white horse which Edward gave him. He jumps to the ground, out of breath.

310

"Beatie, get away quickly! Go at once! Here, take my horse. The soldiers are coming."

I jump up. "Where?" But we can already hear them, approaching fast. "Oh God!" I leap into Cedric's warm saddle. Which way? I turn the horse's head towards the densest part of the woods, but it is too late. The soldiers appear from the same direction as Cedric, about twenty of them. These are not Captain Foreman's tired troops, but alert, battle-hardened warriors in uniforms of blue and green – Lord Allysson's men. The next moment they have surrounded me. They dismount, grab Cedric's horse and pull me to the ground. Two of them grasp my arms in a violent grip. I try to throw them off, but they are too strong for me.

The henchmen come rushing out of the tower, swords raised. Uncle Juniper appears too.

"We are here to arrest Beatrice Garth of Barrowbeck," says the militiaman who seems to be in charge. "Captain Leahy at your service, sir." He looks at Uncle Juniper's henchmen. "I hope we're not going to have any trouble."

Uncle Juniper leans forward and gazes at him incredulously. "Nay lad, what are you on about?" He pushes his way to the lean-to behind the smokehouse where his fighting dogs are kept, flings open the door and with a sharp word of command, sets them on the soldiers.

"Sweet Jesu!" Germaine runs screaming into the tower, and returns seconds later with her six foot longbow loaded. The dogs already have two of the soldiers by the arms, and are shaking them. Some of the soldiers are wielding

311

swords and knives, and others are loading their matchlocks. There is a bang which seems to echo all round the bay, and a dog drops. With a roar, Uncle Juniper comes charging out of the smokehouse brandishing an axe.

"Lord save us!" Three of the soldiers turn and run for their lives.

"Get back south where you belong!" barks Uncle Juniper. "Spineless courtiers!" He swings the axe, bringing down a branch of a tree on the captain's head. The henchmen are in hand to hand combat with some of the soldiers now, and Germaine is systematically shooting swords from soldiers' hands. One soldier stands open-mouthed, watching her. I fight free of the soldiers who are holding me, and manage to get at my knife. I rip the sleeve of one of them with it, but he grabs me again, and twists both my arms behind my back.

Suddenly Gerald arrives. He jumps from his horse. "What in heaven's name...?" He is unarmed except for a knife. He has probably been on watch somewhere. He seizes a sword from one of the henchmen and shouts to Germaine, "Who the devil are these people? Scots?"

She shakes her head, reloading her bow. "They're after Beatrice," she calls back.

The soldier who is holding me is trying to drag me away. Gerald brings his sword up against the man's throat. "Let her go," he orders, tilting it to and fro so that the man can feel its edge. I stagger as I find myself free. "Run into the tower," Gerald commands me, and slashes the sword down the man's front, so that all his buttons pop off. I run. "What are you doing fighting your own people?" I hear Gerald demanding. "You should be saving yourselves for the bloody Scots!"

I glance back as I reach the gatehouse. This is like being attacked by the Scots, but in the nightmare situation of not being forewarned or prepared. It is horrific. It quickly becomes obvious that we are hopelessly outnumbered and inadequately armed. There was no time to set up our usual defences – flaming arrows and boiling oil. There was no time to drag out Mere Point's small, old-fashioned cannon from its cupboard. The soldiers are overcoming and disarming the Mere Point men very quickly now. I can't go in and leave them to it. I grab a bow and arrows from the gatehouse. As I emerge again, I see Germaine fall with a sword wound to her shoulder, and Cedric with a blow to the back of his head. I hear Captain Leahy shouting, "We've no wish to fight you, foolish people. We merely wish to arrest the traitress..." and at the same moment I am lifted off my feet by unseen arms from behind.

It's over very quickly after that. Two soldiers drag me off to where a sleek, military cart stands amongst the trees. The captain and cart-driver race along behind, but all the other soldiers remain, to prevent anyone pursuing us. The cart sets off as soon as I am in it. The two soldiers jump into the back with me, and before I can even sit up, we are rattling away along the clifftop path.

Chapter 33

Here is darkness such as I have never imagined it. The dungeon door has closed behind me. I can hear the bolts being shot on the outside. Now the big iron key is turning. Its metallic grating noise stops with a thud of finality.

I stand quite still in the silence that follows. Outside, I could hear small sounds from the other cells – shufflings and moanings. In here, I can hear nothing.

After a while I turn round in the black soundlessness. I feel as if my ears have been stopped and my eyes blindfolded. In the candlelight, when the soldiers pushed me in here, I could see that no one else was in this cell. Now I am starting to wonder. Perhaps someone else was crouching in the shadows. Or something else.

It is very cold. All my skin is gooseflesh; every muscle

in my body is taut. Where is that hot summer's day, just hours ago, when I lay on the clifftop? There was no time to lace up my bodice or put my stockings back on, before the soldiers took me. What would this place be like on a truly cold day? What was it like when Robert was here, through the winter?

I straitlace my bodice, to try to stop myself shivering. It makes no difference. I wish I had worn my sleeves, despite the heat, which seems so far away now. I wish I had not taken my stockings off. I was not allowed to go home to collect anything. I was not allowed to send word to my mother. No one here at the castle answered me when I asked whether anyone at Mere Point had been killed in the fighting. Perhaps they are all dead.

The stink in this cell is ancient and terrible, thick like fog. I am trembling, and I think I have to sit down. I take a few steps forward. The floor squelches. My shoe fills up with some unspeakable liquid. I jump back, towards where I think the door is. If I can find the door again, I shall be able to feel my way round the cell walls.

I urgently need to sit down now. The shivering has gone to my knees, and my legs do not feel strong enough to hold me. Yet I am afraid to move. At last, the rough wood of the door is at my back again. I start to feel my way round the walls. They are wet and slimy. I recoil as something soft drapes itself across my face, and I realise that huge webs are hanging from the ceiling. The ceiling itself is so low that I can touch it with the flats of my hands.

At intervals I come upon heavy iron rings set in the wall, and other metal fastenings too. I know I am later to be examined by a magistrate. I wonder if afterwards I shall be chained up to these.

I stop. There was a sound, a soft thud somewhere in the cell. I wait, but it is not repeated. I move again. My foot touches something. It feels solid but cushiony. I pause, and reach down with my hand. It is furry. It is cold. It is huge. It is a dead rat.

There's no point in moaning – no one will hear me – but I do anyway. At least the rat is dead, I tell myself. I move more carefully, feeling my way with my foot in its cold, wet shoe. This is a tiny space. The floor is uneven. There are unnameable piles of putrid stuff everywhere.

I realise suddenly that there is a draught coming in. I follow it to a small iron grille near the door, above the level of my head. I reach up and tug, but it is firmly fixed, and far too tiny to get through anyway. Then, as I am holding on to the grille, something warm and furry brushes my hand, runs part way along my bare arm and falls on to my foot. It squeaks. I let go of the grille and scream. A small body knocks against my ankles. Then another and another. Rats.

I scream again, and totter backwards across the cell. I stand shaking against the wall, as far from the grille as possible. I do not know how many rats have come in, or how many were here to start with. The dark is no longer soundless. As well as scuttlings and squeakings, my ears are now attuned to other sounds – smaller sounds like spiders plopping to the floor, beetles' legs clicking, things rustling amongst the piles of filth. I kick and stamp; I find the door and bang with my fists against it; I shout and scream. No one comes.

It is impossible to go on like this. Eventually I have to stop. I stand, huddled against the wall, my arms wrapped round myself. A lot of time goes by. I find I am drifting into sleep standing up. I tilt over as my concentration wavers, and wake sliding sideways down the wall. There are movements against my feet. Something creeps into my wet shoe and wriggles. I shriek, and wrench the shoe off, and shake it. That ensures I am wide awake again. After a while, though, sleep creeps up on me once more. Not seeing makes staying awake more difficult. I walk about, to endeavour to have some sense of place, to stay awake. I take the Dunbar book from inside my bodice, and try to remember the words. It no longer smells of Robert, only of leather and of me. Here, in this foul place, I can hardly smell it at all.

Time becomes an abstraction. I think of John, teaching me to tell the time by the clock which my father stole. I wish I had learnt better, so that I could say, this feels like three seconds, five minutes, ten hours. I think about Robert. He was here in this blackness, this silence, for months. I do not know whether he was in a cell on his own, or with other people. I have never asked him. There has never been the right moment to talk of it, and now we never shall. Does he travel in his nightmares to this exact spot where I stand?

"Robert?" I whisper his name, then call it loudly.

Later, I do fall asleep on my feet, and dream of a green valley under a high, empty sky. There is no sound except for birdsong and the rushing of wind. At the bottom of the valley lies a tumble of boulders with heather growing between them, and there is a pele tower on top of a rise, one of its grey stone walls glowing in the last of the evening sun. It is not any place I know. When I wake, amongst the filth on the floor, it is still clear in my mind, like a bright memory left hanging here in the dark.

Muck clings to my arms and clothes as I haul myself upright. I work my way back round the wall to the iron rings. Webs heavy with dust flap in my face like Lenten veils. I find the rings, and hook my arms through them to stop myself from falling over in my sleep, and I hang there, dozing.

I wonder if Edward will be able to get me out. It would look rather odd if he did, I suppose, since he took me into custody once before, only for me to be found walking free a few months later. I wonder if he will indeed be endangered himself by all this. There must come a point when even the most respectable of justices comes under suspicion, if too many prisoners with whom he is involved end up inexplicably free. I remember Anne Fairweather's words – we mostly need to catch them before they get into the castle, to have any realistic hope of saving them. Perhaps this is it then. Perhaps this is the end of me.

I am hanging, half-sleeping, when the door opens. The light is like a dagger. I have to squeeze my eyes shut, even though there is just one single candle flame flickering outside. "So," says a voice, "you finally see the inside of Lancaster Castle for yourself, Mistress Garth. It is a sorry thing to encounter you so."

"Captain Foreman..." Awkwardly I unhook my cramped arms from the rings.

"I told them there was no call to put you in here. I'm afraid they take a severe line on treason, Lord Allysson's men do." He helps me out into the passage.

"Wait!" I stumble, blinking, and stop him from shutting the door behind me. "Please, shine your candle..."

He doesn't understand what I mean, so I take his candle from him, and shine it into the cell. Somehow I have to have a picture of this place to take with me, to know where I was, all this time. The tiny room is black, crusted, alive with running things: beetles, cockroaches, spiders. Behind a filthy heap in a corner a larger shape shifts, but the rats are mostly in hiding. I wonder if they can climb the walls, to come and go as they do through the grille.

I give Captain Foreman his candle back, and try to walk, but my legs give way. With a faint look of revulsion, Captain Foreman offers me his arm.

"I did not think to see you again," I stutter foolishly. "I thought you had gone home."

He leads me up a stone staircase to a small room. "I'm on secondment until this case is cleared up." He holds the door open for me to enter. "There has obviously been some confusion. Sir Edward Clough says he released you on bail, on the Bishop of Carlisle's recognizance, to appear at the Martinmas Assizes here in Lancaster. No one thought to tell me this, and in the confusion of the changeover of troops, no one told Captain Leahy either. So you have a little stay of execution, Mistress Garth. I am to escort you back to Barrowbeck, from where you are not to travel more than a distance of two miles in any direction. We will leave a man there to guard you. In November, Lord Allysson's men will return for you."

I stare at him. I am suddenly conscious of how I must look – half-dressed and filthy. "How long was I in the dungeon?" I ask him.

"A day and a half. About thirty-six hours."

"Do you know how to tell the time by the clock, captain? I was just learning, before all this happened."

He looks bemused. "I do, madame. I am sorry to think that all the things you might have learnt and achieved in your life are come to naught. That makes me very sad."

"Aye, and me also."

"Sir Edward says you are a silly girl, easily led, and well nigh simple. I do not think I believe him. You do understand that you must not try to abscond, do you not? By standing trial, particularly with the sympathy which

320

Sir Edward obviously has for you, you have a chance of clearing all this up."

"Or of being burnt at the stake."

He looks away. We are both silent for a moment, then he asks, "Were you fed at all when you were downstairs?"

"No. I saw no one."

"That is regrettable. I apologise. I will have some food brought to you now, and then we will ride northwards."

He leaves, and locks me in. I sit down and stare round the little room, which contains only a table, three chairs and some unwashed dishes, yet which feels like paradise compared with where I have been. I realise that I am indeed weak from hunger. I pick a fragment of some unidentifiable foodstuff off one of the plates, and eat it. It is a tiny, dried flake of rabbit. Something strange happens then. For a moment I have the sensation of being once again in the hermit's cottage in the woods, where Robert and I spent so much time – indeed it flashes before my eyes so vividly that for a moment I do not know where I am. It is obviously the taste of rabbit which has done it, and yet, Robert spent months in here, as he spent months in the hermit's cottage. I wonder if something of a person's presence might permeate, and stay, after they are gone. I sit down again, light-headed, aware that I am being fanciful. Captain Foreman returns with a plate of bread and cheese, and when I have eaten it all, we go out into the sunshine.

Chapter 34

After the underground cold, the day's heat is like a furnace blast. One of Captain Foreman's men is waiting for us with three horses. When he turns, I see with dismay that it is Victor.

"You remember Victor?" Captain Foreman enquires cheerily. "He has volunteered to guard you at Barrowbeck. He has a kinswoman who lives somewhere nearby."

"How kind of him." I glare at Victor. "And who might your kinswoman be, Victor?"

He looks affronted at the contemptuous familiarity with which I address him, and I realise that I may be storing up trouble for myself, but cannot bring myself to care. "I believe you are acquainted with her, lady. She also once guarded you. Mistress Brissenden of Hagditch is my aunt."

I almost groan aloud. "Well doubtless your aunt will be glad of your support and comfort," I tell him through gritted teeth, "since she was so lately fastened in the stocks and pelted with refuse. It is most noble of you to advertise your relationship, considering she is so disgraced."

Victor glowers, and seems about to speak, but I turn my back and ask Captain Foreman, without bothering to lower my voice, "Was there truly no one else to take on this guarding duty, captain? Would you not care to do it yourself? We are most hospitable up in the West Moorland."

The captain regards me for a moment. "Madame, this behaviour of yours does you no good. You must learn to be less trouble and more compliant. Now, shall we set off?"

The horse they have provided for me looks as if it should have retired a decade ago. It is bow-legged, and its sidesaddle is frayed and lopsided. Even so, my spirits lift a little as we ride down Castle Hill, towards the outskirts of town. I have a further idea of how I must look, when people point, and one old woman says to another, "She'll be a witch, I daresay."

"God bless you, mistress," I murmur to her graciously, and the two of them scurry away.

I feel I know this route well now, as we pass Weary Wall, then Green Ayre with its clattering watermill. The humid weather has intensified and the sky has clouded over. There is a feeling of thunder in the air as we cross the arched bridge out of town. Captain Foreman rides ahead of me, and Victor behind. I wonder about making a run for it, but the two of them are armed with swords and matchlocks, and their horses look fit and fast. I would stand no chance of getting away.

"Was anyone badly injured in the fighting at Mere Point?" I ask Captain Foreman.

He turns in his saddle. "Several of Lord Allysson's men had arrow wounds. One was killed. I also heard that some local healer was in a fairly bad way, but likely to recover."

Cedric. Fear coils in my gut like a snake. Cedric must not die. I love him myself, but even more importantly, my mother must not be robbed of Cedric when she has so recently lost her sister, and now may be going to lose me. "And the mistress of the house?" I ask him. "I think she was also injured."

"I don't rightly know. It can't have been fatal, anyhow, or I'd have heard. You'll be able to see for yourself soon. I'm sure Victor will be happy to escort you over to Mere Point." He looks round again. "Won't you, Victor?"

Victor does not reply.

In the villages, people come out to watch us go by. We pass the pedlar, travelling south with his two donkeys, as we ride through Kerne Forth. He gapes at us, and calls out, "Greetings, mistress!"

"Stop! Wait!" I call to him. "Have you any news from Mere Point?" but Victor whacks his sword across my horse's rump, sending the poor beast skittering forward so that I am almost unseated.

"Get on!" he snarls. He waves his sword menacingly at

the pedlar. "Get out of my sight, layabout."

The pedlar jabs his heels at his donkey's ribs. "Aye sir, steady on there. I'm going." Above the jangling of pots and pans strapped to his second donkey, I hear his faint words, "None dead at Mere Point, mistress!" and something else, which I can't quite make out.

A storm seems to be building now. The sky is dark ahead, and thunder rumbles in the clouds. Around us, the light has a yellow, indoor strangeness. I reflect on the prospect of being held prisoner in my own home, by Victor. It will be intolerable. It will be far worse than when my father locked me in. Victor will enjoy humiliating me at every opportunity. I wonder if escape will be possible, perhaps through the secret passage under the barmkin, but when I glance back at Victor's grim face I realise that his vigilance is likely to be unwavering. I want to weep and bang my head against the trees.

We make good time, and reach the boggy edges of Mistholme Moss by early afternoon. Herons stand motionless in the reed beds, waiting for the storm. The tension in the air is like a strung bow. Lightning flashes. The rocks on our left glow in the intensified light. Thunder crashes very loud and close. Two hares leap from the bracken and bound away across the hill. In the distance, dogs bark.

"We'll take the way through the woods," calls Captain Foreman over his shoulder. "There's going to be a downpour." He speeds up. "Come along, Mistress Garth. You're ill-clad for a cloudburst."

Lightning flashes again, several times in quick succession, and the thunder that follows is so loud that it hurts my head. The horses are getting jittery. Behind me, Victor keeps up a vicious grumbling, telling me I'd be better off to be struck by lightning, because I'll be back in that dungeon soon. We take the Barrowbeck path at a fast trot. It is so dark where the trees meet overhead that it is difficult to see at all. We cut through Barrow Wood towards Barrowbeck Tower, and I suddenly notice a smell of burning, as if there had been a lightning strike. I slow down and look about me, then call to Captain Foreman, "We might have to go the other way. I think the woods could be on fire." He sniffs, and raises his hand to show that he has heard me.

As far as I can judge, the main storm seems to be heading out over the bay. A few big raindrops splatter on to our faces, then the downpour begins. At once the temperature drops. Captain Foreman leads us on to a smaller path where it is more sheltered. The thick foliage protects us a little, but rain collects amongst the leaves and slides in cold draughts down our backs. This is the path I used to take home from the hermit's cottage. I shiver, suddenly filled with a vivid recollection of Robert's presence there.

At last we reach the edge of the clearing where my home stands. I feel overcome with emotion at the sight of it. The storm is moving away now. Somewhere dogs are still barking – in fact strangely it sounds as if the barking is coming from the tower, though we do not normally keep dogs. Apart from that, there is only the sound of the rain battering the leaves. I halt my horse. Something is wrong. The valley is not normally so quiet, even in the pouring rain. Why are the sheep not calling, the pigs not grunting, the cowherds not shouting and whistling?

Victor nearly ran into the back of me when I stopped, and now he is cursing me. "It'll be the stake for you, madam, oh yes it will. That's for certain, the stake. A good job too. Treason, it's a bloody disgrace, and you can't even ride a bloody horse properly neither..."

I try not to be overwhelmed by sheer misery at the prospect of being locked up with Victor. My hair is drenched and hanging over my face; my clothes are sodden; the filth from the dungeon floor is running off me in rivulets. I can no longer even bring myself to turn round and retort. Then suddenly there is another sound, above the noise of rain. It begins quietly and grows, until it fills the valley, a harsh, blaring bleat, repeated and repeated, even before each echo has died away. My hair prickles on my scalp. I wave my hand behind me at Victor, to stop his blathering. It could be something else. I try to tell myself it is something else – the wind round the tower walls, or seabirds calling – but I know it is not. There is only one thing which sounds like that.

I look up. Remnants of black smoke are straggling from the beacon turret, where the downpour extinguished the warning fire. A smell of burning pitch is in the air. The chilling, unmusical blasts go on and on. It is the ram's-horn, kept in a niche in the tower's gatehouse, and only ever blown for one purpose: to warn that the Scots are invading. We have innocently wandered into the middle of a Scottish raid.

There is just time for me to feel crushingly disappointed. No more raids, he said. No more raids. Oh Robert. Is this his unstoppable Cousin Duncan, or some other border-raiding family, over which he has no control? I draw breath to tell Captain Foreman and Victor to run for their lives, but as I do so, the first Scots ride quietly out of the woods behind us.

I whip up my poor, decrepit horse and try to make it gallop towards the tower, but it is no good. The terrified animal stumbles, panics and throws me to the ground. At once the Scots are all over me. They are hot and sweating, and their patterned woollen draperies smell like wet sheep. I struggle to get at my knife, then remember it was taken from me at the castle. I catch a glimpse of Captain Foreman being overwhelmed, then Victor being neatly toppled from his horse.

A voice shouts, "Surrender, Englishmen, and you won't be hurt. Stay still, ye daft fools." I try to sit up from where I have fallen. Dear God, I know that voice. Inexplicably, one of the Scots assists me with his hand under my elbow. I look amongst the unfamiliar faces, old and young, bearded and clean-shaven, many of them milling about on foot now, as they overcome the two sword-wielding English soldiers. Surely Robert would not have betrayed me to this extent, to take part in a raid again himself. Then I see him, astride a sleek grey horse. He is changed. It is the old Robert back again, his hazel eyes bright and fierce, his lips drawn back in a smile.

"It's plain to see that you Englishmen don't know how to behave in the company of women," he says, and jumps down next to me. I stare at him, and he picks me up and lifts me into his saddle. "Just returning a wee favour," he says softly, and jumps up behind me. "It might be advisable to scream, sweetheart," he adds under his breath, "for the sake of appearances." His hands come round me and gather up the reins.

Obediently, I manage a small scream.

They leave Captain Foreman and Victor tied to a juniper tree, back to back. Robert holds me tightly as we gallop away down the valley. His horse is fast and strong, and carries us both with ease. "I had word of what happened to you," he says against my ear. "We set off straight away, and rode through the night."

We see no one on our way past the Pike. Everyone has run to the pele towers, waiting for an attack which will not come. Then, at the crossroads, where the coast road leaves Barrowbeck, I see Cedric, standing with a basket of herbs in his hands and a bandage round his head. He has drawn back into the protection of a rocky outcrop, to shelter from the Scots. We are almost past him before he sees me, but then he comes rushing out shouting, "Beatrice!"

"Wait!" I grip Robert's hand on the reins, and he slows down and wheels his horse, letting the rest of his companions gallop by. Cedric approaches, leading his white mare. Robert's horse fidgets, not caring to be left behind.

Cedric, the Cockleshell Man, my teacher to whom I have been such a disappointing pupil, stops and looks up at us. "Are you all right?" he asks me.

I nod. "I am now. Are you all right, Cedric? Is your head badly hurt?"

"Aye, but it's healing. You look well enough, Robert."

"I thank you for it. We must go. It willnae be good if you're seen talking to us."

"No." Cedric reaches into his basket and brings out a sprig of herb-of-grace. "For blessing," he says, "and a safe journey."

So we ride north, with Robert's warm body at my back and his breath in my hair. We travel fast for a long time, only stopping to rest when the horses become exhausted. We cross mountain passes, ford rivers and wend through pine forests. I realise that the borderland is familiar to me now. I know the way there, and I know the way back. Our part of the border is safer than perhaps it has ever been, and there are people I love on either side of it.

Cedric will explain all to my mother, and no doubt I shall be able to meet with her, and with other members of my family, at Castle Clough. I may even be able to visit Barrowbeck, once the troops have changed again.

As for John, I cannot think about him. It is too painful. I can only tell myself that he deserves better than me.

So I ride into the unknown with Robert's arms around me. I drift in and out of sleep, wrapped in a Scottish blanket and securely held astride this unfamiliar saddle. When I sleep, I dream of the dungeon, and jump awake in terror. Robert kisses my neck and says, "Poor girl, poor girl, oh God, they put you in that dungeon." Sometimes I do not know if I am dreaming or awake, and I seem to have a fever, although my wet clothes have long since dried on me inside this warm blanket.

When we stop for a rest, deep in the forest, I meet Robert's father, brothers and Cousin Duncan. I am afraid of them at first, because of how they look, armed with so many weapons and dressed in their green and earth-coloured woollen cloth and goatskin coats, the clothing of the enemy. I cannot understand all that the older men say to me, even though they speak slowly for my benefit. We toast oatcakes on sticks over a fire of pine branches, whilst overhead the forest echoes with owls. "We shouldn't stop for long," says Robert. "There may be pursuers – your family or the military."

"My family will understand that I have to go away, Robert. Cedric will talk to them. He will tell them I am all right."

He wraps two more blankets round me and props a fallen log at my back. Unfamiliar fungus, pale and fleshlike, is growing from it. I feel I am in a dream, or in some place not of this world.

"I'm not so sure you are all right, my Bea," Robert says. "You're shivering. I think you've caught a fever." He calls across the clearing, "We'd best get on, Father."

The second night we sleep for a short time on a stony mountain, wrapped in our blankets, with red deer moving silently to and fro just beyond the firelight, and wolves howling to the north. I lie curled up, with the fire at my front and Robert at my back, and burn with fever. In the dawn twilight we mount up again, and on our horse grey as twilight, we cross the Scottish border.

Reality seems far off now. I do not know whether I am in the dungeon or in Scotland with Robert. "You'll be all right as soon as we get home," he whispers, his chin rough against my ear. "We're nearly home now. My mother will know how to make you well again."

We ride through the day. In the light of a golden evening we halt on top of a grassy hill. There is no sound except for birdsong and the rushing of wind. Below us stretches a green valley under a high, empty sky. At the bottom of the valley lies a tumble of boulders with heather growing between them, and there is a pele tower on top of a rise, one of its grey stone walls glowing in the last of the evening sun.

Now I know that I am truly ill, because I can see John coming up the hill towards us, astride his horse. I wipe a corner of the blanket across my eyes to clear the feverish vision.

Robert dismounts. "I ran Salamander's errand, my friend," he says. "You're welcome to stay as long as you wish." He turns to me. "Aye well, Beatrice. I'll be seeing you at the tower, then." Without waiting for me to answer, he sets off down the hill, following his kinsmen. I watch him go away into the dream landscape, this man who was a dream in my mind all these months, whilst my betrothed lover paced and raged.

A screech owl shrieks from the treeline. The vision of John approaches, solid and human, his riding clothes dusty, his hair untidy. He walks his horse alongside mine and reaches out his hand. "Are you all right to ride down the hill?" he asks. I nod. Shadows swoop across the valley. The sun dips behind enemy battlements, and John and I ride down the darkening slope in the tracks of the raiders.

Glossary

barmkin	walled enclosure
blackjack	leather jug
boote	compensate, benefit
broderer	embroiderer
brukle	frail
carretta	small cart, rather old-fashioned by Beatrice's day
cates	party food
chemise-smock	women's light full-length garment worn with other garments on top
cupshotten	drunk
doublet	men's upper garment, sometimes padded, worn with a ruff
fain	gladly or glad
firkin	cask holding nine gallons
fluke	flatfish
forespoken	silenced, forbidden
galiard	formal dance
ginnel	alley
goblin bread	rye or barley bread infected with ergot, a hallucinogenic fungus, used to speed childbirth
grimalkin	old woman
hastening cupboard	warm cupboard where bread was left to rise
hearte raithe	soul
henbane	plant whose seeds were used as an early anaesthetic

jerkin	men's jacket, sometimes padded, often sleeveless
kersey	coarse woollen cloth
kilderkin	cask holding eighteen gallons
kirtle	women's decorative outer petticoat, sometimes padded
Lady Days	four days in the year (one in each quarter) on which the hiring of workers traditionally took place
lanthorn	lantern
mak	mate
mantle	small cloak
matchlock	firearm
mayhap	maybe
mislike	dislike
moss-trooper	border raider
mummer	actor
nightgown	dressing gown
nightsmock	nightdress
pavane	formal dance
pocket	small purse or bag usually attached to belt
posset	drink made from curdled milk, wine and spices
pottage	soup or stew
proving oven	warming oven
rackencrock	apparatus for suspending cooking pots over fire
recognizance	money, or an undertaking, pledged for bail
remove	course of a meal
shawm	woodwind instrument

slee	sly
straitlace	lace up tightly so the edges meet
thirled	open in a snarl
Timor mortis conturbat me	Fear of death troubles me
tinderbox	box in which a spark is struck from flint with steel to ignite tinder (charred linen or dried fungus) creating a flame for lighting candles, torches, fires
venetians	glasses
ypocras	spiced drink made from wine, spirits, herbs and honey

The stanza by William Dunbar (c1456 – c1520) is from his poem *Lament for the Makaris (Lament for the Poets)* written about 1507.